The Hoteliers

A Life of Unexpected Things

Rameez Hattur

First published in 2019 by

Becomeshakespeare.com

Wordit Content Design & Editing Services Pvt Ltd
Unit - 26, Building A -1, Nr Wadala RTO,
Wadala (East), Mumbai 400037, India
T: +91 8080226699

ISBN - 978-93-88930-23-9

For my family.

For all hoteliers.

Disclaimer

This story is not about bosses being wrong, the hospitality field being wrong, or the seniors and juniors being wrong. Instead, it is about teamwork, which is the most important part. It is about how an hotelier's life gets messed up from the first day of college. It is about accepting our faults, instead of blaming someone else.

Every human is riddles with a different problem, but we also have solutions for those problems. Life only gets sweeter when we suffer and prevail.
As a human, I too go wrong.

This novel is entirely a work of fiction. The names, characters, and incidents portrayed in it are a work of the author's imagi-nation. Any resemblance to actual persons—living or dead—events or localities are entirely coincidental.

Acknowledgments

I especially thank all my bosses and colleagues with whom I worked; it would not have been possible for me to write this story without your support. It was a great experience for me to learn from my colleagues, and it was a pleasure to work with my bosses. Both are huge parts of my life, and working with you has been like a book of knowledge, as every stage has taught me new things.

I am grateful for Mannat Lumba, my first reader and editor. Your help, support and suggestions every step of the way made it considerably easy to make the creation of this book a success. I'd also like to thank the entire team of Become Shakespeare, Wordit Content Design & Editing Services for your continuous support.

Google Translate played a major role in writing this book too. Here's to free knowledge!

It is not possible to thank everyone who became a part of my life, as a family member or a friend. I can't reach out to each one of you, but through this novel, I would like to be in touch with all of you. The ones I knew earlier, and the ones I met over the course of writing this book.

Prologue

"Hey bro, how are you?" one of my doctor friends asked, laughing. I looked at him quietly.

"Hey, Manav! Became a Manager, right?" another friend, a lawyer, asked.

"Oh! Manager sir, good morning!" an engineer friend interjected, and they all started laughing at me.

"What happened guys?" I asked, curious.

"What happened? Look at where we are today, and look at you."

"Bro, I am an hotelier," I replied hesitantly.

"Hotelier!" they said together, and started laughing loudly.

Standing in the middle, I felt like a caged creature. It was an embarrassing moment for me. I couldn't understand why they were laughing at me. How does it feel when you meet your old friends after a long time, and all they do is laugh at your field of work? We'd graduated together, and decided to choose a field to pursue. Due to different reasons, today they are doctors, lawyers or engineers - and I am an hotelier. They'd said to me, 'Brother, you take admission and move forward in Hotel Management. We will follow you later.' But, they never did. Had I done anything wrong by choosing to become an hotelier? If not this, what should I be?

Chapter 1

"I'm up, *maa*," I said, hearing a continuous knock on my bedroom door. I was back to reality. It creates a horribly rushed situation when you want to catch the 07:00 o'clock train, and wake up at 06:00 o'clock with last night's nightmare still in your mind.

I ran to the bathroom, rubbing my eye with one hand, and brushing with the other. It took me less than fifteen minutes to get ready.

The person on the other side of the door was my *maa*. She was from Punjab, and my father, from Delhi. They'd fallen in love in college, and got married soon after. I was the only tangible proof of their love. That's all I know about their relationship - *maa* never gave me any more information, and I never asked. Even though dad never hurt *maa*, things between us weren't good. Every time we talked, it felt like a war – zone.

"I am getting really late, *maa*," I exclaimed, while packing my bags.

"Only a minute *beta*, all done," she replied from the kitchen, as she packed some home-food for me.

"*Maa*! What is this?" I noticed some packets of food in her hand.

"Nothing! You just keep them inside and have them during your journey," she said, putting all the packets in a bag.

"*Maa*!"

"What *maa*? Can't I even force you to have more, now?"

"*Maa*! Don't worry; I will be back very soon. It's really getting late, please," I requested.

"I know you are late," she replied, sniffing. "And in some time, you will leave me alone." All Indian mothers treat their children the same way. Here, we don't just go out of town to work. For our mothers, we might as well be joining the army. I looked at her anxious face, so close to breaking down, and gave her a hug. "Please, don't make me emotional *maa*. This is my very first job, and I need your blessings, not tears." I tried to make her understand.

"My blessings will always be with you, don't worry. Now go, or you will miss your train," she replied.

I smiled and started moving down the hall, bag in hand. I could hear her following close, reminding me to have food on time, and call her once a day. I promised I would. In the other room, dad was also getting ready to go to work as usual.

"Dad, I am leaving," I said in a low voice. No reply from his end. "Dad, I am leaving," I repeated, a little louder.

"If I ask you to stay back, will you? Now that you have decided to go, why are you asking me?" he turned towards me and continued. "You still have time to think. You can still change your plans, start a career in our business. What will you do after becoming an hotelier?"

"I want to make a career in hospitality, dad!" I persisted, but he did not seem to listen.

"My business is very big. I meet elite people every day. If they ask me what my son does, what should I say to them?"

"You can tell them the truth. I don't see how that's so bad." I argued back.

"Oh yes, my son, the hotelier. In spite of having a degree, he washes cups and saucers in hotels. Is this what you want me to say? After spending four lakhs for a three-year degree, this is all you're going to do," he continued, disappointed.

"Being an hotelier doesn't end at cups and saucers, dad. You won't understand."

Before he could retaliate, *maa* stopped us both. "Our son is going far away from us for his job. At least today don't fight with him!" I realized his outburst came out of a place of hurt. "I am not interested in his job. He chose this path because of his friends. Don't come to me the day you regret this decision," he said, leaving the house.

I took a taxi towards the Kalka railway station. The train came right on time, and so began my 15 hour journey to Mumbai. My destination was Alibaug. Ninety kilometres from Mumbai, was a certain Zurich Resort and Spa Alibaug, where I was going to be joining as a Management Trainee, in the Front Office department. After my degree in Hotel Management, I'd become very serious about my future. I'd already wasted twenty-five years of my life, and my career was yet to kick-start! Nostalgic already about home, and nervous about what was to come, I somehow made it to Mumbai.

I was to take a ferry from the Gateway of India, to Mandawa in Alibaug. Like a typical tourist, I followed the hotel guide map that they'd sent me. As this was my first day at work, I was dressed in a white shirt, black pants, a tie and a blazer. After reaching the Mandawa jetty, I was waiting for the hotel vehicle, when I noticed a similarly dressed man across the road. When the vehicle still hadn't shown up for a while, I went up to him. "Excuse me, heading to Zurich Resort?" I asked.

He nodded, and thrust his hand forward. "I am Shantanu Chatterji from West Bengal, joining as an Executive Chef." I returned the introduction, "I am Manav Kapoor from Shimla, joining as a Management Trainee in the Front Office."

"Nice to meet you," he replied with a smile. A tall, young guy stood before me. He was around six feet tall, with a French beard framing his face.

By then, the hotel vehicle arrived. We put our luggage on

top of the car with the help of the driver, and made ourselves comfortable. The driver gave us bottles of water, and greeted us amicably. He seemed like an Alibaug local.

"Have you visited this place before?" I asked Shantanu.

"No, and you?" I shook my head.

"This is the first time I've come out of my home-town for work," I smiled.

"Oh really?" he replied.

"This is a very nice place sir. There are a lot of beaches in this city, and greenery everywhere," our driver interjected. We asked him to tell us more about the city.

"During the rains, you will not find any place like this. It's green everywhere. It's unlike anything you've ever seen. So relaxing! Most of the people aren't aware about this city, but it is one of the best cities in Raigadh," he looked back at us from the rear-view mirror. "When you go out of this city don't say you are from Alibaug, or people will make fun of you."

"Why?" I asked him.

"No answer sir *jii*, this is the enigma of Alibaug!" he laughed heartily.

"Tell me something about yourself," I turned towards Shantanu. "I have been in this industry for eight to ten years, visited a lot of places in India as well as other countries. Some places were really good, and some, not so much. But it's all been an unforgettable experience," he replied, with a slight Bengali lilt. "What about you?"

"This is my first job, after completing a Hotel Management course," I replied hesitantly. He was, after all, way more experienced than me.

"Oh yes, don't worry. You will learn everything very soon," he assured me, as we continued down the road. In a few minutes, our driver took a turn away from the main road and towards a road that led to the hotel. There was a huge temple the driver pointed out to, telling us he'd like to accompany us whenever we visit next.

Finally, we reached the hotel, the entrance of which was amazing – with fountains on both ends, elephants on both the sides, and trees flanking the path leading to a golden plaque with the hotel's name on it.

On entering the lobby, we met the Human Resource Manager, along with the hotel manager, who was waiting to welcome all the new joiners. Most of the managers were joining on the same day. I knew the Human Resource Manager, Mr. Kundan Khurana, quite well. He was the one who took my campus interview. I remember him driving me mad with his questions. He had an odd habit of fidgeting with his tie, ten times a minute. "Good morning Chef," he then turned to my side. "Hello, good morning Manav. Welcome to our family!" Khurana sir greeted us with one hand, and fidgeted with his tie with the other. "Meet our hotel's General Manager, Mr. Upendra Suri," he introduced us to the person standing next to him.

"A very good morning, gentlemen," he began, before Khurana interrupted him. "Hope your journey was fine?" We said it was. This was the first time I was meeting a General Manager up close. Mr. Suri looked pretty young. He was around six feet tall, clean shaven, with round spectacles framing his face, and was in a sharp two-piece suit.

As a welcome gesture, they gave us a red rose each, and offered us some snacks along with a drink. We were to meet in the conference hall after a fifteen-minute break.

We entered the hotel lobby and found ourselves in a large room with a shiny white marble floor. Glittering chandeliers hung from the high ceiling. Sofas with teak and glass coffee table sets, sat at each corner of the lobby, upholstered in expensive silk. This was the first time in my life that I was seeing such a hotel. After a long, tiring journey, I finally felt myself relax. After a quick breakfast of samosas and the local favourite - *vada pav*, we'd just started towards the conference room, when I heard a familiar voice.

"Hey, Manav!"

I turned around. Walking towards me like he owned the place, with glasses bigger than his face, and his blazer in hand, was the dumbest guy from my college, Rudra. He was the kind of person who wanted everything, without lifting a finger. He'd wanted to complete the three-year degree in a year, and become a General Manager soon after. He was a typical know-it-all.

"Rudra! What a surprise. What are you doing here?" I feigned civility.

"Forget about me," he countered, "How come you're here?"

"I passed the campus interview and the managers chose me as a Management Trainee."

"Campus interview!" he laughed, "And you got selected! How is this possible? You know, only talented people get selected in campus interviews. People like me, not fools like you. Did you bribe the manager? Or did you beg them to take you in? But anyway, since you are here, you will get to see me as the best General Manager this hotel has ever see, very soon."

"Okay, of course. Why not?" I humoured him.

"Not only okay. Say, 'Yes, sir!'"

The chef was confused with our conversation. He was looking at Rudra like he'd never seen anyone like him before. I was used to his antics, but to Shantanu, this was unbelievable.

"Can you introduce yourself please?" Rudra asked him cheekily. I introduced him as the Executive Chef, Shantanu Chatterji.

"Oh! An Executive Chef! How are you, Mr. Chef?" he smugly put his hand on Shantanu's shoulder and continued.

"Mr. Chatterji! Do you know how to make egg *bhurji*? I like it very much! If you don't know how to make it, ask me. I will teach you!" he chuckled and walked away.

"Who is this clown?" the chef asked me, slighted.

"Leave it, he's been like this since college. He was my IHM batch mate," I replied. "Very nice!" Shantanu laughed, "You have a good friend!"

The conference hall had been arranged to seat 10-15 people, three to each table, all facing a small stage. Each table had cards with names of different managers, written along with their designations. On every table was a small book named 'Guide to Alibaug', with local information about the city. The hall was almost packed, with new and existing managers. None of us new joinees seemed to know each other, apart from Rudra and I. Between us was an empty chair, with '*Joy Dharmarajan, Housekeeping Manager*' written on it.

Thousands of questions were running in my mind. Who will ask what? What will I have to say? What will happen next?Rudra sat behind us. Shantanu pointed this out with a grumble. Soon, Khurana came on stage. As the HR Manager, he was to arrange and be involved in all activities.

"Good morning, guys," Khurana said, still fidgeting with his tie. "I hope you all know me. I am Kundan Khurana, your HR Manager. My door is always open for all of you, and I hope you don't hesitate to ask me for anything, at any time."

"Today, we all welcome you as a part of this organisation. This is like a small family. Just how we greet all our family members every day, we do the same here too. We have to meet each other every day, so we all have to work as a team," he continued, "So before we move forward, introductions are a must. Let me start the introductions with our organisation's youngest, most talented and dynamic person, our General

Manager, Mr. Upendra Suri." Khurana waved his hand towards Suri, and requested him to come on stage.

Standing in front of the mic, Mr. Suri looked at us all, and urged us to introduce ourselves instead. One by one, all the new managers started introducing themselves, right from their college, to their work experience. During their rounds, I remember feeling very embarrassed, for everyone seemed to have more experience than me. Some had ten years of experience, some eight, and some six. Then came Rudra's turn. He began, "I am a very hard worker. It has been my dream to work in good hotels and be a professional hotelier. I have struggled a lot to get my degree." This was all a farce.

By the time my turn came, I was trembling. This was the first time I was going to be talking in front of such experienced people.

"Good... good morning sirs," I said, looking towards Suri and Khurana. "Good morning to all. I am Manav Kapoor, from Shimla. I have completed my degree in Hotel Management from Dehradun, and am now joining you as a Management Trainee in the Front Office. I will need your help, time and motivation to settle down. It has always been a dream to work with such talented people. I'd like to thank all of you for giving me this opportunity, and a special thank you to Khurana sir who selected me." I tried my best.

Khurana smiled, looked at me, and urged me to take my seat. Suri, however, looked like someone was forcing him to smile. Now, it was his turn to introduce himself. "Hello everyone!" he waited for a second before continuing, "I don't want to introduce myself. My work will speak for me. I consider myself a passionate hotelier and I have been eager to work for an organization that is the future of this industry. I have wanted to build this hotel's reputation for leadership and am passionate to bring about outstanding business results. I have been a part of this industry for the last fifteen years. I started my career as a waiter in Calcutta, and today I am the General Manager of this hotel."

I was hooked.

"Fifteen years ago, I had asked my senior what I should do to be a successful hotelier," he continued. "He didn't reply to that question, but asked me to work honestly, patiently and work hard, for one day I would get my answer. Today, after fifteen years, when I think back to that question, I feel the answer is right in front of me. For the last fifteen years, I have worked by my own rules and regulations. Thousands of people are connected to the hospitality industry, and every day our industry grows a little more. As it does, it also increases jobs in the world."

Everyone was listening very carefully.

After a few seconds of silence, he said, "Let me ask you a question. What does it mean to be an hotelier?" He looked around at us. While everyone started giving their own opinions, I was just looking around, waiting to hear the right answer. For, of course, I didn't know what it was.

"Someone who cares for others. That's what it means to be an hotelier," Shantanu answered.

Rudra poked me from the back, "You don't know the answer? Then why did you come here?"

"If you know the correct answer, then please, go ahead," I grumbled. He stood up and said, "The world's most professional and talented people become hoteliers."

Suri still wasn't impressed. "Okay, let me tell you," he began, just as a voice echoed from the hall's entrance.

"Excuse me! Good morning! Good morning all." A tall, good looking guy strode in, with one small bag in hand and another on his shoulder.

"Yes, gentleman?" Suri asked him.

"Hello, I am Joy, sir! Joy Dharmarajan! The new Housekeeping Manager," he introduced himself as he walked down the hall.

"Don't you think you are too late?" Suri half-sneered, "And hoteliers are always punctual."

"Actually, sir, if I'd gone to my room and come back here, it would have been too late, and I didn't want to miss this meeting. So I decided to come here directly." His eagerness was evident.

"Anyway, let's welcome this gentleman as our new team member." The hall erupted in obligatory claps. The newcomer kept his bags in one corner, and came towards our table where the empty chair was waiting for him.

"Mr. Dharmarajan," Suri continued, "I just asked them all a question. Let's see if you have the answer."

"Of course, if it is related to being an hotelier, I definitely will," he smiled confidently.

On asking him the same question, he took a deep breath and began, "When people of the old world sacrificed their families, friends, and happiness, we called them *Rishi Muni*. In today's generation, we call them hoteliers."

His answer shocked everyone in the room. Khurana could not stop laughing, and fell off his chair. One by one, all the managers started laughing. Of course, it was meant to be taken as a joke, but Suri's face had turned red.

"What is this, Joy?" Suri thundered. The hall became silent all of a sudden. We all held our breath - what would happen next? "How can you make a joke on hoteliers like this? We are all hoteliers here," Suri rambled on, clearly hurt.

"I am not joking, boss. I am also an hotelier like you all. I am just stating a fact," Joy replied. "Facts like working more hours than required. No holidays. No personal life. Like we exist only to keep others happy and solve their problems. We keep others happy, but aren't happy ourselves. No sooner have we solved a single problem, than a second problem arises. An hotelier's life depends on a hanging sword that can come and cut our neck anytime."

Mr. Suri went red in the face. He quickly finished his bottled water in one gulp, and left the stage.

The introductions had finished.

Chapter 2

I was avoiding Joy after the meeting. Twice he came to me, trying to shake my hand, but I ignored him.

"Why are you ignoring him like this? We must work together. We can't afford to be like this. You are in Front Office and he is in Housekeeping, the closest departments of this hotel," Shantanu tried to convince me.

We were all waiting outside the hall for the HR's assistant to give us our accommodation keys. After a long time, Khurana's assistant finally came with a list of names, and a bunch of keys. The management was providing accommodation to all of us. Everyone started shouting at him together, for their room allotment.

We read the name on his lapel – Bheem Singh – a slim, dark complexioned man with greasy black hair. "Shut up!" he shouted, "Do not behave like school kids! You are not kids, and I am not your teacher. So don't you start clamouring or you'll end up having to sleep on the beach!"

"Give us the room keys. We've been here since morning, and we are all exhausted. And don't try to be over smart, this is your job," Joy jumped in.

Bheem pretended to not have heard him. "Don't talk too much and listen carefully," he waved a hand to calm the ruckus, "We have divided all the flats according to their names. We have Club House, Merteen House, Versoli house and Valenki Villa. You can choose your room as per its availability."

"Club House," me and Joy said together. Just the flatmate I didn't want! Joy looked over to me and smiled. "No, no, I want another accommodation!" I cried, looking at Joy.

"There's only one last room available. If you want it, take it. Or go look for an accommodation yourself," Bheem replied, still looking at his list. "All names and staff rooms have been allocated by the senior management. Manav, Joy and Rudra - you three will stay at the Club House," he counted us on his fingers.

This was unbelievable. I was going to have to stay with Joy and Rudra! How horrible! Two of the biggest idiots I'd ever met! My life was going to be hell. With no other choice remaining, he handed us the keys. I looked at him for a few seconds. The chef was also going to be staying with us for a few days, until his family arrived, after which he'd be moving to another flat.

"Hey, give me Valenki Villa, please! The room must be as good as its name!" Rudra requested.

Bheem caught hold of his ear and said in a low voice, "Valenki Villa is reserved for girls coming from Uttarakhand, not for duffers like you."

At this, all the boys looked at Bheem, some of them asking him the names of the girls and the location of their accommodation. He was not going to tell this very easily.

We picked up our stuff and put it in the staff vehicle. We had the occupants of Club House, Marteen house and Versoli house sharing the ride with us. It was one of the best moments of my life. With so many new faces, some of who were freshers like me, and some with good experience. We were a mix of all.

Finally, after a twenty-minute drive, we reached the Club House. It was a two-storeyed bungalow, surrounded by greenery. The construction of which looked straight out of the 1950s - natural colour on the outside, chandeliers hanging from the ceiling, with an entrance like a Maharaja's *haveli*, and two huge doors. There were no other houses nearby, except one white bungalow around 500-meters away.

"He's brought us to a jungle," Joy mumbled.

"C'mon everyone, listen carefully. The management has come up with some rules and regulations for the accommodation."

"Rules? For what?" Joy looked around at us.

"Rule number one," Bheem continued, "Outside friends are not allowed at the Club House, number two - no drinking allowed in the Club House, number three - no one will enter the Club House after midnight, number four - no fighting in the Club House. And finally," he spoke a little louder, making sure we understood, "No girls allowed in the Club House. No sisters, no friends, no cousins allowed. If anyone is found disobeying these rules, the management has the right to terminate him without any prior notice." He looked around, silently challenging us to counter him.

"What about a *girlfriend*?" Joy interrupted, feigning innocence. For a minute, both of them looked at each other. "You mentioned sisters, friends and cousins, but said nothing about girlfriends," he added cheekily.

"Shut up! Your girlfriend is also someone's sister, cousin and friend, right? No need to act smart here," Bheem sneered.

"There is nothing around," Shantanu changed the topic.

"The whole world is around this bungalow, Chef!" Bheem replied, "See that bungalow over there?" he gestured towards the white bungalow, a little distance from ours. The bungalow was shining in the hot sun. "The bungalow that you are looking at is Valenki Villa."

All of us went quiet for a second. With our mouths wide open, we stared at it. In that moment, the Valenki Villa was comparable to the Taj Mahal.

"Don't look too much, and don't even try to enter that bungalow." Bheem broke our reverie.

"Is there anything we can do that isn't punishable?" Joy smirked.

Chapter 3

We entered the Club House and found ourselves transported back to the fifties. Antique furniture, old construction. There were two rooms on each floor - Joy, Rudra, Shantanu and I took the rooms on the second floor, accessible from the corner staircase.

"Ooh, nice room!" remarked Joy, "Need some sleep now. Way too tired after a 12-hour-long journey." While Joy and Shantanu lay on their respective beds, and Rudra busied himself arranging his stuff in the other room, I too started unpacking. I could see Joy trying to speak to me again, but I hardly responded to him. He offered me a cigarette from his pack.

"I hate smokers," I spat.

"Those who don't smoke always hate smokers," Joy laughed.

"Oh really, if you already know the answer then why ask me?" I countered.

"You know, all this is part and parcel of being an hotelier. We smoke, drink, and hardly ever sleep. A real hotelier is one who accepts this as a challenge!" Shantanu piped in, taking a drag from the cigarette. As they continued talking, with occasional wisps of smoke escaping their mouths, my phone rang. It was *maa*.

"Hello *maa*," I moved away from the others.

"Where are you? Have you reached safely? How was your journey?" One breath, multiple questions.

"Yes, *maa*. I reached safely. I am in my room now, and I will have food on time," I pacified her. She then scolded me for not having called on reaching.

"*Maa*! I reached in the morning and attended a meeting straight after. I've just come to my room," I replied, tired.

"Yes, he's reached," I heard *maa* say to someone. I did not ask her, but realised immediately who it was. Dad. He was the last person I wanted to talk to, so I said my goodbyes soon, and hung up.

"*Maa*, right?" Joy asked, stubbing his cigarette. I nodded. "You are very close to her, aren't you? Didn't speak to dad?" he enquired.

"Why? Must I tell you everything? Whom I speak to, and whom I don't?" I snapped. He kept quiet. Meanwhile, Shantanu was talking to someone from home in the corner. I could only make out a few Bangla words.

"You don't speak with m*aa*," I pointed out to Joy.

"She is no more." I apologised, genuinely sorry. Shantanu disconnected the call, his white cotton dhoti slipping down his waist. After a struggle, he finally held it in place.

****

Since none of us knew much about the city, we forced Shantanu to cook for us. We took out the old crockery, kept in a small kitchen next to the hall. All the pickles, chutneys and *papads* that *maa* had packed, I brought out. We finally sat down to eat. We opened the piping hot bowls to find fish curry and rice cooked, specially made by Chef Chatterjee.

"Such good food on the first day! Thank you, Chef!" I exclaimed.

"This is a specialty of Bengal," he replied. "West Bengal is famously known as the land of *maach* (fish) and *bhaat* (rice). Bengalis share an irrevocable relationship with these two foods, which are a staple in almost every household." He spoke so fast, I could hardly keep up with what he was saying.

"I cooked in a hurry though, so don't give me bad feedback!" he looked at us, grinning.

"Good or bad, doesn't matter. You cook, and that is more than enough. Also, now that we have such a good friend in Hospitality, we don't need to worry about food anymore!" Joy laughed. I nodded, serving rice.

"Nothing like that okay, our GM is very strict, you know that?" Shantanu said.

"Don't call him sir, let's call him *boss*," Joy quipped.

"He doesn't like it," Shantanu pointed out, "I know him well. We met a few years back, and worked together for a couple of months."

"Bosses anyway don't like anything. They always think they are right, and we are expected to just follow their instructions. If they call the night, day-time, then we need to go along with it. But if it isn't right, why should we?" Joy made a face. "You know what? I never liked bosses."

"You don't know him," Shantanu sighed.

"And he doesn't know me!" Joy chuckled, and turned towards me. "So, what do you have to say?"

"Well, this is my first job. I don't know much compared to you guys, but one thing I'm certain of is that I want to work honestly, work hard and become a successful hotelier. Not for myself, though. The three years of my life that I spent on getting my degree, need to be repaid. I need to help *maa* and dad recover their money." They both put their forks down and stared at me in disbelief.

"Where were you till today, bro? Why did you not meet me before? You are a great man. You are a genius!" Joy shook his head. I remained silent.

"Don't worry, you will be successful in this industry very soon," Shantanu assured me, "And for any kind of help, I am here." I smiled at him in gratitude.

"So you are like the next genius of this industry, right? All bosses tend to like people like you," Joy pulled my leg.

"Why you are so against them?"

"I hate the word - *boss*. Because they hate your sleep. They hate it if you do well. They don't like it if anybody says they are wrong. A boss thinks he is always right. That's why I hate them. You know what? A boss is such a creature, who you will never be able to satisfy, even till your last working day."

"He is right," Shantanu interrupted. I was still looking at Joy.

"You are just starting your career, don't behave like a baby or everybody will take advantage of it. Try to be smart. I will help you with that." I was confused. Was he teaching me the right way, or not?

"Do you know the true meaning of *boss*?" he angled his head towards me and said in a low voice. I shook my head and let him answer.

"The true definition is – Beware of Short tempered Seniors!" he laughed.

"What?" I shook my head in disbelief, supressing a smile.

"If you say this in front of Mr. Suri, he will fuck you!" the Chef gestured wildly, and lost his balance on his chair.

We heard someone laugh on the other side of the door. I angled towards a side, and saw Rudra, who was listening to our conversation.

"What happened?" I asked him.

He started walking towards us, smirking, his patent Baba's *Churan* in one hand. He'd take those tablets over twenty times a day. The result of which, no one wanted to be close to him in college – he was an actual fart machine.

"Having food, guys?" he asked, popping another tablet in his mouth.

"No! Dancing on the dining table!" Joy mocked, scraping his plate clean.

"Fish. Rice," Rudra noticed.

"Have something?" offered Shantanu.

"No thanks, this is my *churan* time," he said, popping another tablet. "I heard you talking about bosses. You shouldn't talk this way, they are like our college teachers. We should respect them too." Rudra emptied the entire bottle in his mouth.

"Have you worked with any of these bosses before?" Joy asked.

"No, but I will be one of them very soon," he replied, walking out of the dining room.

I have always found a way to attract such problematic people in my life. I knew Rudra in college too – he was still the same. Another problem was Mr. Joy Dharmarajan – someone who had created a scene in the meeting hall a few hours back, and was now seated next to me. I would've liked to tell him, 'I am very serious about my job and life. I have a lot of dreams I need to fulfil, but if I stay with you for a long time, I might miss my goals.'

"Hey bro, what happened? Where'd you go?" Joy put his hand on my shoulder. I snapped out of my daydream and shook my head.

"Don't be so serious in life. Try to take everything easy," he said.

"What's easy? Nothing is easy in life," I replied, solemnly.

Joy looked at me thoughtfully for a second, then said, "If the world would appreciate such honesty, every donkey would be seen as faithful." Joy explained to me the difference between hard and smart work. This intrigued me.

"Then you tell me how to work?" I asked Joy, since I did not have as much experience about the various styles of working.

"Well, since you're asking for my opinion, we should work hard 25% of the time, work smart 25% of the time, and the remaining 50% should come out of your passion. Without passion, you can't be successful in your life." Someone who I'd wanted to stay away from a few hours back, was now giving me tips on being successful!

"You are a great man!" Shantanu said in Hindi, folding his hands in the traditional *namaste*.

"You know what the toughest job in the world is?" Joy asked me. I shook my head.

"Keeping a smile on your face," he waited for a second before continuing. "Especially in this industry, you have to keep a smile on your face at all times. Have you ever seen an unsmiling receptionist? They always keep a smile on their faces for the guests, even if they are not happy themselves. You should learn from them! This will help you more," he explained. That bastard brought a little smile on my face. I hadn't laughed since I left home.

This changed my perception about Joy; he wasn't as bad as I'd thought. We could become friends.

"How come you're in this field?" I asked him, taking a sip of water.

Still smiling, he began, "After graduating, I had no other choice left. I'd been trying my own business with friends during college, but it failed. I didn't try again. They said, 'If you are failing in everything else, you should join hospitality.'"

"Oh, yes!" Shantanu jumped in, "80% of failures from other fields are in hospitality, because this industry makes a winner out of them."

"Were you a failure too?" I asked Shantanu.

"I am the only man in my family. Before I could complete my Hotel Management degree from West Bengal, I unacceptably, became an hotelier." After a nano second of silence, he continued, "But I am happy today! I reached here after years of struggle." So this is what the life of an hotelier looked like.

"So, you don't have a degree, then?" He nodded.

This was a surprise to me. It got me thinking. Shantanu had an experience spanning 10 years, with 3-years' worth IHM degree. As for me, a graduate with a 3-years' worth degree, after spending 4 lakhs, I joined as a Management Trainee. The person next to us was just a normal graduate, but he became a manager purely out of experience. How was there such a big difference between him and me? I asked him how he got his break.

"I'd been waiting for 2 consecutive days," he replied, "Waiting in queue for an interview. I was rejected by ten interviewers. I had to visit more than 50 hotels to get a job." Ten years of frustration was evident on his face. "It is not important to get the job; what's more important is how you can prove yourself in front of such talented, experience people." He took a deep breath. "I believed in myself. I don't think any degree is required to be a successful person, you can create a way by yourself also."

I started comparing myself to Joy. After graduating he joined this field, and after ten years he'd become a manager. There was a big difference between us. Even without wasting three years and lakhs of rupees on an IHM degree, he'd achieved a lot. Was there luck behind his success? Or was it simply a result of hard work? I was confused. Did I waste three years to get a degree? Did I waste my dad's money? Or was it just a wrong decision?

"How did you decide to become an hotelier?" Joy asked me now.

I chuckled at his timing. What would I have said, was it my decision? Or did I follow a friend's advice? My dad was against my decision, and yet I joined IHM. He'd wanted me to join his business after graduating, but I'd refused to do that.

I waited for second and said slowly, "It was a decision made by Mahatma Gandhi's three famous monkeys. Don't say bad

(Rohan, the doctor friend), don't listen to bad (Krishna, the lawyer friend), and don't see the bad (Sameer, the engineer friend).

"What?" they both shouted together, stunned.

Chapter 4

A Few Years Back

Rohan, Krish, Sam and I were a group of best friends. We'd spend all our time together. Our families always assumed we'd do nothing in life. Especially my dad, who was against my friends from the word go. He never liked them. But when you're young, you don't want to lose your friends at any cost. All three of them hailed from middle-class families. Rohan's father was a doctor, Krishna's brother an engineer, and Sameer's mom, a lawyer.

Much like other Indian families, their families were the same. Their parents wanted them to follow their path. But we can't all be the same. Everyone has different dreams about what they want to be, but nobody wants to listen. No parent wants to understand. They expect us to sit tight and listen as they plan our lives for us.

After graduating, we were faced with a big question. *What's next?* On one hand was the happiness we felt on having graduated with great marks, and on the other, anxiety about our futures.

****

Ever wondered what it feels like when your friends come up with an idea for your collective futures, when you're fast asleep at night? This was the first time that I was experiencing something like this. Rubbing my eyes, I looked at the clock on the wall.

What were they doing now? I stumbled to the window and saw Rohan, Krish and Sam trying to enter the house. I mimed at them, asking them to wait.

"What happened so late at night? Is everything okay?" I asked, worried.

"Nothing is okay, that's why we came here!" Sam replied.

"Oh, really! What happened?"

"We've got an idea for our futures," Rohan said.

"Idea, at this time?" I shook my head, "I think you guys are taking life really seriously."

"Yes, we are," they said together. Rohan continued, "After finishing studies, everyone starts dreaming of the things they can be - some people wish to join the Indian Police Services, some think of becoming a doctor or an engineer, but we will do something different. They say, if you want to create history, you have to think bigger and think differently." I was dumbstruck. Was this really an option?

"What it this *something different*?" I asked. If they had a way of getting out of the routine fields, I wanted to know!

"Can you please tell me, what this 'something different' is?" I repeated, impatient.

"Let's take admission in IHM," Sam said.

"What? What is IHM?" I'd never heard of it before.

"Yes, IHM." Rohan nodded.

"Yes, we will take admission in the Institute of Hotel Management, and become successful hoteliers!" Krishna grinned. "It's the perfect place for people like us. There are tons of different courses available." We'd just graduated at the age of twenty, and now they wanted to study more! By the time we'd finally start settling down, we'd be nearing twenty-five. This was all too confusing.

"What are you thinking? See this," Rohan flipped open a magazine he was carrying. The front cover flaunted a good looking manager with a headline that read – 'When hospitality equals Success!'

"Brother, just listen," he urged, "There is good scope of work in this field. A lot of people are joining this course, becoming successful and getting posts with high salaries. Some of them are even moving abroad. I think we should give this a shot." Sam and Krish also nodded in agreement.

"Have you asked your family?" I asked them.

"Once we are ready, then we'll discuss it with them. Are we ready?" Rohan looked at all of us. He sighed impatiently. "Listen, don't think too much. It's time to do something, and not to think." He thrust his hand towards us. Slowly, Krish and Sam came forward and put their hands on top of his. I stood staring at them, wondering whether this was right or wrong, whether dad would accept this or not. Sameer took my right hand and kept it on top of theirs.

****

The worst moment for me was when I had to discuss this decision with dad. Of course, it wasn't only me; three of my friends were also involved. Dad seemed no better than Hitler, during his rages. He was in his bedroom, getting ready for office, and *maa* was busy searching for something in the cupboard.

"I've told you a hundred times to keep my things ready. Now I can't find my tie!" he screamed, as *maa* searched every inch of the cupboard. "I have to attend an urgent meeting with some high profile people, and can't afford to be late!" I entered the bedroom and looked at them. They couldn't see me.

"Dad," I said in a low voice.

"Hmmm?" he replied absent-mindedly, looking into the mirror running his fingers through his hair.

"Actually, I wanted to talk to you about my new career," I hesitated.

"I am in a hurry to attend an urgent meeting. We'll discuss this later." He turned towards me, "But please don't come to me with a new story."

"No dad, I have already taken a decision. I'm just informing you." I stood a little straighter, trying to prepare myself.

"What? What is it?" he held my gaze.

"Dad... dad I...," I stuttered.

"Can you tell me so we can stop wasting each other's time, please?" he started walking towards me, much like a tiger walking stealthily towards his prey.

"Dad I've decided to join IHM for further studies. I'm going to be an hotelier." I hurried through.

"Are you mad?" He looked at me, then at *maa*. "I have built a big business for you, and you want to do Hotel Management now? No! No, you can't!"

"But dad, I want to stand on my own two feet. I also have a dream. Please let me do it? Because I will, with or without your permission." This was the first time I was ever standing up to dad like this, because of which I also got into the biggest argument of my life.

"Shut up!" Dad went red in the face, as he took another step to stand between mom and I. "Your pampering has made him mad!" he said to *maa*.

"Dad please just speak with me," I looked down.

"Look how he is talking to me now," still looking at *maa*. "I know very well why you have taken this decision. If you fail, don't come to me." He glared at me and left.

Even though this conversation shook me up, instead of being dissuaded, it strengthened my decision. Dad had never tried to understand what I wanted. All he'd thought about was how I'd help him in his business after graduating. But what about what I wanted? What about my dreams?

****

"Good morning, Rohan," I smiled, once at our meeting point. "Hey buddy, what happened? We're starting something new in our lives today!" He looked so morose!

"Rohan, is everything okay?" I repeated when he did not reply. "Rohan please, what happened? Say something!" He pursed his lips and shook his head.

"Rohan please, don't be quiet. Tell me what's wrong."

"The thing is," he started, "My father thinks I can be a good doctor. He said I should make a career out of it, instead of becoming an hotelier. My dad being in same field would also be helpful."

I was instantly taken aback. I withdrew my hand from him, shocked. "What? Have you gone mad? It doesn't matter to me what your dad thinks! Tell me what you think!" But before he could answer, Krish strolled in.

"Krish! Thank God you're here. Just look at what he's saying. Has he gone mad? He doesn't want to join IHM with us!" I half-screamed, frustrated. But Krish looked at me blankly.

"Guys, what happened?"

"Listen, I'm so sorry, but I can't take admission with you either. My brother wants me to become an engineer. He thinks I can be a good engineer, and will help me get a good job." Krish said. I was quiet for a second. I was remembering my dad's dislike towards them, when I saw Sam coming towards us. Before he could say anything, I blurted, "Do you also want to say something?" He kept quiet.

"What happened, does your mother want you to become a lawyer too now?" I demanded. He nodded.

I turned around to face them all. "Your father wants you to become a doctor, your brother wants you to be an engineer and your mother wants you to be a lawyer. But did no one think about what I want to be? I fought with my dad for you guys, and now you are all backing out!" I was beyond angry.

"Bro, I'm really very sorry. We didn't think this would create problems for us," Krish said.

"What problems? You've already made your decision. I don't want your apologies now." I removed Krish's hand from my shoulder.

"Listen, there still is one thing we can do," Sam said.

"What is it?" I asked, rudely.

"You go and take admission, move ahead in this field, and we'll follow you after some time," he suggested.

"Yes of course!" Rohan jumped at the suggestion. "I think this is the best for all of us." With this, apologising again, they left.

****

If your girlfriend breaks up with you, it hurts for a while, but you bounce back. But if your close friends do the same, it hurts so much more. And this wasn't just one person, but three people who'd deserted me. I was inconsolable. I'd keep reminiscing about old memories, and thinking about my fight with dad simultaneously. I didn't know where to go from here. *Stop! What are you thinking? Mad boy!* A voice inside my head said.

"I am fed up with all of this," I sighed. "I am all alone, lonely, and sad. I fought with dad for these guys, and they turned their backs on me. Now I can't speak to either of them."

It's okay. It seems hard right now, but all will be fine. What do you want to do? The voice whispered.

"I don't know," I shook my head, defeated. "And please leave me alone."

Yes, you have to be alone. Because you were alone when you came into this world. When you walk in the dark, your own shadow doesn't walk with you. Through this loneliness, will emerge a new perspective. Be patient.

"So, what should I do now?" I asked.

Don't think too much, just ask your heart what it wants, and move ahead!

"My heart doesn't say anything."

I was still for a moment, absolutely still. I looked within just as the voice whispered, *Manav, don't look back. Just keep moving ahead.*

I opened my eyes and looked around. The voice vanished. This was just the sign I needed to forget everything and move on. Life never waits for anyone, and it definitely wasn't going to wait for me.

****

It wasn't easy getting admission in IHM. There were two-three other colleges near Shimla, but I was fed up with the city. Not because of the city's flaws, but because of the friends who'd betrayed me there. Thanks to the voice inside my head, I forgot to miss them.

Maa and dad were in a deep sleep. I slowly opened their bedroom door and took dad's laptop from the bedside table. I closed the door to my room slowly, keeping in trying not to wake dad up or there'd be another fight to tackle.

This was dad's office laptop, and all his passwords were *maa*'s name, so it was easy for me to unlock it. I logged on to the internet and typed, 'Good IHM colleges near Shimla.' Two decades back, people relied on good friends or colleagues for ideas and suggestions. Today, no one had the time to listen to anyone. We're all busy in our own lives. Search engines like Google have replaced people. Ever since the internet has become an extension of ourselves, we've replaced real friends with social media. For me too, Google and the voice inside my head filled the void.

I suddenly saw someone turning the knob on my bedroom door.

"*Maa*, you're still up!" I exclaimed as she entered my room.

"My son is disturbed at 2:00 a.m., he isn't asleep yet, so how can I be?" she walked in slowly, and sat at the edge of my bed. "What happened, *beta*? What's bothering you?"

"What to do *maa*, I really can't understand. I don't want to join dad's business now. I want to do something of my own."

"Don't worry so much. Just do what your heart says. It will always try to show you how to be strong, and will tell you what to do," she held my face in her hands, her words mirroring the voice inside my head.

"My heart tells me to do Hotel Management."

"Then go ahead, don't overthink it." After a pause, "Would you like to have some coffee?" I nodded.

Within the next five minutes, a piping hot cup of coffee was in my hand, and a search result with ten answers in front of me. As I scrolled through the page, I read bits and pieces of all the colleges. Suddenly, out of the corner of my eye, I read *Institute of Hotel Management, in Dehradun.* I clicked on the link. I'd never been to Dehradun before, and had only heard of it from others. A hill station in Uttarakhand, it was around 230 k.m. from Shimla.

The new tab opened, with options like news, images, and videos to choose from. I clicked on images, and a beautiful collage opened, with information on the side. In the last row was an option to know more information about the college. I clicked on it, sipped my coffee, and read.

"The campus provides complete theoretical and practical training specially designed for future hoteliers. This focuses on the profession as it is today, and prepares the students for their futures as hoteliers. The institute provides high class education to

meet international hospitality standards, and works with a group
of talented professionals from across the country, and abroad.
We will be happy to have you join us to experience quality
education in a unique, motivating and inspiring environment,
which will prepare you for a successful future."

Draining the lees from the cup I was holding, I scrolled down
to where the courses were mentioned.

Course	Duration	Fees (Yearly)
1) Diploma in Hotel Management	1 year	INR 1,25,000/-
2) Degree in Hotel Management	3 years	INR 1,50,000/-
3) Bachelors in Hotel Management	4 years	INR 1,80,000/-

There was a note under the course details, saying how
students could join any of these courses after completing
high school. But I was a graduate. Was this going to benefit
me? There was yet another option for me. I could apply for a
post-graduation program.
My next task was to choose the right course. What would be the
perfect course for me? The long duration course looked like a
good option. For graduates, there was an option of opting for the
post-graduate diploma course. As I clicked on it, more information
popped up. This program was known as the B.H.M. course. It was
a regular fully-residential 4 year-long undergraduate program,
divided into eight semesters. During which, students would
have to undertake different sets of theoretical subjects as well as
practical classes. I completed the online application process - the
college would be contacting me shortly.
The night had almost passed; it was 5:00 a.m. There was no
use trying to sleep now. I kept tossing and turning in bed, but
eventually, sleep took over.

****

I was in bed when I heard my phone ring.

"Hello?"

"Hello. Hello. Am I speaking to Mr. Manav Kapoor?" said the person on the other side of the line.

"Yes, speaking," I responded.

"Hello, I am Professor Chandra from IHM College, Dehradun. I am the Dean of the college," he introduced himself.

"Hi, good morning sir, good morning," I said, my voice breaking slightly.

"Very good morning, how are you?" he asked. I replied and asked him the same.

"Good," he said. "We received your admission form for our college. Are you ready for the further processes?"

"Yes sir, I am ready." I was under the impression that my admission process was already complete and I could go join the college directly. "When can I come for the classes, sir?" I was in such a hurry to get started with college.

"Wait, you have just finished the application procedure. Your admission is still pending. You have to complete a few more steps before we can decide whether you can join or not."

"Okay, sir," I said slowly, a little nervous now. "What is the next step? I will complete that as soon as possible."

"Don't hurry. Wait, I will tell you," I kept quiet as he continued. "I am mailing you a letter and sending you a hard copy through post on your given address. Please read it carefully, and appear for your personal interview on the date mentioned in your letter. Please check all the details and be on time. See you soon."

I thanked him and disconnected the call.

When my ex-best friends barged into my house a few weeks ago and suggested me to join Hotel Management, I'd thought it would be an easy task. But it wasn't, as I realized after this call.

****

"Manav! Manav! I heard dad shouting my name. I got out of my bedroom. At the same time, *maa* also came out of the kitchen.

"What is this?" he had a letter in his hand. '*IHM College, Dehradun,*' it read.

"A letter from college has arrived, and nobody's bothered to inform me!" dad started shouting.

"Leave it *na*! Let him do what he wants to, please. We should help him with his decision. We should be happy about it. After all, he is our son. He is *my* son. So, please?" she requested.

"If you want to help him, go ahead. But I will not help in any way, I am not happy with his decision at all. What should I tell the people who ask me what my son does? Mr. Karan Kapoor's son is an hotelier, not a businessman like his father! No. I will accept anything but I will not accept my son as an hotelier." Dad threw the letter and left the room.

I picked the letter up, and quickly ran to my bedroom. Sitting down, I carefully opened the fateful letter.

To
Mr. Manav Kapoor,

*Welcome to the family of **IHM Institute & the Hospitality Industry***

Subject: Admission Letter

You have received this letter since you showed interest in the Institute of Hotel Management, Dehradun. We are glad to welcome you to our family.
Please keep in mind a few steps mentioned below, which are extremely important to undertake before the completion of the admission process. The student must have completed high school, class XII (10+2)

Have you completed the registration procedure?
Are you reading up on current affairs to keep yourself updated
on the events in the world?
Are you equipped and prepared for the group discussion?
Are you ready for your personal interview?
Are you ready to write your own statement of purpose?
Are you sure you have chosen the best professional look?
Are you ready to fulfil your ambition in this exciting industry?
Are you ready to meet talented people from across the world?

Your personal interview has been scheduled for the 25th of
September, 2011 at 10:00 a.m. in the college campus.

Note: Be on time for the interview to adhere to the punctuality
principle of the hospitality world.

Best Regards,

Chandra Prakash Rao
Head Principal of IHM, Dehradun

This was the first time in my life that I was reading a letter
addressed to me, from such a reputed college. I looked at my
reflection in the mirror, and smiled.

Chapter 5

As decided, I reached college on time on the day of my interview. In reality, the college was very different from the pictures on its website. It was love at first sight for me. Surrounded by hills on all sides, the college seemed huge. More than five hundred students from different cities were present for the interview. I understood the importance of Hotel Management after seeing such a huge crowd. A few students were in groups, and a few were alone. Maybe they were all like me - came to college after high school or graduation. But reasons can be different for all.

I was feeling very alone amidst all of them. I checked my name and signed the sheet at the entrance. My name was somewhere in the middle of the list. I was terrified; you could see it on my face. I asked a few students about this interview, but they were giving an interview for the first time too. Everyone was new here, eager to find hope for their futures.

I was dressed like all the others. The dress code was strictly mentioned in the letter. One by one, all the potential students started going to and from the interview hall. Some of them looked nervous, and some seemed happy. This was my very first interview. I didn't know what they would ask me. I was little bit, actually very, disturbed.

Hey there, how are you? God, damn it. My inner voice was back. I could actually hear him chuckle.

Wherever you go, I will be with you. I am a part of you, and will not leave you alone, don't worry.

"I am worrying because you're back! I am already very nervous, don't disturb me anymore, please." I felt silly for talking to myself, but irritated too. "And don't start your lecture here; I'm here for my interview, not for you."

Why are you still nervous? Why are you still feeling lonely? He whispered. *Nothing is permanent in life. Everything will disappear once we stop breathing; everyone will leave you after some time. Only one thing will be with us till our last breath, our confidence. Just trust yourself, don't lose your confidence. Only listen to your hear. What is it saying? Believe me; if you listen to your heart you will never be alone.*

I suddenly felt him disappear. I looked around, but he'd left. I was completely alone.

****

"Manav! Manav! Manav Kapoor!" The security guard announced my name for the third time, standing at the entrance of the interview room. I came from behind ten to twelve students, telling him I was present. He looked at me angrily, from top to bottom, like he wanted to say something but mumbled within instead. He waited for a second and gestured at me to enter.

I entered the room, fixing my tie and wiping my sweaty face. It wasn't the heat, but nerves. The room was silent. An old man, Mr. Rao, the Dean of the college was seated opposite the table. I remembered his name from the letter I had received. He was wearing a cream coloured plain shirt, a black blazer and trousers, and a red tie. Round spectacles sat on his face.

"Good afternoon," I greeted him in a trembling voice.

"A very good morning, gentleman," he smiled.

"Good morning, good morning sir," I corrected myself.

"Please, have a seat," he gestured to a chair. I thanked him and sat down. "Oh! Manav Kapoor. You are the one with whom I spoke on the phone, right?" I nodded.

"If I am not wrong, you are in a huge hurry to join Hotel Management, right?" he asked while going through my certificates. "So, since you are very interested in this course, can you tell me one reason why you want to join?" By asking me this, he put me in a fix.

"No sir, not any special reason for it. I got an idea and I decided to choose this field."

"Oh, so you mean to say Hotel Management is just an idea! Anyone can take advantage of this idea."

"No sir, that is not what I meant...," I stammered.

"You just said so, my dear," he smiled.

"Sir, actually!"

"Yes, go ahead, gentleman."

"Nothing sir," I fumbled.

"Forget it. Let me tell you the definition of Hotel Management. It is very different in reality. Let me explain something to you," he was looking at me like I was an idiot to have come there without a proper reason. He looked at me and continued, "You are wrong, you know? To be a part of Hotel Management you should have a big heart. You should have guts to fight problems. You should have the patience to accept challenges at every step. The course is very tough to listen to, tough to write about and very difficult to understand. Every year more than a thousand people get connected to this industry, and that number is only increasing. Showing our talent and to be present in front of the world, that's the reason people choose Hotel Management. People are making a passion out of it and it has become a successful career path for the new generation. Now do you understand, gentleman? Hotel Management is a passion! not an idea." I nodded. I was not left with any other choice, because of his explanation.

"Can you tell me something about yourself?" he asked.

"I am Manav Kapoor from Shimla. I completed my 12th

grade and graduated in 2nd class, but after graduation the biggest question I had was, *what is next*? I spent two to three months just thinking about what could be next. I wanted to do something by myself. So, I got the idea of IHM."

"Gentleman! This is not an idea...," he began.

"Oh! Sorry, really sorry sir. Passion! From today, IHM is my passion, not an idea." I corrected myself. He laughed. Was he is laughing at me or at my decision?

"Where did you hear about this for the first time?" he asked.

For a minute, I went back to the past. The faces of my ex-best friends started twirling in front of me. *I didn't know about this. You bastards showed me this way! Where have you left me? I will never forgive you. I will kill you bastards if you come in front of me. Come!* I screamed internally.

"Excuse me? Are you okay?" The Dean asked, looking at my disturbed face. I came back to reality. The Dean offered me some water. I took the glass from the table and drank half the glass in one go.

I nodded. "Yes, I am okay. Thank you for the water."

"So, what do you know about hospitality?" he asked.

"Not much more," I replied in a low voice.

"Before you choose any field, you should have more knowledge about it; you should know its pros and cons. The field that you have chosen, think about where it will take you, or where you want to take it. You should know all this very well, otherwise you will fail." The Dean seemed to have decided what I will do in future; he had given me the results of three years of education in the interview hall, without me having to give any exams.

"Sorry to say, Dean..., Rao sir," I looked at his name plate on the table as I'd forgotten his name.

"Sorry for what?"

"How can you assume someone will pass or fail in an

interview? How can you decide whether I will be a success or not in a few minutes? When a child is born, does he or she know the rules of world? Does he or she know who is good and who's not? Does he or she know who their *maa* and dad are? I am just like that baby. I am just entering this world. This world is new for me; I want to be a part of it. Today I am not capable but I want to be. Why can't I do this? Sometimes in life we need to take something to go ahead, why not this? It is an unexpected choice that's come into my life. I want to see where it leads me to, and achieve it. That's my goal." My voice echoed around the empty room. The Dean looked at me like he'd never received such an answer before.

"Really, I want to join," I continued. "I want to make it my passion. I have to fulfil my dreams. Sir, please give me one chance. Please." I stood up and started requesting him with folded hands, almost in tears. He waited for a second while looking at me, and finally broke into a smile.

"In my entire career as a Dean, I have never seen a person like you. I have never seen such interest like yours. I have never seen such confidence in any student. I think you have a bright future as a Hotel Management student. Keep it up. Don't lose your confidence, keep it as it is. Go and live the IHM life, best of luck." I was stunned. I ran out of the hall thanking him profusely, happiness radiating on my face. I was feeling crazy. All around me students were looking at me.

I called *maa* and said, "Hey *maa*, your son has confirmed his admission in college!" She was ecstatic.

"God bless you *beta*," she gave me her blessings.

I stopped running at the college gate. The voice inside my head came alive again. *See, I told you! If you listen to your heart, you will be the solution to your problem.*

I smiled in immense gratitude.

Chapter 6

Present Day

It was our first working day. As usual, some members of the Housekeeping staff were busy cleaning the lobby and the area around it, some of the Front Office staff was busy with guests at the reception, and Shantanu and I were crossing the lobby to attend our morning meeting.

"Good morning, good morning, good morning," I saw one of our hotel staff members wishing everyone as much as possible. I hadn't seen him at the introduction meet. He was moving from one corner to the other, wishing people non-stop. His behaviour was like a salesmans. Aged around thirty-five – forty, not a single hair was visible on his head, much like what a person looks like in old age.

"Who is that?" I asked my reception staff.

"Godwin sir," the receptionist replied.

"That is fine but which department is he from? Stop him! We can't tolerate this type of behaviour in front of our guests. He is wishing people peculiarly."

"Sure sir," the receptionist said and moved towards him.

"Forget him! He is a sales person," Joy said coming from behind me, keeping one hand on my shoulder and the other on Shantanu's.

"Sales person! So what?"

"Sales people always behave like this. Ignore him."

"He is from the sales team. Leave it. What he is doing is correct," the receptionist stopped himself after listening to the Chef.

"I don't understand. If he is from the sales team, why is he behaving like this?" I asked, trying to get more information.

"Lots of work pressure, less sleep and never achieving the month end target," Shantanu explained. I wasn't convinced.

"Look at his head, all gone. Not a single strand of hair left," Joy pointed to his head.

For a minute, I was confused about his behaviour. I left it for the time being though, because we were getting late for the morning meeting.

"Oh! I forgot my diary in the office. I will be back in a minute. Please wait for me," Godi said to us and ran to his office. Shantanu and Joy laughed at his behaviour and I looked at them and smiled, as we moved towards the meeting room.

Everyone was already present before us, except for Suri and Khurana sirs. As the given time was 09:30 a.m., everyone had reached fifteen minutes earlier, to attend the very first morning meeting.

A 20 by 30 square feet room, with a clean, shining wooden wall with yellow coloured LED lights in a box on the ceiling, clashed greatly with the hall's walls. There was a long table in the middle of the hall. Exactly above the table, was a translucent chandelier with small crystals, giving the room a lavish look. All the managers' chairs had been placed around the table, with Suri sir's chair in front to see us all easily. This is where most of the bosses like to be seated, because they want everyone to listen and look at them when they speak.

"Good morning, everyone. Sorry for being late." Khurana sir entered the hall, moving towards his chair faster than an express train. When he realised Suri sir was not in the meeting room, he slowed down. He sat down, smiling at me and Joy, fixing his tie. I smiled back.

"Don't smile too much," Joy mumbled into my ear.

"Why? You have a problem with me smiling also now?" I replied in the same tone.

"I don't have any problem with your smile, but you know who you are smiling at, right? He is from the Human Resources department; you know what Human Resource means?"

"Please don't start with your *gyaan* again," I requested him with folded hands.

"But you have to listen."

"No please."

"You should." He was behaving like instant glue; once stuck between your fingers, then it's very difficult to get rid of.

"Okay tell me," I gave in.

"Human Resource means high risk people, and these people never smile at you without a special reason. They smile only at two instances, one is when they make someone too happy and the second, when they make someone cry."

"What?" I shouted. Everyone looked at us. I gave them all a fake smile to show them nothing happened, and continued, "Why? If someone says good morning, I can't even reply?"

"Yes, of course we should reply! But beware of dangerous people, you are a fresher in this industry, understand people before forming any relationship."

"I have that much sense." I laughed.

"Sorry, I wasn't aware," he grinned.

"For your information, we are at the morning meeting. Please behave yourself and don't try to explain everything to me all the time," I smiled back.

Before, he could say anything, everyone stood up.

"Good morning, sir!" everyone chorused.

Suri sir had arrived. The cacophony of the meeting room had transformed into a silent movie scene in a split second.

"Good morning guys," Suri sir smiled obligatorily. The very first meeting of the very first day had started with a fake smile. I looked at Joy. *'See, this is the fake smile of fake people,'* he seemed to be saying with his eyes.

"If you guys are done looking at each other, can we start our meeting?" Suri sir looked at us.

"Yes! Yes sir, we can! Good morning sir," I replied, somewhat fearfully.

"Thank you, gentleman," he replied.

"Okay, before you all start working with me, let me tell you something more about myself. As of now we've just come to know each other through introductions, but apart from that, the most important thing is, we have to work together. Something might match or not but between two hoteliers the work should always match. Your working style should be a match, and most importantly, you should know what my requirements and expectations are." For a second he stopped himself and looked to us before continuing, "As a General Manager, I have some of my own rules, along with those of the company. These I have been following since my first job as a General Manager, and I feel that every manager of mine must know about every rule. The rules are mandatory for you, as well as the other staff. Rules are rules; there will not be any compromises with the person who breaks them. If you have any queries, don't stop me in between. After I finish, you can put your query in - but it must be meaningful.

If anyone has anything to discuss, please," he motioned and looked to us. We were totally quiet for a while. He continued looking at us, "Nothing?"

We were all quiet.

"Okay, so let's move ahead," he opened a diary and started explaining the rules, and we all quietly concentrated. "Rule number one, morning meetings will be held at 09:30 a.m. sharp on all working days. Daily activity will be discussed in these meetings and it's mandatory for all managers to be present. Everyone should be punctual, for delays will not be accepted, except for during emergencies," he looked towards Khurana sir and said, "Note down all activities of every manager." He turned to our side, "Please keep in mind, your activities and performance might affect your appraisal. It depends on you and how you want your appraisal to be. Only you will be responsible for it.

Rule number two, Operation Service meetings will be held on every Wednesday at 03:00 p.m. All weekly activities and major issues will be discussed in this meeting. The reason for this meeting on a weekly basis is, for example if any work was given to you at the first meeting it should have been completed by the next one. We will all be ready for the next week's achievements and it will kill our laziness as well. We will be fit and fresh to go ahead." "Does anyone have any questions?" he stopped to ask, as if we had the guts to speak to him during the meeting.

"No sir!" two or three managers replied, the rest busy writing down the rules.

"Rule number three," he continued, "Each and every staff member of this company is responsible for all the good and bad things which will happen on the premises. Everything on the premises belongs to our company; it is every individual's responsibility to keep all things safe and secure."

"Rule number four, increasing the company business. It's not only a sales person's or my job, it's everyone's. So before we think what this company's value is, let's understand our value first. Everyone in this meeting room is with good experience from different reputed hotels, and good knowledgeable IHM colleges. This is the most valuable thing for an hotelier, so put all your hands together to grow along with the company. From my perspective, a manager's value is in lakhs, and if you all put your heads together then our value will increase. If our value increases then surely the company's value will also be on top at all times."

"Rule number five. All managers' leaves will be sanctioned by me only. I don't like managers bunking or absenteeism. As everyone knows the rules of hospitality, we have a fixed time to come in, but no fixed time to leave at, so please keep in mind we are not government servants to leave our jobs after nine hours only. Complete your work, your tasks for the day, and then leave."

"Excuse me Mr. Suri, I want to say something," Joy interrupted after a long time; I was wondering why he was quiet until now. Except Joy no one had the guts to ask him a question.

"Yes, gentleman," Suri sir said reluctantly. He didn't seem to want to listen, but in the meeting room, the situation couldn't be helped.

"Sorry to interrupt, but this is very important," Joy said.

"Yes, yes, everything is important in this meeting room. Please go ahead," Suri said, impatiently.

"Mr. Suri! A banker does a billion rupees worth business every day, and yet leaves office on time. Engineers with businesses worth millions close on time. All government workers complete their work in nine hours only. Everyone wants to complete their work and finish office on time to reach home and spend some time with family. So, why can't we close our office on time? We also have families, we also have a personal life," as he said this, everyone looked at him, shocked. What was he saying? Especially to Suri sir! Suri, meanwhile was wondering what to say. His pen moving from his left to right hand showed his impatience.

"We are hoteliers! And we work for the private sector," Suri sir replied after a few minutes.

"So what if we are hoteliers? So what if we work in the private sector?" We looked at Joy, shocked.

"What do you want to say?" Khurana sir interrupted.

"We are hoteliers but we're also human beings. And working for such late hours doesn't stick with us. Work is a never-ending process. Interest of a client is important, but so are our families. We didn't study hard and struggle in life to work late nights in office. If we fail in our lives, neither the company nor clients, nor the bosses will offer us a helping hand; our family and friends will." Joy was not ready to stop. All of us were looking at him like he'd lost his mind. Suri's face was steadily getting redder, and yet Joy continued, "Life is not only about work, office and clients. There is more to life. We need time to socialize, entertain, relax and exercise. We should not let our lives become meaningless."

"What the hell is this?" Suri sir was finally losing control.

"Mr. Suri, this is not hell, there are more benefits of leaving office on time," Joy started. "Three benefits of leaving office on time - efficiency, good social life and quality family life. Three downsides for leaving late - inefficiency, no social life and less family life."

"What do you want from me?" Suri sir finally asked Joy, losing his temper.

"Nothing, Mr. Suri. The greatest man in Indian history once said, 'A person who stays late at office is not a hard-working person. Instead he/she is a fool who does not know how to manage work within the stipulated time. He/she is inefficient and incompetent in his work.' I just want to say that we too should learn to manage our work in the given time and should be free for other activities. That's it."

There was pin-drop silence in the room. Joy was taking deep breaths, looking at Suri, and Suri stared back, almost as if he wanted to say something.

"We will think about this. And very soon we will improve it," Khurana sirinterrupted them and stopped the conversation before it created a bigger issue. Everyone remained silent.

Khurana mumbled something and started talking, with Suri sir's permission. "Okay guys, let's move ahead. As we are all new here, it is a must for us to understand and learn more about our brand. Our head office in Zurich will be conducting training sessions for managers from tomorrow for the next three days. I request everyone to please attend the training sessions to understand more about our brand. It is mandatory for all managers. The morning meeting is now over for the day."

****

"What are you doing?" Joy asked. I had started removing my IHM books and clothes from the cupboard.

"I am doing what is right for me," I replied.

"What are you saying? What happened now?"

"If I stay with you for one more day then surely I'll have to return to Shimla. It is better to stay with Rudra instead of you," I said and started taking my stuff to Rudra's room.

"It's okay *bhai*, nothing has happened," Joy said, stopping me between both the rooms.

"Nothing's happened? You start fighting, arguing with the General Manager in the first meeting in front of everyone, and you're saying nothing's happened! I don't think you need your job, but I don't want to lose mine because of you. I had decided not to stay with you on the first day but I don't know how the hell I got taken in. I was mad to not realise what a headache staying with you is!"

"Listen! Listen!" he stopped me again. He took a last drag of his cigarette. I looked at him and the cigarette smoke in disgust. He passed the cigarette to the Chef and continued, "Listen, whatever I said was an answer to his questions, not an argument. See, these bosses are very typical, and very smart. Short tempered, they're like a different kind of creature. A boss' temperature always reaches more than 150 degrees in a second without any reason. And if you get into the habit of listening to them, then you have to listen to them until your last day of work. These bosses are more dangerous than anything in the world. We have to be smarter than them. If you don't stop them at the start, then you're finished. I know these bosses better than you." The huge grin on his face made me angrier. He was taking everything as a joke. "Look Joy, I am here to be a good hotelier, I need some good people to help me. I need people who can teach me good things, unlike you."

"Oh, really?"

I nodded.

"I can help you better than him, trust me," he gestured towards Rudra.

"If you can't teach someone good things then don't teach bad things either."

"I am a fool! I am a bastard! But with whom you are going to stay, what is he? He is just a blank IHM book. He has zero knowledge of this industry. He is like a classroom's black-board. You can write anything on it, read it and later, erase it," Joy pointed out. I looked at Rudra, who slowly was getting worked up after listening to Joy.

"Hey don't crack jokes on my professionalism. Don't judge me by my body language, okay?" Rudra retaliated.

"Oh! Can you tell me what can be done with a blackboard?" Joy mocked him.

"One classroom's blackboard brightens a thousand students' futures." Rudra went up and held Joy's collar.

"And you think you are one of those thousand people?" Joy laughed loudly, thumping his hand on Rudra's shoulder. Rudra's spectacles fell down and shattered. His face became hot, as Joy continued grinning.

"Don't hurt my ego," Rudra said seriously. Joy still did not understand his emotional upheaval, and laughed at him. "Joy. Please don't hurt my ego," Rudra warned. Joy laughed even louder.

Thad! Thad! A loud sound resonated within the Club House. Rudra had slapped Joy. Suddenly, the house became completely silent. Joy stood shocked, with his mouth wide open, glaring at Rudra. Rudra stared back at him, unblinking. Both the Chef and I were looking at them. The fact that I was moving to Rudra's room had started a fight between Rudra and Joy.

"You can do anything, but you can't hurt my ego. This is the first time in my life that someone has done this to me."

"Hey, Rudra," I said softly, keeping my hand on his shoulder. He quickly removed it and stopped me where I was.

"You hurt my ego; you made me doubt myself. Every dog has his day. Don't forget this," Rudra said, and started towards his room, taking the broken pieces of his spectacles with him.

"I will call you back," the Chef said into his phone in Bengali, and joined us. "Hey guys, what's happening?" He was holding on to his dhoti, which was on the verge of falling.

"Shantanu please, you continue with your phone call," I said.

"That was my wife. She cut the call. I can't even talk to her properly with you both fighting in the background. What happened to him?" He looked towards Rudra.

"Ask this gentleman," I pointed towards Joy.

"Shantanu please make him understand. He is not listening to me," Joy said to him.

"I will tell you one fact about hoteliers. If someone is not listening to you and you try to make him understand, he will never understand until someone shows it to him the hard way. Once someone does that, then he'll realise. Don't force him, he will come back in his own time," the Chef smiled sadly.

I collected the rest of my clothes and went into Rudra's bedroom. He had kept his broken spectacle fragments on the bed and was staring at it.

"Rudra! Are you okay?" I asked.

Without a word, he put his finger on his lips, asking me to shut up.

Chapter 7

Training Session

I hadn't spoken to Joy ever since I'd moved to the other room. In the training room, my chair was next to Joy's. I moved it to next to Chef instead. Rudra sat with Joy, with his broken spectacles on. He'd fixed it temporarily for the training. He also wanted to move but all the seats were occupied.

A training session is the most enjoyable learning experience for anyone, especially for hoteliers. In our lives, we undertake training at least once. We hotelier never pass a single day without any form of training. And the most frequent question to be asked in interviews is, 'How much time do you spend on training daily?' There are a lot of things that come under training. Focussing on listening is a part of training. Learning something through someone else, teaching something to someone, correcting the wrongs, all constitute as training. But this training turned out to be even more special for all of us, especially for Joy.

"Hi guys," a beautiful voice entered the hall. Everyone turned around to see who the voice belonged to. A five and a half feet tall lady, with light brown hair, donning a short black skirt as a part of her uniform, was at the door. She was the most gorgeous foreigner we'd ever seen. She walked down the hall to a table nearby, capturing our hearts with every step. Everyone was busy staring at this gorgeous trainer. It seemed like no one had ever seen such a lady before. Rudra was the most excited to see her, with his mouth half-open, eyes unblinking, he stared. Joy closed his mouth and said, "She is our trainer. Don't look at her with lust. Respect women."

"Hey! You shut up! Don't teach me whom to respect. I know this better than you," Rudra snapped, offended.

"Oh, really!"

"Yes, of course."

"I didn't know," Joy sniggered.

"Hello, everyone! Good morning!" she said, in a voice sweeter than honey. All of us replied energetically.

"Oh, thank you so much guys, I like your team work," she laughed happily. Ten to twelve people shouted louder than a hundred people. She didn't know it wasn't team work, but the craze Indian boys had for foreign women.

"How are you all?"

"We are good, how are you madam?" some of us replied.

She smiled, "Well, before we start the training, let me introduce myself. I am Ketaki Salvianes from Zurich, and am here as a trainer for you guys. I will be conducting the training for the next three days. I hope you enjoy it. It will be great if you guys learn from and understand the sessions. As a trainer, I like to speak more. I like to ask more questions. I like to listen to more answers. I like to teach new things and learn new things. If you guys have any questions please don't hesitate to stop me at and ask. I will like it and will be happy to answer." We all had our name badges, and everyone's positions had been printed and kept on each table, to help her understand who was who.

"So, should we start?"

"Yes," we nodded in unison.

Training session – 01, she wrote on the board.

"Let's start the session with a small game," she said and looked to us for approval. "Are you ready?" A few of us replied in the affirmative. There really was no reason to reject a game where we were to play with her!

"Okay, very nice. I will provide a blank paper to everyone. Write down one thing that you like the most and one thing that you don't like about your life. Without showing anyone or discussing with each other, fold it and give it back to me. I will open it on the last day of training and will share it with you all." She handed out small pages to us and we became busy writing. Some of us got done very fast, and some were writing slowly. I got done last. Till then, she was busy watching us, lest someone tried to copy or discuss.

"Is anyone left? Please help me drop all the papers in this box," she carried the box to each one of us, and we all dropped our letters in.

"Thank you so much," she said after reaching her place. "Well, this was just a small part of the training. Let's start the official training with some general knowledge about the hospitality industry. You guys are all from good hotels and colleges, so I hope some of these questions will be easy for you guys. And whoever will give the most number of right answers will receive a special surprise on the last day. Is that fine for you guys?" We kept quiet and started looking at each other.

"Guys, I have a surprise gift for the winner. It can be anything!" she tried to excite us.

We replied together, "We are ready!"

"Okay, let's move on. Which is the world's very first hotel, and when was it built?" She wrote the question on the board and moved towards us. The question was not easy. I don't know about the others, but I'd never come across this question in my three-year degree. Everyone went into deep thoughts and started closing their eyes. Some of them started thinking of their past experiences, and some were searching for the answer in their IHM books. But such a general knowledge answer wouldn't be found in books or history.

"Yes, anyone?" she was expecting the answer from us, but no one had one. "Guys, I am not here just to ask questions. I will require you to answer as well, even if it is wrong. But please say something."

"The Hoshi Ryokan in Japan is the world's first hotel to be built in the year AD 717." After a long struggle, finally Joy answered. Yes, only such a genius could have had this answer!

"Very good! Joy is right! The Hoshi Ryokan is in the village of Awazu, Japan. The world's first hotel was started in AD 717, and the Ryokan has evolved through the centuries. Today the hotel's capacity is a hundred rooms with 450 guests. Today, all the guests are given a garb called *Yukata*, on arrival, which is a part of the traditional Japanese cotton kimono. And the most important thing, this hotel has seen 46 generations of owners. Joy's answer was really good, and this makes him my first winner." Ketaki started clapping for him, and in a minute, we joined along. Involuntarily, my hands also started clapping, and I sat with a small smile. Except Rudra, everyone else had liked the answer.

"Okay! Question number two. What is hospitality?" she wrote this question on the white board as well, and moved to our side. Some of her hair fell on her face, but it just added to her beauty. Instead of thinking of the answer, some of us were lost staring at her.

"I am here for the next few days, you can see me later. Let's get some training!" she laughed. She was looking at us one by one. I was ogling at her with eyes wide open, when she stopped her patrolling and looked at me for an answer.

"Yes, you have something, Mr... Manav!" she read my badge.

"Hospitality is one of the leading industries in the world, which is only growing every year," I said, thanks to what my Dean had explained to me at my interview.

"Okay, good," she said, and moved on to the next person.

"Hospitality is a second home for those who are associated with it," the Chef said.

"Hmmm, very good," she said and looked at Rudra for an answer.

"*Hospitality* is a Roman word. The definition of which is only hard work. This is the place where we can achieve our goals faster, show our talents to our colleagues and be a boss," he completed his answer in one breath and wheezed. He took a sip from the glass on his table. Ketaki seemed to have liked his answer.

"Very good! Very good! How for one question, I am getting different answers, it'll help me understand better. Thank you, guys," Ketaki clapped for him. We did the same, and Rudra sat a little straighter, proud.

"I think you also have something to say. As trainers, we immediately get to know what's going on in the minds of our attendees," Ketaki looked at Joy. Joy was quiet for a second.

"Joy, are you listening?"

He nodded, and began, "Hospitality is home away from home," he gestured, "When people come to stay with us, we make them feel at home. This is hospitality, and it is a bundle of joy. Every person who is connected with this industry knows exactly what happiness is. This is one of the world's best places to meet new people every day. We can work with different kinds ofpeople. We can see their good and bad habits. This is the place that shows us our capabilities. There is no other definition for hospitality." Ketaki became happier than ever.

"Joy, I can see your passion for hospitality and you seem to have good experience as well!" she smiled at him and turned to us. Rudra's face hardened when he saw Ketaki happy with Joy's answer.

"Joy is right. There is no fixed definition for hospitality," she said and smiled. "Okay guys! Jokes and laughs apart, let's come to the point. What are the three most valuable things to keep in mind for your company to grow, and give perfect service to our guests?" She went on to write this on the board too, along with - Management, Boss and Employees.

"Who does what, is extremely important in a company," she explained. "Management is the first point of contact in the company; this includes hiring good bosses or managers for the company, which is the most valuable and important part."

"Bosses – they have the authority to hire their staff, so they should hire good and educated employees who can make their work easy. A boss should be cool, open-minded, positive and motivating."

"Employees – they are the most important for any company. If a company takes care of their employees, they will take care of their customers and guests. If their customers and guests are happy, then automatically the company's business will grow. An employee is more important than management and bosses, because an employee is the only one who comes in contact with your guests and customers every day. So, please understand that an employee is the foundation of a company, and every management member should first think about their employees." Ketaki's way of explaining things was amazing. It included smiling at, and motivating everyone. Joy seemed to be giving her more importance than the training.

"Does anyone have any questions?" Ketaki asked.

"Yes," Joy raised his hand.

"Yes, please," Ketaki motioned.

"If employees are more important than anything in a company, then why are the employees here not valued? Why does this company think of an employee at the very last?" Joy asked.

"No, where do we not value employees?" she looked around at us.

"If you take history as an example, it's always a higher authority who becomes famous, and not the employee. Only a few of them share their success with them. I have never seen any employee on the cover page of a newspaper or a magazine. We should think about them first, if an employee is as important as you say. Why is their value not higher than the management?"

"Are you against bosses?" Ketaki asked.

"No, I am with employees."

"No I think you are against bosses," she argued. "Don't forget, you are also a boss for someone," she smiled.

"I am an employee first," Joy smiled right back.

"Manav! Do you have anything to say about this?" she suddenly turned to me.

"No, no," I said, taking a sip from my glass.

"What do you think, who is more important?" Ketaki asked.

"I think both are equally important," I said. I didn't understand why she'd suddenly moved from Joy to me. Joy always wanted to fight; he always wanted to show people how right he was. Why would Ketaki think I am a friend of Joy's? I am no longer his friend. I wanted to say this to Ketaki, but kept quiet.

I looked at Joy and thought to myself, '*Mr. Joy Dharmarajan. Understand! Not everyone is like you. We have to manage ourselves. If you can't manage yourself then at least don't put others in a fix.*' I wanted to tell this to him in front of everyone, but I controlled myself.

"Now we will talk about guest satisfaction," Ketaki continued. "Guest satisfaction is close to the hearts of every hotelier who has entered this training room. Telephone companies call their customers and take their service's feedback, bankers call their customers and take feedback, but how will we hoteliers ensure that our guests are happy? Can anyone tell me?" she asked us, looking at us one by one expecting an answer. We were quiet.

"Guys, please answer me. We are here for training, and not for watching a horror movie. I don't like silence in the training room, so please don't be quiet."

"Shantanu, you please," she said, looking at him.

"We will take personal feedback from all the guests," he replied.

"Okay, good!" she said, and moved on to the others.

Rudra raised his hand and said, "If our guests are happy with our service, then definitely they will promise to come back again, or they will suggest this place to others."

"Very good," after listening to Rudra, her eyes rested on Joy again. "Yes Joy, would you like to say something?"

"Yes, of course," Joy replied. "If we take feedback from a guest, only a small percentage of them will say good things. Guests always promise to come back, but that happens very rarely."

"Then you tell us, how will we ensure that our guests are happy?" she countered.

"If a guest tips any staff member, that means he is happy with our service. Because this is what generally happens. I think we should recognise guests by this easy way. If we take an example, we also tip waiters based on their service. I think this is the best way to come to know whether a guest is happy or not," Joy said.

Along with Ketaki, everyone in the training room erupted in laughter. Sometimes the things he says are well and good, and sometimes, not so much. Like right now, this was like a joke to everyone. *Really? Was this a good idea?* I was thinking the same. "You mean to say, the ones who don't give tips are not happy with our service," Suri sir interjected. He felt personally attacked. Wondering

"No, that's not what I meant...," Joy started.

"No, you meant it. If someone is not giving a tip, that means he is not happy. Only the one who gives a tip is happy, right? You said it just now. You should not judge a guest by the tip he gives. We are in the hospitality industry, and we should think like hoteliers," Suri sir said.

"Mr. Suri, I am thinking like an hotelier only."

"No, you are not."

"Yes! I am."

"Mr. Suri, I think Joy is correct. Please come and join the training with us," Ketaki interrupted as she sensed the conversation moving towards an argument.

"I would like to meet you in my office after the training," Suri looked at Joy in anger and left. There was pin-drop silence was in the training room, everyone was busy looking at each other. Really! Did he call Joy to talk to him or to screw him over? *'Bosses always call juniors to their office when they've done something beyond their expectations.'* I remember Joy telling me this earlier. *'Mr. Joy, now you will come to know what the value of bosses is,'* I thought.

"I think Joy has a different way of seeing the hospitality industry. Like with every new generation come new ideas and thoughts, these new things will always help us grow and reach greater heights. I always welcome and encourage new ways of thinking. I request Joy to please come join me, and share some of his knowledge and experience," she invited him up to the stage with her. Joy was refusing, but when she forced him, he gave in.

Rudra chuckled and said, "Hey see, he was talking too much

earlier. Now you see what he will say. Anyhow, you took the right decision to change your room. He is useless, he is an uneducated man." I shushed him so I could concentrate on Joy. "Umm," he smiled nervously and started, "When I was a kid, I wished to grow up as soon as possible, and when I did, I wished to become a successful man. They say your dreams can change if you don't solidify them at a small age. As I was growing up, my dreams were taking a different turn every step of the way. I was confused, what do I have to do? And what will I have to be in life? But all my 'what' questions are still where I have left them. One day, I became a part of the hospitality industry. Today, when I look back I don't know what I have lost, but after becoming an hotelier, I have learnt a lot. I can at least say to myself that this is my dream, because whatever I have achieved from here, I wouldn't have reached from anywhere else in the world. I just want to say that this platform is for us to show our talents. It is a great opportunity for us to shape our goals. The work is full of challenges, and what I earn from here can't be explained in words." No sooner had he completed his speech that Ketaki and all the others started clapping. The Chef forced me to clap too, but I was busy thinking about Joy. Whether he was a good or bad person, his behaviour was very risky.

The first day's training session had ended, and everyone started moving from the training room to their respective departments. Joy and Ketaki were walking down the corridor outside the training room. Khurana's assistant, Bheem, came from behind us and said, "Hello Jai, Suri sir is calling you to his office." "Are you Khurana's assistant or Suri's?" Joy roared, "And don't call me Jai. I am Joy! Joy Dharmarajan." He stopped walking and asked Ketaki to move ahead without him. I also moved to the Front Office.

Chapter 8

"How was your first meeting with our dearest boss, Mr. Joy?" the Chef asked, taking a drag of his cigarette. The Bengali lilt was ever-present; sometimes giving his sentences a sing-song tone.

"Good, not bad," he replied, taking the cigarette from Shantanu. "Was it good or did he screw you?" Rudra interfered making a lewd gesture, and we all laughed out loud.

"You, shut up, I will kill you. Disciple of Suri," Joy said to Rudra. Rudra's face turned red. No laughter this time. He kept quiet as Joy continued, "I know who you are. You are a disciple of Suri. I saw you in his office. I saw how you were behaving with him. Don't mess with me," Joy shut Rudra up.

"Leave it! Leave it, don't waste your energy on this fool," the Chef said to Joy, ignoring Rudra. I also was interested to know what happened in Suri's office. After much forcing, Joy started his story.

A couple of hours back.

"May I come in?" Joy asked while opening the office door after knocking. Mr. Suri and Khurana were both in the office, waiting.

"Yes, yes, please come in. Welcome the new generation's great man," Mr. Suri made a big show of welcoming him. Before anything could start, Rudra knocked at the door, accompanied by a waiter. Both of them entered with Mr. Suri's permission, carrying some snacks and refreshments. Keeping the tray on the table, the waiter left the office, yet Rudra stayed.

71

"Would you like to have something more, sirs?" Rudra asked both of them. Khurana looked at Suri asking him if he wanted anything, as if they hadn't eaten a single bite since the morning. "Some hot *pakoras* with ketchup and green chutney would be great," Suri said.

"Sure, sir. Why not? Definitely. When would you like to have it, sir?" Rudra asked. Mr. Suri looked at Joy as if trying to figure out how much time he'd be in his office. "Send it in the next thirty minutes." Rudra left, thanking him profusely, eyeing Joy.

'*Bastard you never asked us for food. How are you asking him?*' Joy grunted.

People in Human Resources always try to be ally-pally with the bosses; they always try to maintain a relationship with them. It helps them clear their work faster compared to others, and most importantly, it helps them keep their jobs safe. The bosses also like to keep people from Human Resource close, as they come to know the good and bad things about all the employees.

Joy sat quietly, watching the scene unfold, as Mr. Khurana started loosening his tie to have some snacks. He moved the plate with the snacks towards Joy, and gestured at him to take something. Suri instantly took the plate back and looked at Joy as if asking him whether he'd come to the office just to have snacks. Joy chuckled. He felt like going to the restaurant to order some more snacks for them.

"What do you think of yourself?" Suri started.

"I think of myself as Joy! Joy Dharmarajan, Housekeeping Manager."

"Oh, you are such a genius, aren't you? Don't be over-smart in front of me. I know exactly who you are, Joy Dharmarajan," Suri paused before taking a bite from the puff on his plate.

"Don't forget, I am your boss."

"I know that,"Joy mumbled.

"What? What did you say?"

"Nothing, nothing, Mr. Suri," he emphasised each word.

"What is this, 'Mr. Suri'? Every time you call me that. Can't you call me *sir*?"

"Mister is always better than sir and more respectful. The world uses this word so why can't we? Respect should be from the heart, Mr. Suri," Joy replied, knowing full well Suri was arguing with him. Suri looked at Joy first, like he wanted to say something but controlled himself and looked to Khurana instead.

"What does this mean?" he asked again like he did not understand.

"This means, Mr. Suri, that if anyone is respecting you, it must come from the heart and not just as a formality. Most people pay their respects for the heck of it, but keep abusing you from afar."

"What do you think about your bosses? You think we are fools? Or are we mad?" Suri spat, rudely.

Joy kept quiet, much to Suri's annoyance. "Hello, I am talking with you, answer me," he said, banging on the table.

"No, I've never thought like that," Joy replied.

"Then, what do you mean? What do you think about your bosses?" Suri stuttered as his rage came dangerously close to spilling out. Meanwhile, Khurana was trying to fit a whole sandwich in his mouth at once, spilling some tomato and cucumber slices on the table. "Sorry," he mumbled to a disgusted Suri.

"Don't stand like a statue, I need an answer, Joy Dharmarajan," Suri said, taking half a sandwich from the plate. Joy remained silent.

"I said don't be quiet! Tell me what you think of me. I am your boss, so what do you think about your boss?" Joy still remained quiet.

"Hello! Are you listening?" Suri said, much louder.

"Yes, yes boss, I am listening," Joy finally said.

"Don't just listen. Give me an answer. What do you think about your bosses?" Suri looked like he'd erupt at any moment.

"Bosses? Mr. Suri, bosses should be like captains of a cricket team," Joy said with a faint smile.

"So according to you, I should start playing cricket in the hotel and become the wicket keeper!"

"That's not what I meant, boss. It doesn't matter where you're a boss, but your attitude and behaviour should not be like the others. I said a boss should be like a cricket team's captain, since he must get involved only at the last minute. A boss is one who takes the right decision at the right time, and most importantly, someone who enjoys success from behind the stage. He gives a whole lot of benefits to the team, but he is worth more than the teams." Joy knew what a big risk he was taking, talking to him like that. Khurana's half closed eyes were on him continuously.

"Are you listening to what he is saying?" Suri turned to Khurana.

"Listen Joy," started Khurana, but before he could continue, Joy stopped him and said, "The Human Resource Manager is like the Umpire - no one can and should cross him. His decision should be final."

Khurana closed his mouth and slumped back. "What nonsense are you talking?" Suri shouted.

"I am not talking nonsense."

"Shut up!" his fist banged on the table and echoed across the room.

"Fifteen years of my career and no one has ever argued with me this way! And you, someone who's joined just a few days back, are standing in my office trying to play cricket with me!" he bellowed.

"I just...," Joy began.

"Get out of my office, bastard! You're mad!" Joy waited there for a moment, and looked at the both of them.

"What are staring at us for? Waiting for us to start playing cricket? Get out of here or I will kill you! Khurana send him out of the office right now," Suri screamed. Khurana looked at Joy and motioned at him to go out. Joy moved towards the door, and turned back to facethem again.

"Get out!" he was so angry he could barely breathe. Joy opened the door and left.

Chapter 9

The Present

Laughter, fights and jokes. Life was going smoothly for everyone in the Club House. Sometimes, our Martin House colleagues would come and join us. We'd all go to dinner together, to a local *aunty* nearby, where we'd get home-made food at rupees 50 each. It became our regular dinner joint, only to be missed when Shantanu would cook in the Club House. Godi was a resident of Martin House, but we'd all spend time in the Club House only. Some were new, and some were experienced guys. Joy became like a teacher to everyone and we were all trying to learn something or the other from him.

Everyone had a different story, so if I had to count, there were innumerable stories in the Club House. Some of them shared their love stories, some their college stories, and some shared their work experiences. All of us were busy sharing some part of our lives with each other.

Joy was busy on his phone, laughing. His phone was beeping non-stop, and he was replying constantly.

"Guys, let's go to Alibaug beach," Joy suddenly stood up and said.

"What happened to him?" Godi asked looking at us. "Are you okay?"

"Do you want to come or not?"

"Of course, yes," Godi replied.

"So, keep quiet and come."

"Yes, I am ready."

"Chef, are you ready?"

"I am always ready man," he laughed. We'd started going to the beach every alternate day.

"Sorry, I don't want to come," I said when Shantanu looked towards me. "Hey, c'mon man. Don't come up with stories now. We have to go," he said.

"No, please."

"Don't take us for fools, and don't try to become like Suri or Rudra, the greatest people of our industry," Joy snorted.

"Joy please?" I implored. They didn't listen, and took me along with them.

The distance from the Club House to the beach was around thirty minutes by foot, with a local market, a temple, a mosque and a bus stand in between. We reached the beach in the evening, when the tide was high. The waves were hitting the coast at enormous speeds. The sun was half-hidden behind a fort in the middle of the sea, waiting to set. Because of this, the sea and the area surrounding it, was drenched in yellows and oranges. It was beautiful. Ever since we'd come to Alibaug, this was the most colourful evening we'd experienced.

There were some small stalls selling *pani puri, bhel, pav bhaji,* and the likes around, absolutely crowded. Everyone on the beach was soaking in the colours of the evening. Some of our hotel employees and couples were at the beach too. After a day of hard work, everyone liked visiting this place for some peace.

"Hey guys, it's too late!" a girl's voice called out. We turned around to see Ketaki, who seemed to be shining as the last rays of the sun hit her. I wondered how she'd come to know where we were.

She headed over to Joy and hugged him. "How are you, Joy?"

"I am good, and you?"

"Very good," she said. "Hey guys, how are all of you?" She finally acknowledged us. I remember how at the Club House, Joy was chatting with someone on the phone and had suddenly stood up and insisted on coming to the beach. Ketaki was the reason behind it.

"Hello Ketaki," I said, a little put off.

"Hey Manav, what happened? Are you okay?" she read my face.

"Nothing, I am okay," I composed my reaction instantly.

"Don't worry, I am only a trainer inside the hotel. Outside, I am a friend. Let's enjoy this beautiful evening together. There's nothing quite like the beaches in India. So, shall we?" she asked.

"Yes sure," I replied with a smile.

"Let's walk on the beach," she said moving towards Joy. We came in step just behind them.

"Are they dating each other?" Rudra interfered, shocked.

"No, she thinks of him as a brother and they're both discussing the stuff siblings discuss. You really are daft. You don't have any sense. She is a beautiful girl, and he is a champ. Of course, they are dating," Godi replied.

"Shut up, he is not a champ."

"So, you tell me, who is he?" Godi asked.

"Leave it."

The colours of the evening, the occasional spray of water from the ocean, and the sand under our feet - this was soon becoming an unforgettable moment, especially for Joy and Ketaki, the newest love birds. Slowly, Ketaki was trying to hold Joy's hand, and Joy was trying to do the same. We looked at each other awkwardly, and one by one, started changing our direction. In a little while, they were both far ahead of us. Joy looked back, but saw no one there. He noticed Shantanu and me at a distance. We left them to enjoy the evening alone, and gathered together, all bachelors to one side. Joy and Ketaki's love story had officially started, and I couldn't help but be jealous of them.

****

"Is this the time for dinner? This is not your house," *aunty* shouted at us when we reached her shack at 11:00 p.m.
"Actually *aunty*, we were at the beach with our new friend, so we got late," Joy said, calming her down, and moving towards Ketaki. "*Aunty* please meets our friend. Ketaki, this is *aunty*, and *aunty*, this is Ketaki."
"Hello *aunty*, how are you?" Ketaki asked politely.
"Oh, *gori mulgi!* I don't understand English," *aunty* replied, looking at Ketaki and grinning. "Come inside. This is the last time," she warned, "If this happens again, then you look for another aunty to get your food."

The loveliest Marathi spread was served in front of us. There were more than ten different dishes in front of us, adding to our confusion as to what to eat first. As it was not a restaurant, and aunty was running a small business within her house, we had to eat sitting on the floor. However, this was a first for Ketaki. "Nice dish! I really liked it," Ketaki said as we started eating. This time *aunty's* smile changed.
"Do your parents know about this girl?" *aunty* asked Joy, then looked at me and in turn, Shantanu. "Does your wife know?" Shantanu stopped mid-bite, and looked at her. We were completely quiet, out of respect for the care she'd taken of us. "*Aunty*, she is just our friend. Nothing else," Joy replied, breaking the long silence.

"I know what type of a friend she is. Coming from the beach this late at night and having food in my house. At this time, almost half of India is fast asleep and you say she is just a friend."

"Chef, give me your wife's number. I want to talk to her," she turned to Shantanu.

"Aunty, I was sleeping in my room when these guys came and woke me up for dinner. I don't even know who she is." Shantanu looked at me.

"*Aunty*, the food is too good. I love it. Really, thank you so much," Ketaki smiled.

"What did she say?" *aunty* asked Shantanu, as she didn't understand English.

"*Aunty...*"

"What *aunty*? Tell me what she said in English!"Aunty said louder.

"*Aunty*, she said the food is very good and she loves it," he explained in Hindi.

"She said a lot of words in English, and only this much has been translated." We were quiet.*Aunty* looked towards Ketaki and us.

"Should I give her some poison?" she said in Hindi, stressing her words. Ketaki look at aunty and turned to Shantanu for translation. "Tell her," she said to him, but he looked at us. "What are you looking at them for? Tell her!" she repeated.

"Would you like to have dessert?" Shantanu asked nervously, since he obviously couldn't ask her the truth.

"Yes, of course," Ketaki replied, happily nodding her head.

"Oh God, she's gone mad!" *aunty* exclaimed, "Have you fallen in love with someone?" she asked Ketaki directly.

"Yes," Ketaki replied, without understanding what was being asked. Shocked, we looked at them.

"With whom has she fallen in love?" Joy and I concentrated on our food, as Shantanu still stared at her.

"Chef, is it you? Give me your wife's number. I want to talk to her right now," *aunty* repeated.

"No, no *aunty*. It's nothing like that. You are misinterpreting what she said."

"I am misinterpreting? She is the one coming from the beach with you guys at midnight, ready to have poison for the sake of love, and I am the one misinterpreting things. Keep this in mind. Your family thinks you are doing something for them, but you're shattering their dreams. And you, Chef, you are married, right? Still you like to do such things?"

"*Aunty...*"

"Shut up. What *aunty*? This is the last time I'm serving you. If I see you guys again, then see."

We winded up soon, and moved out.

****

The second day of training was pretty normal, since not much training took place. By noon, everyone was bored, tired and sleepy. We moved out of the hotel in the evening, on the coach meant for employees.

After the training, both Joy and Ketaki were missing. We looked all around but couldn't find them. On reaching the Club House, Shantanu was getting ready to cook dinner, and Rudra and I were helping him. I ran to open the door after the doorbell rang continuously.

"Good evening Manav!"

"Ketaki!" I mumbled.

"Hello Manav, how are you?" she asked.

"Ketaki! You!"

"Yes, I am Ketaki," she grinned.

"But..."

"But what, Mr. Kapoor?" I looked behind her to see Joy walking towards the door.

"Joy, what is this? What the hell is going on?"

"What hell?" he grinned, "Ketaki, this is Manav. Manav, this is Ketaki."

"Of course I know her!" I snapped, "You know very well that girls are not allowed in the Club House."

"Where is the girl? She is our trainer and we are here to be trained," he said, as they both entered, smiling throughout. I called out to Shantanu.

"What happened? Why are you shouting?" he asked, coming to the door.

"*Ore baba! Ei sundar meye ki bhabe ekhane elo!*" he exclaimed. Ketaki laughed at his Bengali.

"Hello Chef, how are you?" Ketaki asked.

"Hello, *ami bhalo achi, tumi?*" Shantanu said in Bengali, before realizing no one could understand him, and repeated himself in English.

"Chef, what are you doing? You know very well girls are not allowed in the Club House. It is against the rules, right!" I said, thinking about Bheem's rules.

"Hey, shut up! This lady's come here for the first time and you are talking nonsense," Shantanu reprimanded. Thanks to our loud voices, Rudra came out as well. I thought he'd do something to make her leave.

"Hello Rudra, how are you?" Ketaki asked him too, as he stood looking down. He didn't reply and went back inside.

What was going on? I wanted to stop Ketaki from entering. I wanted to tell her to go away. This accommodation was only for bachelors. What was Joy doing, breaking the rules? And no one was telling him off! Shantanu was taking Joy's side, but what happened to Rudra? Why weren't Shantanu and Rudra realising what Joy was doing was wrong, and must be stopped?

"You don't worry, I will handle it," Joy said, shaking my shoulder.

"Why not to worry? We all should be very worried," I said, removing his hand.

"Really! I will kill your worries. You go eat your food." Ketaki entered the kitchen and started helping Shantanu. During their conversation, Shantanu used some Bengali words which no one understood, but they all laughed nonetheless. I stood like a statue, watching quietly.

"Manav, please don't be quiet. Say something," Ketaki said from the kitchen, looking at my stony face.

"You please leave from here, and then I will speak," I said, standing in one corner, requesting her. "Ketaki, please, at least you should understand. You are a trainer. You know the rules better than us. Please understand and make them understand too, whatever is happening is not good for all of us, and no one is listening to me."

"Don't say anything. Everyone will say the same to you," Joy said, pulling out two large beer bottles with four glasses. I stood shocked.

"What is this?" I asked.

"This is an energy drink. Would you like some?" Joy offered.

"You shut up! You don't say anything. This is all happening because of you," I said harshly.

"Hey, calm down. Don't be angry. This is just an energy drink. Finish one glass in one sip, then sleep and feel the magic."

"Guys, at least understand *now*," my face scrunched up, like a crying baby's.

"What happened? Why are you so angry?" he asked.

"What is this, Joy?" I pointed at the bottles.

"This is beer, and we are all a part of this. You know, beer is the third most consumed beverage in the world after water and tea," Joy said, taking a bottle in hand.

"What is happening here? Just because I am not saying anything doesn't mean you will do whatever you want! Ketaki, Ketaki!" I shouted.

"Yes guys, I am here. Snacks are ready," she brought out a plate from the kitchen.

"You are too good," Shantanu grinned, looking at the beer. Chefs have always liked to drink. They become thirsty just looking at alcohol.

"What happened, Manav? Why are you so tensed? Just relax and forget the outside world. Come and chill with us," Shantanu said.

"Joy, please. Don't do this, please!" my voice was breaking.

"Hey Manav, don't worry everything will be fine, all is okay," Ketaki said.

"Nothing is okay, Ketaki. Please try to understand. We will all be in trouble. Please don't drink here, please! You don't know Rudra. He is not a good guy. He will tell someone everything, and I will lose my job! Please," I begged them but they didn't listen.

"If Rudra drinks with us, will you?" Joy challenged me. I knewRudra was not a drinker. In our three years together at IHM, I had never seen him touch alcohol, much like me. He was from a very strict and reputed family. His entire family was against alcohol, and was vegetarian. As for him, he was definitely avegetarian. He wouldn't even share water with a non-vegetarian.

"Mr. Rudra, can you come here please?" Joy called. He came and stood in front of us, his head down, nervous. Joy filled the same quantity in all the glasses. Ketaki picked one glass up, the second glass was taken by Shantanu, and the third by Joy. A fourth glass was left on the table.

"Would you like to drink?" Joy asked Rudra, looking at me. I looked at Rudra for a moment, then looked at Joy.

"Joy, he doesn't drink," I said.

"Can you be quiet, please?" he glared at me and moved towards Rudra. "Would you like to drink with us? Now don't be too formal. Come. Come and just enjoy. See your future is calling you. C'mon Rudra. Come and finish it. Come," Joy insisted. I couldn't believe what I was seeing.

I was busy looking at Rudra's face. He looked up slowly, at me, then turned towards Joy. Rudra took theglass from Joy's hand and gulped it down in one go. I looked at the slowly emptying beer glass, unblinking. After finishing, Rudra banged the glass down on the table.

"Now, enough. Or do you have something else, Mr. Dharmarajan?" Rudra shouted, his face a few inches away from Joy's.

"Oh my God," I exclaimed, my mouth open.Joy closed it with his hand. They all said their cheers and started drinking. After a few sips, they returned their glasses to the table.

"Mr. Dharmarajan," Rudra mumbled angrily, his face flushed.

"Rudra, are you okay?" Shantanu asked, and Rudra gestured at him to be quiet. "You destroyed my relationship with my religion. You made me ashamed of myself. You are a sinful man and I will never forgive you. Don't forget this day, Mr. Dharmarajan. You will have to remember this day."

"Rudra, it's fine," Shantanu said softly, trying to pacify him.

"You, Chatterjee! Don't you for a minute think that I am helpless. It's your day today, but soon it'll be mine. Don't forget this," Rudra slurred, and left.

"Rudra! Rudra!" I ran after him, shouting his name. He started vomiting in the wash-basin. I patted his back trying to comfort him. After cleaning up, he relaxed and sat on the floor near the window facing Valenki Villa. I brought him some lemon water and sat with him.

"Rudra, what happened? Why did you drink?" I asked. He was busy looking at Valenki Villa.

"Rudra, are you okay? What happened, why did you drink?" I repeated, shaking his shoulder.

His silence spoke volumes. Something must have happened between Rudra and Joy which none of us knew of. Still, I asked him again. He just looked at me quietly, and looked back at the Valenki Villa.

"Rudra," I repeated.

"Nothing," he shook his head. I knew he was lying, I knew he wasn't a drinker. But what was the reason for him giving in today?

"Rudra, if you don't want to tell me, it's okay. I'll leave you if you wish," I stood up, ready to move. He held my hand and requested me to sit with him.

"As a human, I too have a right to dream, I also have the right to love someone. But, no one loves me, no one gives me a chance to either. I am almost 32 years old, and no one has ever come up to me to tell me she loves me. My life has become a living hell. I feel like something is killing me. What's the use of such a life? After so long I have found something to keep me happy, yet God gives me people like Joy. People, who don't understand my happiness."

"Rudra what happened, can you tell me?"

"You tell me, what should I do? I have not done anything wrong and I haven't broken anyone's heart. I was just enjoying myself and was feeling like a normal human being," he said, his eyes wet. I realised he was in the depths of love with someone. But, with whom?

"Rudra, can you tell me please?" I repeated, and he started telling me what happened last night.

Rudra, the night before.

It was 02:00 a.m., and he was lonely. He wanted some sort of magic to happen, and God must have heard his prayers, for magic did happen.

Joy never slept before two or three in the morning, as most of the time he was busy messaging or talking to Ketaki, or spending his time smoking the night away.

It was around 02:00 a.m., and Rudra was looking at Valenki Villa, waiting for something tohappen. For his love was there, inside the Villa. He'd only ever read about it or watched movies about it, but this was the first time he was watching a *real* girl undress. He forgot the world outside, as he stared in.

The window in his room faced the bathroom of Valenki Villa. Anyone could see what was going on, on the other end, if the curtains were not drawn. The light in the bathroom came on, and the girl entered. She opened the window slightly to let the fresh air in. She removed her shirt, and he glued himself to the window. As she stood under the shower, his breath stopped. He was so absorbed in ogling at her, he lost track of time. He didn't imagine anyone would be awake at this time, so lost in his own world was he.

"What is the time now?" Suddenly, Joy entered the room and switched on the lights. As the lights turned on, Rudra's bubble burst. They both looked at each other quietly. Joy looked down at Rudra, as he hurriedly covered himself with a towel.

"This is not the time to barge into rooms, asking people the time," Rudra fumbled awkwardly, still recovering from what he'd witnessed.

"Sorry, I didn't know. And I will never ask you the time again," he pointed at Rudra's groin. He quickly covered his exposed self and blushed. With all this commotion, now the girl in the shower also looked at them, and screamed.

"Bastards! Rascals! Who is that? What is your name? It is two in the morning and you're peeking into the girls hostel! Don't you have manners? Meet me tomorrow and I'll thrash you!" She was rightfully angry.

"It is 02:00 a.m.," Rudra said to Joy after hearing her.

"I know," he laughed.

"Please, don't tell anyone," Rudra sat on the window sill, holding the towel tightly.

Joy laughed and went out of the room, shutting the lights and the door behind him. Rudra sat frozen in the same spot, as Joy continued laughing outside the room.

****

During the last few days, Ketaki and Joy became very close. They were sharing a lot of things with each other. Chatting late into the night, having dinner together in the Club House, and even going to the local *aunty's* mess. Ketaki was in love with her food. "I will miss this food when I will leave Alibaug!" she'd always say. But we knew she'd miss Joy more than anything else.

"Should I open and read everyone's likes and dislikes?" she asked, taking out a couple of letters from the box, at our last training session. One by one, she opened and read all of them. A few were good, some of them very good, and not one person wrote anything negative. She read all the letters except Joy's. Afterwards, Shantanu and I were in the corridor outside the training room, discussing something.

"Manav," I heard Ketaki call out.

"Yes?"

"Excuse me, I was just leaving," said Shantanu.

"I want to talk to both of you," she stopped him.

"I know you don't like Joy. You don't like him much. Maybe it's because of his attitude, but believe me, he is not what he shows himself to be. He is very different. He is very sweet. He cares about you guys. He thinks he will help you grow in your lives. He wants to make you both his good friends." She was talking like she knew everything about Joy. Why was she telling me all this? Why was she taking Joy's side? She hadn't known him long.

"Manav?" she asked, shaking my shoulder.

"Yes, yes, sorry."

"Today is my last day in this hotel and in Alibaug. I have conducted many training sessions in my life, but this training was very special for me. I have never before met a person like him. He is very nice. He is very talented. I suggest both of you be with him, and I know the three of you will be good friends," she said, handing me a small letter that we'd given her on the first day of training. "You know, I read everyone's letters, but I did not read Joy's. This is for you. It will help you understand what Joy is," she closed my hand around the letter, and started leaving. She turned around after a few steps. "I leave for Zurich today evening. If you guys have the time, please come with Joy to bid me goodbye. It will make me very happy."

Her tone made me feel something different. She turned around and walked away. I watched her leave, with my heart telling me to stop her.

That was the day I realised how close she'd become to Joy. Was I feeling jealous of them? If this was love, then why didn't I like it? I could feel their love, I could almost touch it. I realised

I was missing *my* love. My IHM love, my love in the college corridors. I was missing this one girl I'd felt something for, for the first time in my life. I'd never shared this with anyone. No one knew my story. I still didn't know if it was one–sided or not, but it was something remarkable.

Chapter 10

First Day of College

Everyone had different reasons for joining IHM. Some became students listening to their parents, some came in hopes of achieving something in life. Some of them joined this field as a last resort, and some didn't have any other choice. Somesaw the course as a platform for success, and some of them came grudgingly. People like me. Everyone's choices were right, all their reasons valid.

A Hotel Management degree is unlike any other degree. Here, you have to build connections with people. You have to understand what the world needs, and fulfil it. You have to learn the standard operating procedures, and make them a part of your daily work.

"Excuse me, can you help me reach the first-year class?" Someone stopped me as I was rushing through to class. I looked up. Wearing a light brown coloured lipstick, with her hair tied with a bow, stood the most beautiful girl I'd ever seen. The happiness radiating on her face mirrored mine. I couldn't take my eyes off her. I don't have words to explain her beauty. It felt as if everything else dimmed in front of her.

"I am also looking for the same," I said, trying to compose myself, returning her smile.

"Oh, really! Let's find it together," she said, and we started walking together.

"By the way, what is your name?" she asked me, while looking into the classes around.

"Manav, Manav Kapoor," I replied.

"I am Suhani Rawat," she turned around and held out her hand to me, "From Dehradun." I shook her hand.

As it always goes, everything seems to become more beautiful when a beautiful girl gives you her hand. The way she held my hand, made me more comfortable. They say if you start your day happy, your entire day will go smoothly. I was sure my day would be excellent.

"I have five members in my family," she continued, "Mom and dad, an elder brother, an elder sister, and me. I am a very friendly person, but I like my friends to keep a particular distance from me. I like to be very clear with all my relationships. I don't believe in love at all. I hate it when people say they love me because I want to be remembered for who I am, and not just as an idea. I like ice-cream in winters, travelling, and playing basketball. I like to make new friends, and my favourite colour is pink, even though most girls like the colour. Sometimes I like to have non vegetarian-food, but my family is purely vegetarian." Without a moment's thought, she rattled off about herself. I just kept looking into her eyes. After a moment's silence, she looked into mine and said, "11th November, 1992."

"What is that?" I asked, still looking at her.

"My birthdate," she laughed out loud. I was taken aback. This was all new and strange to me.

"What happened?" I asked her as she continued laughing at my confused expression.

"Nothing, just the look on your face, I...," she burst into giggles again.

"I didn't ask you anything, why'd you tell me all this?" I asked once she'd stopped laughing.

"People take six months, or sometimes a year to tell all this to others. One year is the time we'll take to complete two semesters, and a year of college, so better not spread it over such a long time!" she grinned. "What about you?"

"I am an only child," I replied.

"Oh, really. Well," she continued, "and your hobbies?"

"I like…," I mumbled, looking around.

"What are you looking at? Tell me what you like," she repeated.

"I like reading biographies of successful people," I replied.

"Oh nice. Very nice."

"I think we should go to class now," I said, as we reached the door. She nodded.

There were more than fifty students in the class, each with a different dream. Most of the students were busy searching for answers to their futures in the books in front of them. We took our seat. She sat to my right, still smiling at me. To my left sat a guy I introduced myself to. He told me his name, Rudra.

Professor Chaturvedi was the first IHM teacher we met that day. He looked down at all of us, as if we'd asked him for something. The class had become silent.

"Good morning," the professor said, in a low, rough voice.

"Guys, I said, good morning," he repeated forcefully. This time we all replied equally loudly. Rudra shouted a little louder than the others.

"Do you know who you are?" the professor looked at us. "Guys, do you not know who you are? My dear students, you are future hoteliers. You will have to be a fire fighter, an iron man. You will have to be a lot of things, which will only be possible if you concentrate in this hall, and adhere to being a part of this. You are here for an IHM degree, and not anything else. I don't know what you know about being an hotelier, but I will tell you exactly how one should be. Hospitality is dependent on good hoteliers. You should be street-smart, knowledgeable, and have a strong work ethic." He paused for emphasis and continued, "IHM is a very important aspect of becoming successful hoteliers. It is very important to be sharp and clean in your life. Understand the standards that have been set." We looked at him in rapt attention, as he scanned our faces. "Did you understand?" he asked.

"Yes sir," only Rudra replied.

"Very nice, great student," he looked at Rudra and continued. "If you want to be a part of this world, if you want to stand tall amongst such bright people, then you have to be present in this hall for the next three years. You have to forget the world outside. You have to forget everything else for the next three years. Just keep reminding yourself why you came here. You are a part of IHM, and want to be good hoteliers." His way of talking was very different from what I'd experienced earlier. On the very first day I understood how I'd have to compromise a lot in the coming years.

"So, what is the hotel industry?" the professor started walking down the aisles, towards the blackboard, then turned back to us. "According to British laws, a hotel is a place where a bonafide traveller can receive food and shelter, provided he is in the position and condition to receive it…," he paused. "I hope you understand."

"Yes sir," Rudra replied.

"I think you are the only interested student here," he said to Rudra and looked at us. "Take initiative here, my dear students." Rudra chuckled, and slowly all of us started laughing as well.

"Do you know, in short, how the hotel industry works?" he asked, waited for a reply and continued, "Okay, as it's your first day today, we will just go through the basics. I will read out a few points, listen carefully and keep them in mind. The hotel industry is divided into different departments. Here are the major departments along with their responsibilities."

He opened the book in front of him and started listing the points. "There are four major departments – Front Office, Housekeeping, Food Production and Food & Beverage. You must understand that every department has different roles."
After reading out and explaining all the departments in detail, he shut the book and looked at us. "Thank you for today. Read and understand the points we've discussed, and we will resume very soon."

****

I had almost fallen in love – one-sided love. I had started doing crazy things that I'd never done before. I tried ice cream in the winter, willingly got wet in the monsoons, started day-dreaming. This was all happening for the first time. I was getting addicted. I could see nothing else in front of me except Suhani. Every moment with her was special.
"Let's go for a long drive," she said when her red Mercedes arrived at the college gate. When a normal guy suddenly gets invited by the world's most beautiful girl, someone he secretly loves, there's no reason to refuse.
"Suhani, you hail from a rich family, so why did you choose to do Hotel Management?" I asked her, as we sat on a small bridge next to a lake, our legs splashing in the water. She was in a red half-sleeved kurta with black leggings, which suited her so well. Her Mercedes was parked behind us. It was a starry evening.
"Whatever we have today belongs to my dad. I know it is enough for me, but I don't want it. I want to liv my life on my own terms. I want to explore the world after struggling, live an unprivileged life. I want to face problems. I don't want to inherit an easy life that has no meaning; I want to make my own life meaningful with my own struggles. What will I do with my dad's property? If I just sit in it, then what is the meaning of my life?" she replied.

"I think the same. I feel the way we both think is almost the same," I smiled.

That day, I saw a new side to her. She wasn't the same Suhani I'd met a few days back. This new side, I really liked. I was damn sure she was not like any other girl. She was the kind of girl who knew exactly what she wanted out of life, like me. All her thoughts and dreams mirrored mine. To me, she was perfect.

"Who are you very close to in your family?" she asked.

"*Maa*," I replied. "What about you?"

"Of course, my mom. My dad is always busy. He never gives his family any time. He mostly uses his time to make more business and money, so my mom is the only one who takes care of all of us. What about your dad?"

"He is Hitler," I said, making a ridiculous face.

"Hitler!" she repeated and stared at me, then burst out laughing. "Why are dads like this?" she sighed.

"Maybe only Hitler knows," I smiled.

She sat straighter, "You know, life is not what we think it is. Life always shows us the right way but we choose the wrong path anyway. If we pass, we say it is due to luck, and if we fail we say it's a part of life."

"So, what do you want out of life?" I asked.

"I want to be like that star," she pointed to a cluster of stars above us. "I like to shine at night, I like to be quiet for some time, I like to walk under the light of the moon."

"If you want to be a star, then I will have to be the moon," I said emotionally. She looked at me and we laughed, her hand slightly touching mine. I felt a flutter inside. I was watching her laugh, her happiness lifting my spirits.

"Manav, are you in love?" she suddenly asked.

"Yes," I said.

"With whom?" I fell silent.

"Tell me, whom are you in love with?" she looked at me, smiling. I stared back, seeing my reflection in her eyes. "Please tell me."

"Don't you know?"

"No," she said, softer than before.

"What do you think? I teased.

"How would I know!"

"Take a guess," I said, coming slightly closer to her. Our surroundings became silent, the cold water still splashing against our feet. We were both lost in our own world. I thought she felt the same way, and there would be no better time to tell her.

"It's you."

"Really," she said after a minute, then came closer, so she was almost whispering. "How much do you love me?"

"Madly, no one could ever love like me." She kept quiet. I waited for her to reply with bated breath. All of a sudden, she started laughing at me. I laughed along with her without understand why.

"What happened?" I asked her once she'd calmed down.

"Nothing," she said seriously, but burst out laughing again.

"Suhani, what happened? I really do love you."

"You are really mad, you idiot. That was a nice joke," she grinned. She didn't realise how serious I was. She was taking it as a joke, and eventually, I gave in too.

****

After every session, conducting a practical class was mandatory for any subject. It was to be attended by all the students. Everyone gets to work in their choice of department. I was interested in the Front Office department, and Suhani didn't choose any, since she liked them all.

"What are you guys doing here?" Professor Chaturvedi stopped us as we were coming out of the practical hall.

"We are just coming from the practical session sir," Suhani said, looking from me to the professor.

"Oh, really! Very good! Which particular session did you attend, my dear students?" he asked, staring at me. Suhani kept quiet and looked at me too. "My dear student, can you please tell me what session you just attended?" We remained quiet.

"Gentleman, please explain," he said a little louder. We didn't understand what to say. Because he'd guessed we hadn't attended any session then, he was forcing us to say something. "Food & Beverage, sir," said Suhani quickly. She looked at me. I was still quiet.

"Oh, Food & Beverage, that's my favourite department. I am very close to it. I have a different kind of relationship with that department. Anyway, if you were in class, that means you learnt something, right?" We nodded. Since that was his favourite department, I was damn sure he'd ask us questions about it. The way he was smiling said so.

"Can you please tell me the five basic rules of the Food & Beverage department? Something that every hotelier should know," he asked.

"Actually sir," Suhani started, before he stopped her and looked at me. "You, gentleman? Do you have something to say?" I was still looking down.

"See, you say you have attended a practical session, and yet you don't know anything about it."

"Sir! But...,"Suhani stumbled.

"Shut up!" he silenced her. "Don't waste time here! You are here to be good, hoteliers. Your families are under the impression that you are doing struggling and working hard, but here you are, wasting time. You are wasting your parents' money and your time."

"We are not wasting our time here, sir," Suhani said politely.

"Then tell me the five rules." Again we were quiet.

"See, you don't know anything and you want to be good hoteliers. You know what?" he said with gritted teeth, "To be a good hotelier in the future, you have to be a good IHM student first. The world only values great IHM students. If you continue to behave like this, nobody will give you a job, and your life will become meaningless."

"But sir, it will take us time to understand all the subjects. The entire IHM syllabus is not in one book. We can't just read one and get the degree."

"What? Keep quiet. Now are you going to teach me how to study? I am your professor. Have some respect!" he shouted at Suhani, his face turning red. "You can't be a professional hotelier." I motioned to Suhani to be quiet.

Rudra was crossing the path behind sir, but stopped on seeing us. "Good morning, sir," he said politely.

"Good morning, gentleman. What is going on?"

"Only studies, sir. Nothing else," he deliberately shifted the books in his hand. Was he reading all of them at the same time? Or was he already done with them? Naturally, his boot licking worked. The professor got happy as soon as he heard his reply, and smiled at him.

"See, now this is a novel student. We can even call him a real hotelier." Rudra had finally impressed him "If I asked you something, will you be able to tell us?"

"Of course, sir, it'll be my pleasure."

"Can you tell us the five basic rules of Food & Beverage?"

"Sure sir, why not," he readied himself. Suhani and I looked at each other.

"Listen carefully. And be like him," the professor glared at us. Rudra started, "Always serve the lady first, because we give more respect to ladies, and as usual, ladies are always first.

Dress professionally. First impression is the last impression, so why not take the chance to impress a guest on the first contact. Be confident. If you are working in a hotel and are not confident enough to handle a guest, then it will reflect in your work and the guest won't be satisfied. Maintain eye contact. Proper eye contact will make your guest feel that we are listening to him properly. Pay immediate attention to your guest. Every guest wants your full attention. So, if you are busy then you have to be smart enough to pay proper attention to your guests. Sometimes if you have to cover two to five tables at a time, it may become impossible to concentrate on all the tables equally. So, if another steward is free then they should help their colleague cover all the tables together. After all, we are all part of one organization and we have to work as a team."

The professor couldn't stop grinning. The answer he got far exceeded his expectations.

"Sir, are you okay?" I asked him.

"No, I am not," he said, tearing up. I quickly looked at Suhani. "My dear student, you have made me cry today. I don't have anything to say to you. You are the future of hospitality." Rudra became deliriously happy as soon as he heard him. Professor Chaturvedi was the kind of teacher who'd hardly appreciate anyone. For him, Rudra had become the ideal student.

Chapter 11

We were to attend eight classes every day, from 7 a.m. to 5 p.m., with half an hour breaks between them. One thing I could never understand was how if one teacher couldn't teach all the subjects, then how were we expected to understand all of them in one go? I had come to experience the real life of an IHM student only after I joined. I was feeling the pains and pressures of a student's life. We'd study the entire day, with no time to spare. How to keep your guests happy? How to understand what your guests need? How to fulfil their requirements? How to provide the best customer service to your guests? What exactly is to be done in college and then, on the job? Every single day we were busy trying to answer such questions. If we were to be successful, then we'd have to constantly keep thinking about our goals. Till we didn't become passionate about it, we wouldn't be successful. Success, passion and craziness, these words had got stuck in our minds like a mantra. I had made this as much a part of my life as I had Suhani.

With so much happening, I didn't realise when we completed a year in college. And yet, my love was still one-sided. Throughout the year, I had tried hard to express my love to her, but couldn't. One-sided love was definitely more painful than a heartbreak. Suhani Rawat. A perceived spoiled child of a rich dad from Dehradun had become a good friend of mine. I was from a medium class family in Shimla, but she thought of me as a good friend to her, regardless. As the days went by, we become very close to each other.

I saw Suhani laughing in the college garden. I looked up, and stopped behind a pillar in the corridor. Both her hands were in the air, and she faced the sky and smiled. She looked so happy. I found myself praying she'd always remain this happy. The whole world seemed to fade away, as I immersed myself in that moment. As everything else dimmed and quieted, I could hear music fill the garden. In that moment, it was just Suhani and I. Before I could stop myself, my legs had automatically started moving towards Suhani. It was magical. I had nothing but her in my mind. Slowly, steadily, I made my way to her. Suddenly, almost as if it were pre-planned, it started raining. As the raindrops made their way to Suhani, she was drenched from top to bottom, her red coloured *salwar kameez* completely wet. Now she looked even more gorgeous. It was almost as if the Gods were with me too, they'd created the perfect romantic moment for me. Now, as I stood in front of her, she stopped dancing and looked at me with such intensity, like she wanted to kiss me. I put one hand on her back and held her hand, bringing it back from the sky. She started smiling even wider, now that she found herself in my arms. I just kept looking into her face, as she came closer. The distance between our lips was slowly shortening. I removed my hand from her back and held her neck, and then kissed her. In that moment, we'd forgotten the world.

Hey, snap out of it. Suddenly, the voice inside my head came back and shook me. I was shocked and angry, for he'd just broken the best daydream. I blinked and looked at Suhani. She was busy talking to another student in the traditional IHM dress code. That's when I really understood it was all just a dream, never to be real.
Do you love her? The voice inside me asked. I kept quiet. *Does she love you?*
"That's what I want to know, which she will now have to tell me," I said and started walking towards Suhani.

Wait. You are a good friend to her. You are a good partner to share life's pains with. You are a good buddy to help each other out, but that doesn't mean she loves you. Have you asked yourself what she thinks about you? Did she reply when you asked her, that day?

"Of course, she loves me."

This you are saying. She is not. Has she ever told you she loves you? This is your decision, but what about her?

I immediately stopped myself. Really, she'd never said she loved me. Was the voice inside my mind right? *Instead of changing what you have, let her remain your best friend. Friendships are anyway always better than relationships.* So she was only meant to be a friend.

My love story ended at the garden, without ever starting. I had never felt alone or unhappy with Suhani around. The bond we had was stronger than that of lovers, and I knew she'd always be available for me.

As the year came to an end, it was time for us to go for our industrial training. When your luck is bad, then you can't do anything to stop things from unfolding. We'd tried so hard to be in one place, but our training was to take place in different cities. I got Shimla, which was my home town, and she got a place in Goa.

"Are you going tomorrow?" I asked her, back at the bridge. She nodded without saying anything. My heart was begging her to stay.

"Where are you going?"

"You've asked me this a hundred times, and every time I have said, Goa." She was losing her cool, her eyes glazing over with tears.

I kept quiet once I noticed her tears. She started crying, her head on my shoulder, and her hand in mine. I had a horrible feeling that I was about to lose something precious today.

"Will you will miss me?" she sniffed. I remained quiet. She asked me the question I'd wanted to her. "I asked you something."

"Of course I will, and you?"

"Very much. Why you don't come to Goa with me? For your training?"

"Don't worry, I will come to meet you there."

"And if after I reach Goa, I need you, what will you do then?"

"I will be available on the phone all the time."

"If I really, terribly need you, then?"

This time, I become completely quiet. I don't know what capacity I needed her in, but as friends, we both needed each other.

As the day went on, this thought of being in separate cities became a wall between our relationship. Batch by batch, all the students moved to different parts of India for their own industrial trainings. The time you get close to someone, is also the time you end up having to move away. That training divided us. We said our goodbyes, and headed our own ways.

Chapter 12

Present Day

It had been over a week since Ketaki had left for Zurich. Sometimes she'd call me on my mobile, and Shantanu and I would speak to her when free. We had become good friends. Joy and Ketaki's love story had also become famous.

The deadliest time for all of us lay between five and eight in the morning. It felt like a World War between Club House, Versoli and Marteen House, since Shantanu's rooster alarm would wake everyone up at five o'clock.

Thrice a week there'd be water shortage in Marteen and Versoli Houses. Every time this problem arose, everyone would come over to shower and use our facilities. Club House was their only option. But here, there was just one wash basin for shaving and brushing, with a half-broken mirror on the wall, a shower and a toilet. Only one person could use the facilities at a time, but in times of emergencies, we'd have to close our eyes, noses and mouths and share it. Where one would be on the toilet, someone would be shaving over the same basin that a third person was brushing over. On those occasions, the three of us would take full advantage of the VIP toilet and wash-basin. That toilet was designed by some Japanese company with a pencil-sized jet spray under the seat cover. We'd end up spending hours there just for that.

Rudra would never use any of the washrooms in the morning. According to him, one should get done with everything the night before. Considering our profession, we don't have the luxury of time to keep waiting for our turn in the morning. After dinner, we have nothing special to look forward to. We have to go to work the next day, whether we like it or not.

So just before going to sleep, he'd brush, shave himself with an expensive-looking shaving machine, relieve himself, and change into his night wear. This way, the next day, as soon as he'd wake up, he'd just have to throw on a shirt and run to work. He'd also do this since Mr. Suri appreciated him reaching earlier than anyone.

Our daily routine work had started. We'd leave the staff room at 08:15 a.m. and go wait for the coach at the local circle point (Club House point). That was the fixed time for pickups. Some of us would reach before time and manage to catch the coach, and some would miss it by minutes. The ones who'd miss the coach would have to travel on their own expense. But most of us would reach around ten minutes before time. These ten minutes we'd then spend making fun of each other. Some would start deep, serious discussions in a group of three or so, and some guys would stand in the corner, smiling at everyone. During this time, Godi would go up to and wish everyone good morningnon-stop, as if he were   meeting us for the first time. Once he'd finish, he'd put his phone on speaker and play the latest love songs. Soon we knew them all by heart too. Our latest favourite was a Punjabi song called*Hiriye*.

Bheem Singh would always sit next to the driver, as it was his job to be present at all the pick-ups. By eight thirty, we'd reach the hotel, and head to the meeting room. Nobody had the guts to be late for the meeting, except Joy. But whenever he'd come late, he'd always have a valid reason. Sometimes it was fixing some department's problems, and at times, tackling a complaint or an issue. Suri sir wouldn't say anything to him, but it was obvious how much he wanted to.

Our morning tea break was from 10:00 – 10:15 a.m., the lunch break from 12:00 - 14:00 p.m., and the evening tea break from 04:00 – 04:15 p.m. Once a week we'd go play cricket on the local Versoli beach, or sometimes in the hotel itself. The games too were a part of our job. The reason behind this was to better the staff's teamwork, and spend some moments of leisure.

An hotelier's life balances on five bamboo sticks, each complicated in its own way. Guest complaints was the most important, most prioritised aspect for hoteliers. This is what created fights among the best of hoteliers, for this decided how capable we were.

"Please, can you start?" Suri sir pointed at me to start the morning meeting. He looked hot and unhappy, a sure shot indication that everyone's morning was going to get worse.

"Good morning everyone," I looked at Suri sir and started reading from a logbook, like a school student. As usual, the meeting started with the Front Office team, since this was the only department that kept an eye on all the other departments at night, in the absence of the General Manager.

"Number of arrivals today – 45, number of departures - 40. Last night's closing was 80% with ARR (Average Room Revenue) 5500/-, VIP (Very Important Person) Rooms – 5, HWC (Handle with Care) rooms – 4, problematic guests – 6, and regular guests – 8." Everyone was listening to me with full concentration. I looked at Suri sir again and continued. In the first few minutes of every meeting, we'd all get to know what everyone else was doing, and who was performing the best. All the managers in the room had now set their minds and eyes on me, and were listening to every word I was saying.

"The most common guest complaint at the time of check-out, was how the breakfast was pathetic and not up to the mark." Before I could continue, Suri sir stopped me and looked at Shantanu.

"Pathetic! Not up to the mark! What is this, chef? What is going on in your department? How and why did this happen? Can you explain?" Shantanu kept quiet, his face turned down.

"Chef, I am asking you something." Suri shouted.

"Sir, actually…," he started before falling silent again.

"What *actually*? What do you want to say? Speak clearly so we can all understand you. You know very well how I don't like people who don't speak up. Please explain yourself, give me a solution and assure me this won't happen again."

"Sir, I was short of staff," Shantanu said in a low voice.

"What? Is this your answer and solution? Is this the assurity you are giving me as the Executive Chef?"

"No sir, but…"

"You are the chef of my hotel. This excuse doesn't suit you. Shortage of staff is every hotelier's problem, that doesn't mean they stop giving their 100%. If they can do it, so can you. I will not tolerate such answers and excuses. Better yourself, put in more efforts to avoid guest complaints.The guests who are with us at the moment, must leave the hotel happy at any cost."

"Yes sir."

"Don't just say 'yes sir'. What you will do about this, please tell us?"

"Sir, I will concentrate even more in the kitchen,' Shantanu said.

"Yes, and you will meet all the guests as they come for breakfast, speak to them as much as possible, and sort out these issues."

"Sure sir." Do or die but your guests should be happy. I was absurdly, a little happy about Shantanu's situation.

"Why is there staff shortage in the kitchen department?" Suri sir turned to Khurana sir.

"I was not aware of it," he replied nonchalantly.

"I had informed you earlier," Shantanu interrupted.

"Have you knocked on my office door even once, to share this issue?" Suri sir asked angrily.

"No sir."

"Then keep quiet and listen! Do you understand?" Suri sir snapped. It was better to be quiet instead of creating a bigger issue. "Yes, Khurana. Can you please look into this matter on an urgent basis? And tell me when I can expect new staff in the kitchen."

"I called three - four people for an interview today, and will hire them if they are suitable for the available position. I will update you on the same by the evening, sir."

"Please update me before the end of the day." Khurana nodded vigourously in reply. Every problem here is connected to each other. One problem has to be explained by more than two people because no one wants to take the resonsibility on their head. Everyone wants to shift the cap from their head to another's.

I weighed the pause, and continued reading aloud. "Room numbers 2020, 4023, 1060 and 6060 had complaints. They said the rooms were not cleaned properly. The guests found hair on the beds and the floors. The shower area was dirty. Tea cups were dirty. The rooms' cleaning was not up to the mark. Mr. Mehta from room 2020, and Mr. Reddy from room 1060, have both stayed here for long and they are not happy with the housekeeping services." On one side were the guest complaints, the second had Suri sir, and yet another side had Joy. I couldn't hide the complaints even for the sake of friendship. It could backfire on me.

"Can you explain this, Joy? Why did this happen?"

"I was not aware of this, Mr. Suri. Let me check and I will get back to you," Joy answered.

"But why were you not aware? This is not a cricket pitch where you just hit the ball and don't see where it lands, Mr. Dharmarajan. You are working in the hospitality industry. You are responsible for all your department's problems and are answerable for all of them. You have to prepare yourself before coming to the meeting."

"Of course, Mr. Suri. But we should get some time to prepare ourselves," Joy replied.

"You have to manage yourself. Whether you have the time or not is not my problem!" Suri shouted.

"Yesterday, I came to work at 08:45 in the morning, and left the hotel at 11:00 o'clock at night, and again reached before 08:45 in the morning today. If such a situation continues, how are we expected to manage ourselves?" Joy argued.

"Joy! I am warning you, don't argue with me! I will fire you!"

"I am not arguing, Mr. Suri. I am just explaining myself. If we work for more than 14 hours at a stretch, and don't give our 100%, you only tell us how to make that possible." Joy was never happy until he fought with Suri. He always liked to go against him.

"You have to concentrate on your work. You have to do something out of the box." Suri turned towards all of us. "Listen to me. You have to give your 100% at any cost. I don't know how you will do it, but I don't want a single complaint from any department." Do or die, but give it your all. It always came back to that.

As for cost-cutting, this was something we couldn't do because we had a fixed budget. We couldn't afford to buy a lot of things because they weren't in the original budget. So, we had to improvise. Like how often our dreams would have us flying in the air, trying to touch the sky, but then we'd wake up to our collective reality. This was the same at work – we'd want to give a lot, but that'd never happen. Every day, we'd wake up at 05:00 a.m. and reach the hotel before 09:00 a.m. By the time we'd return, it would be well past 10:00 p.m. If someone works for more than 12 hours a day, non-stop, where the hell will he receive satisfaction from? If all went well, we'd get one off a week, on Sundays. But if a special corporate person, an owner or a VIP would come to stay, our Sundays would automatically get cancelled without informing us. Suri sir was a sucker for punctuality – he hated it if anyone ever took an off. Sometimes days would go by before Joy, Rudra, Shantanu and I would get to see each other, since we were all busy with work, and the few times we got free, we'd be fast asleep in our rooms.

The only time I'd get to speak to *maa* was at night. After an entire day's work, speaking to her became my only reason to smile. Our work was a never-ending process. Unlike our bosses, who wanted us to give our 100% at all times, we realised doing less work, but doing it perfectly, was way better. Recent industry surveys showed 70% of the existing staff preferred not to continue in the same hotel after more than six months. This was because everyone received instant increments and promotions in lesser time, when shifting from one hotel to another. That's the reason why recruitment too, was a never-ending process.

"Hey, look. Look!" Joy exclaimed, pointing at Khurana sir running from the Back Office to the General Manager's office, across the lobby.

"What happened to him? Why is he running?" Shantanu asked.

"Excuse me, Mr. Khurana!" Joy shouted.

"Shut up! Are you mad?" I shushed Joy. "We are in the lobby!"

"Sorry sir!" he laughed.

Shantanu, Joy and I looked on as Khurana sir almost ran to Suri sir's office, with an envelope in hand. Khurana sir didn't realise we were staring at him. Joy dragged Shantanu and me behind him. We were walking some distance away from him, hoping he didn't see us. Once or twice when Khurana turned around, we hid behind pillars. When we finally reached outside Suri sir's office, we hid behind a glass partition and peeked inside.

"Excuse me sir," Khurana sir knocked twice and opened the door. He looked so excited about something. He seemed to be bursting with the news. I doubt he even took a breath from his office to Suri's. He started wheezing. Seeing this, Suri sir handed him a glass of water.

"Thank you, sir," Khurana sir said, without touching it.

"What happened, Khurana? Why are you so tensed? Calm down."

"Sir, please see this." Khurana handed him a DVD from the envelope in his hand.

"What is this?"

"Resume, sir, for a receptionist." Joy and Shantanu looked at me and raised their eyebrows, asking me if I knew anything about this. I shook my head.

"What? Resume in a DVD?"

"Yes sir."

"Who sent this to you? And when did you receive it?"

"I don't know who sent it sir, only that it has 'Application for Receptionist', written on it. I received it today, by courier."

"Are you sure this is a resume?" Suri sir seemed unsure. "A DVD can have anything on it. Do you understand what I am trying to say?" We stood outside, mouths agape. Khurana sir seemed really excited to watch it, but Suri sir's apprehension put him in a fuddle.

"I don't think that is a resume. What do you guys think?" Shantanu looked at us.

"We don't know anything. Now just shut up and watch," I said, and we turned to the office again.

"I am not sure, sir. I received this by courier so I have no idea who sent it. There isn't even a name on it," Khurana sir said, clearing the air. Suri sir held the DVD and looked at it from all angles, but he couldn't find anything.

"Really, nothing is mentioned," he said.

"What do you think we should do?"

"I think we should watch it, what do you think, sir?"

"Yes, I think we should watch it and see who this person is."

"Yes sir. Sure sir," Khurana sir said, and looked around as if to confirm that no one was watching, even as we stood hiding just around the corner. Suri sir tore the DVD's cover and looked at Khurana oddly. He then inserted it into a slot in his laptop, pressed play, and waited. Outside the room, Joy and Shantanu were equally curious. After a few seconds of blank screen, the video started. A beautiful woman, around 22-25 years old, came on screen. She was wearing a pale red-coloured sari, with minimal make-up.

"Namaste. I am Neha Tandon. I first want to explain why I sent a DVD instead of a couple of pages of my resume. The most important reason was, this is more environment-friendly. If I'd sent this on a few pages and you hadn't liked it, or if you'd thought I wasn't capable enough for the position, you would have thrown it in the garbage, which would have harmed the environment, or my personal information could have been leaked or misused. I don't want to mess with the environment and I like keeping my personal information safe.

I am from Delhi. My date of birth is the 25th of September, 1990. There are four members in family - my dad, mom, elder brother and I. We are from Gujarat, but we move cities basis my job location. I am unmarried. The languages I know are Gujarati, Hindi and English. I completed my B.Com., then got an IHM degree from Ahmedabad, in 2011.

I have basic computer knowledge. I worked with Hotel Grand Lee in Delhi for two years, as a Front Office Associate. Then, 18 months as a Receptionist with Sun Paradise in Kolkata.

My hobbies include spending time with my family, watching Hindi movies, and playing Chess. I can only work in the 9 to 6 shift, as I have responsibilities at home too. I like to work in a friendly environment. Don't expect too much from my side apart from work. I am a straightforward kind of girl, and I don't like politics in the work place. I like people being truthful, as I am a truthful person too.

My strength lies in my ability to adjust to new situations easily, and learn the requirements of a new job. I can socialise and mingle with guests and colleagues with ease.

Thank you so much for taking the time out to watch my DVD resume. If you feel I am a good fit for your organisation, please call or email me on the details given.

Thank you so much again!"

The video ended with her email id and mobile number on the screen. There was pin-drop silence inside the office as well as outside.

"Oh no, what is this Khurana?" Suri sir shook his head, taking a glass of water from the table, and settling back into his chair. He drained the glass in one sip. "What an amazing lady."

"Sir, you like her?" Khurana sir asked.

"No, I didn't like her. I like her thinking, her confidence and her attitude," Suri sir replied.

"Oh really? Me too sir."

"Yes, of course. There are very few people in industry who think this way," Suri pointed out.

"What should we do next, sir?" Khurana asked.

"Without wasting time, we should call her and give her the opportunity to join us."

"You are right sir, we should call her immediately."

"Yes. So, what are you waiting for?"

Khurana sir started dialling her number from the office telephone, which thankfully, had fantastic speaker volume. A dialling tone and the phone start ringing. She picked up the call in four – five rings.

"Good morning, Mr. Khurana. How are you?" She said from other side, her voice, now on speaker, resonated in the entire office, reaching us as well. Suri sir looked at Khurana angrily, wondering how she knew his name.

"Khurana what is this? You know her personally and you didn't inform me? Why?" Khurana put the phone off speaker.

"I don't know her! Really sir, I don't!" Khurana looked as shocked as him. Outside, we were also confused about what was happening.

"What a man," Shantanu chuckled. "I know this well. These Human Resource people always do things behind your back. They never tell you how things really are."

I looked at both of them. Joy looked at me, hit me on the back of my head and said, "Go closer. See, I warned you about this."

"Neha, can you please tell us how you know my name?" Khurana sir asked.

"Oh. What happened sir?"

"Nothing, we just want to know how you know my name."

"I just know sir." Suri sir's eyes widened threateningly, as Khurana tried to reassure him. Everyone fell silent, and suddenly, the lady started laughing.

"I am just joking sir. Don't worry. It was very easy. I noticed your name and number under the job vacancy post in the newspaper, and saved it." The room let out a collective sigh of relief.

"See, sir. I was right. I told you I didn't know her," Khurana mouthed to Suri. I looked to Shantanu and Joy to see how they were reacting to this.

"What?" Joy asked. I shook my head and turned back.

"Hello, sir, are you there?"

"Yes, yes Neha. I am here."

"Sir, I hope you have seen my DVD, and liked it."

"Yes, I really liked it."

"Apart from the information on the resume, would you like to ask me anything?"

"Actually no," Khurana sir said, and looked at Suri sir who was nodding his head vigorously. "Yes, yes. I want to ask one thing."

"Yes, please sir."

"When do you think you can join us?"

"Sir, really? You liked my resume?"

"Yes, of course. Our General Manager also liked your resume. He only selected you. Now we are just waiting for your confirmation, so we can send you the offer letter."

"Oh, really sir! Thank you so much for giving me this opportunity! Could you give me one day though? I will confirm with my family and give you the joining date in a day's time."

"Yes of course. We will wait for your call," Khurana sir said, and kept the phone down.

This affected me more than anyone else outside the room. As the acting Front Office Manager, and as per the hierarchy of the department, this interview should have gone through me, or least of all, they should have taken my opinion on it. But without my knowledge, they were recruiting staff for my department. This was the first time after I'd joined, that I became a little nervous.

"Don't worry, everything will be fine," Shantanu said to me on sensing what I was thinking.

"See, I told you. People in these high positions are dangerous, especially people in these two designations. You will never get to know when they go behind your back," Joy said, looking at both of them inside the office.

"Shut up, what are you saying?" Shantanu said to Joy, and turned towards me. "You don't worry, we will handle it."

"What will you handle?" snorted Joy.

"This situation."

"She's already been recruited. She will join us very soon, my dear chef. You can't do anything now."

"C'mon *yaar*, don't talk nonsense," Shantanu replied.

"I am just telling you a fact. You also know this very well."

"I know, but can't you stay quiet for even a minute?"

"Shut up *yaar*! Shut up!" I shouted at both of them. "I am already very tensed, please won't make things worse."

"See how tensed he is. Help him relax," Shantanu mouthed to Joy.

Chapter 13

We would sit on the terrace of the Club House whenever we got the time. Twice or thrice a week Shantanu, Godi and Joy would like to drink in silence. I'd be there too. I wouldn't drink, but I liked having snacks and Red Bull with them.

"This is ridiculous, they shouldn't behave like this," Shantanu said to me. "Sorry bro, we couldn't do anything for you."

"Oh, Chef, what are you talking about. These people are like this only, it is all just political drama," Joy said.

"Oh really," I said, looking at them. "By the way, why is this hurting you guys more than me?"

"Because you are our dude!" Shantanu clapped me on the back.

"I think you've had enough to drink. We should go and sleep." I started getting up.

"Where you are going? Sit here," Joy pulled me next to him, took a drag of his cigarette and blew the smoke in the air.

"You made me sit for this?" I gestured at the fast evaporating smoke.

"Take every step very carefully. If you don't understand then listen to your seniors. It will only help you," Shantanu said.

"I know."

"You don't know anything, this is your first job," Joy said dismissively.

"Can only an experienced person understand things? I know I am a fresher but I am not a fool. I have some common sense as well."

"Yes, you have sense but you don't have experience which is the most important thing here," Joy replied.

"Oh really, so it's better if you only explain your different sense and experiences to me."

"Now you want an explanation from me!" he laughed.

"What happened, why are you laughing?"

"The feeling when we get without spending anything, and the experience we get after exhausting ourselves. But the things and experiences we get after spending is more valuable than anything else. I have an experience of eight years. That means around 2920 days I have spent in this industry, which is now a big part of my life. Wherever you go in the world, everyone wants to climb the ladder kicking someone else down in the process. No one here listens to anyone. We are the ones who work hard and someone else reaps its benefit. We work over ten hours a day, and someone else gets recognised for it. We pool our knowledge together and someone else becomes successful." I think it was his frustration that was finally coming out, but what he said, I'd felt to be true too. He had incredible knowledge about his work, but one thing that I needed to learn from him was what jobbers wanted and what their lives were like.

"What do you want me to do?" I asked.

"Always be happy."

I smiled. Suddenly, Shantanu's mobile started ringing. He started fumbling with his dhoti where it'd got lost. I took it out and gave it to him, seeing the caller id: Boss – 2.

"Oh, what happened? Why is Suri sir calling you now?" I asked, shocked.

"Relax, relax. This is not Suri, but my wife," Shantanu grinned. "You have one boss in your life, but I have two! One's your Mr. Suri and the second is her. Where one fucks me in the office, the second fucks me back home. One makes my whole day a living hell, and the other makes my entire night hell. I don't understand what to do. My life is becoming too complicated."

"Think later, pick up the call now or your wife will come to the terrace and catch us," Joy said.

"Right, right." Shantanu picked up the call, but before he could say anything, his wife started shouting.

"What were you doing till now? I've been calling you for such a long time, can't you see? You've forgotten your wife and children. You wanted this only, and that is why you left us alone. You only want freedom. You are selfish. You are a rascal!" Her words echoed across the terrace and all of us grimaced. She cut the call in anger.

"What happened?" Shantanu asked, looking at our faces. We shook our heads.

"What to do, this is my life. Whenever she expects something from me, I use my job as an excuse. Whenever she demands something, I remember my job's responsibilities. When she was pregnant, I was abroad. She was expecting me to be with her at the time of delivery but I couldn't quit my job and come back home. Even today, when she needs me, I am still not with her. She misses me and I am just sitting here with my responsibilities. My son is seven years old, and my daughter is five. I don't even know when they grew up. I know nothing better than work, work and more work. After passing out of IHM, I only listened to people and worked. Even for my wedding, my first boss gave me leave only for fifteen days. He screwed me that one time, and since then, all the bosses I've had only come to get their work done." That was when I realised how every hotelier had their own internal battles that they kept hidden.

"Chef, this is a part of our life. Try to be happy," Joy said soothingly.

Shantanu smiled, "You know, we can tell how much salt a curry needs to make a guest happy, but we forget to keep our own people happy. We always seem to be trying new things for our guests, people we have never met before, but we don't do a single thing for our families. We make special dishes for special guests but we don't take out time to create special moments with our loved ones. We can serve food to a hundred people but we don't have the time to sit and eat with our own people."

"Enough chef, please don't make us cry now!" Joy exclaimed.

"Think positively, this job is also a part of our life. I think it is very important. Almost all our families have to keep a smile on their face because of this job. A lot of their survival depends on this."

Joy's phone started ringing. It was Ketaki on a video call.

"*Gori* madam *ka* phone *aa gaya.*"

"Hey darling," Joy answered.

"Hello guys, how are you all?" Shantanu and I said hello, coming in front of the camera.

"What are you doing still up?"

"Just chilling with these idiots," Joy replied, as Shantanu came in front of him and started talking to her, beer glass in a hand.

"Hey Ketaki, how are you? We are missing you so much, we three…," he turned to me and mumbled, "You don't drink *na*?"before turning back to the screen."No, just the two of us are waiting for you, having fun on the terrace with beer. When are you coming back?"

"Oh really, I will be there very soon!" she laughed and looked at the Red Bull in my hand. "Hey Manav, still just a Red Bull?" Before I could answer, Shantanu rambled on, "Ignore him, he is just an energy drinker. When you come, don't forget to brink a special energy drink from Zurich!"

"Of course, why not!" she smiled. "Okay guys, now please go and enjoy."

"Okay madam, bye," Shantanu said, as she waved back at him.

"Bye, darling," Joy said.

"Bye Joy, talk to you later." They sent each other flying kisses via the phone, and cut the call.

"What happened?" Joy asked Shantanu when he noticed him staring.

"Nothing."

"Then why are you looking at me like that?"

"What was that?" Shantanu giggled and mimicked their kiss.

"It's called a flying kiss."

"I have never given my wife any such kisses in over a year. I want you to teach me how to do this."

"Oh my God, he's started again. Now I think we really need to move."

"Before we leave I want to try it once," Shantanu insisted.

"Okay, we will try it tomorrow. Now let's go back," Joy said calmly.

"But I want to try it right now!"

"Chef, please," Joy started, looking at me for help.

"What are you looking at him for? He is still a baby boy. No girlfriend, no wife. His life is too complicated bro, too much!" Shantanu started laughing again. He took out his mobile and started video calling his wife. He told us to move to one side so we don't come in the frame. I lifted all the glasses and beer bottles and moved them to another side.

"Chef, what are you doing man," Joy sounded exasperated now.

"Shush! My boss two is on call now."

"What happened now?" Shantanu's wife asked rudely, answering on the first ring.

"I want to say something."

"What?"

"No, sorry. I am sorry. I want to give you something."

"First you decide what it is then tell me."

"I want to give you something."

"What?"

"You will recognise it."

"Whatever it is, say it fast. I have a lot of work to do."

"Okay, okay. Look here," he said and slowly puckered his lips, giving her a virtual kiss.

"What is this?" her voice had softened.

"A flying kiss."

"What?" she sounded a little angry again.

"That was a flying kiss darling, especially for you."

Without waiting for a single second, she started throwing utensils around and shouted, "Bastard! You keep us at home just so you can go do all these things! You don't spare a moment of thought for us and you have the audacity to send me flying kisses now! You just wait. Mom!" She called out to Shantanu's mom and continued, "See this, your son is giving me flying kisses on a video call. See what he is doing!" He quickly cut the call and shut up. I looked at him silently, sensing the awkward situation.

"Sorry," he said to us, sheepishly.

Joy started laughing, and I joined in. Shantanu looked at us seriously after a minute, and we stopped. In spite of feeling miserable from the inside, his mood suddenly changed and he started laughing with us.

****

"Excuse me sir, we can't allow madam here," I said, stopping Mr. Singh at the reception. He was one of our regular guests, but would come with a new girl every time. He was also a VIP guest according to our records, which meant we had to give him the best service.

"Why?" he asked, shocked.

"Sir, actually madam is not eighteen yet, so as per the hotel's policy we can't allow her to check-in," I said, checking her identity card.

"How is this possible? She is above eighteen," his tone hardened.

"No sir, you can check for yourself," I showed him her identity card. "Actually sir, we don't even allow this identity card, but since we know you, you're a regular guest of ours, we've overlooked it. But the age limit is a mandate for all."

"Oh really? Let me check." He snatched the ID and went to speak to the girl sitting in the lobby, who was glaring at me. She looked prettier than she did in her photo, and her name, Sarita, didn't suit her one bit. They argued back and forth for a minute, the girl glaring at me throughout.

"Excuse me gentleman, how is it possible that I am not eighteen? Please check my ID properly," she said, now at the reception counter.

"Yes ma'am, you are not yet eighteen," I verified.

"But how is it possible?" She took the card from Mr. Singh and said, "Look, my birthdate is 20/11/1998."

"No ma'am, you are not eighteen yet. It's August right now, and you birthdate is November's."

"But how? Can you explain?"

"Sure ma'am."

I took out a calculator to explain this to her easily. I kept it on the counter in front of her and started, "The current year is 2016. 2016 minus 1998 *is* 18, but ma'am look, we're still 3 months away from your eighteenth birthday."

"What are you talking about?" she looked thoroughly confused after my explanation, and looked at Mr. Singh.

"I don't understand his calculation. Dear, can you please look into this?"

"Okay darling wait, let me handle this. You sit and relax here," he gestured at the sofa in the lobby.

"Listen Mister...," he looked down at the name on my badge. "See Mr. Manav. Actually, we came in a hurry so we didn't know better. But now that we are in your hotel, leave it and give us the room please. I am your regular guest; you know very well how frequently I'm here. Leave it for now and I promise I will not bring her the next time, I will bring someone else who's of age."

"Sorry sir, I really can't. I can't go against the policy, and I don't want to break the rules."

"What you are talking about? What rules are you breaking and which policy is this? Dude it is just a matter of a few hours. We are here to attend an urgent meeting for my office, and have to make a presentation urgently. That's why we are here. We'll be done with the presentation in two to three hours, and will leave once done. Don't worry, we don't want to stay here the entire night."

"Yes, I agree sir, but I'm sorry. I can't do this," I replied.

"Now don't say anything, keep this for yourself and I will take good care of you. I will give you good reviews regarding your duty as well as the hotel," he discreetly held out some money.

"Sorry sir, I don't need this. I am not that type of a person," I said, returning his money.

"Hey dude, it's nothing. Keep it."

"Sorry, sir."

"Manav, please understand we are in a hurry. Please," he requested again.

"I am really sorry sir."

"Should I speak to your seniors?" he threatened.

"Of course, sir. You can if you want to, but I don't think anyone will agree to this."

"C'mon buddy, don't say this. Now where will I go to make my presentation? I have an important meeting in the next five hours, and you're not trying to understand."

"Sir, the most I can do from my end, since you are our regular guest, is if you want to, you can sit in the lobby and work on your presentation. You will only need a laptop's plug-point, and that we will provide."

"Here! In the lobby? Are you mad?" he laughed incredulously.

"Sir, we are providing you whatever you require to make your presentation. We're giving you a free AC zone, a power plug. I don't think any private area is required just for this," I reasoned.

"Dude, you know very well how some presentations need to be done in silence and in private only. You understand what I am trying to say, right?" he smiled and winked.

"That I don't know sir. I'm sorry, but…"

Before I could say anything else, the girl on the sofa suddenly stood up and started walking towards us, exclaiming, "Wait, wait! I remember now. My office identity card has the wrong date of birth, but I have my driving licence with the correct one. See this." She held out her driving licence with the valid date. I was shocked. My receptionist looked at me equally confused.

"Sarita, you are great! Excellent! Amazing!" Mr. Singh said to her, taken aback himself.

"Thank you, dear," she smiled.

"By the way, you saved our presentation!"

"You are most welcome. And dear, now we can concentrate on your project even better. So, without wasting another moment, we should move to our room, as we have less than four hours remaining," she said with a sort of finality.

"Yes, yes, you are right. We should move," he looked at me triumphantly. "So, gentleman, can we go now? I hope you don't have any problems now?" I couldn't possibly stop them after this, so I gestured to my reception staff to allot them their room. Completing their paperwork, they took their room keys and proceeded to their room, smug. I watched them in stunned silence.

"That's a nice presentation they have going on." I turned around to see Joy standing in the corner, watching all this calmly. "No laptop in hand, no computer in the room, and not even a single sheet of paper in hand. Yet they have to create a good presentation in four hours for their company's future. Nice, very nice. I think we hoteliers should learn how to make a good presentation in such a short time, from such people," he smirked at us.

"Oh really, you'd know best."

"Do you honestly think they came here to make a presentation in a private hotel room?" he laughed at my alleged naivety.

"I don't know anything, but of course you know better than me."

"Yes of course!" He straightened up and came forward, "You know, these corporate sector people don't work like us. Almost 90% of them don't work on the weekends, but their families think they do. In actuality, what their families don't realise is that their weekends are reserved for four-hour presentations in hotel rooms."

He came to a halt in front of me. "Do you want to listen to what *presentation* they are making?"

"What, are you mad?"

"I am not mad, but we can see this madness of a presentation," he offered.

"No, thanks."

"Don't worry, I am here," he assured me.

"You are really mad!"

"No, I am not mad, I am Joy Dharmarajan," he grinned. "As the Housekeeping Manager it is my responsibility, and I have the authority to enter any vacant room without anyone's permission."

"So, what do you mean? Should we go and sit behind their bed-stands, and ogle at their live presentation?"

"No, but we can *listen* to it!"

I looked at him unbelievingly, as he forced me along with him. Their room was 4012, and the room next to it, 4014, was vacant. The wall between the two rooms was only six inches thick, so anyone could listen into the other room easily. We entered the vacant room and he gestured at me to keep quiet. We slowly tiptoed across to the wall that served as a partition between both the rooms. He put his ear against the wall and gestured at me to do the same. We immediately heard someone scream. I was shocked. I stood away from the wall and looked at Joy with eyes wide open.

"What was that?" I whispered.

"Nothing, it's just some English channel." I felt myself relax as the channel in the other room changed.

"Oh my God, please switch off the television. My mom's calling! You don't make a sound, please." We could hear the girl shout at Mr. Singh. Both the rooms fell into complete silence, broken only by the ringing mobile. After letting it ring for a bit, she picked it up.

"Yes mom," the girl said. She waited for a reply and continued. "I don't know mumma, I am very busy today!" Pause.

"Mumma so what if it's a Saturday! People don't work on the weekends or what? My boss has given me a lot of work to finish in four hours. He said I can't leave before completing it." Pause.

"Ow!" The girl shouted, and we heard her push something away. Pause.

"Nothing mumma, something bit me." Pause.

"Mumma, I can't tell you the exact time, but once I leave office, I will let you know." Pause.

"Mumma, I am not a small baby," she sounded exasperated now. "I am mature now. Don't worry I will be home on time." Pause.

"Mumma, do you doubt me? Would you like to speak to my boss?" Pause.

"No mumma, wait, speak with my boss."

"Sarita, is it done?" Mr. Singh asked from a muffled distance.

"No sir, give me some time I will finish it soon. See, now do you trust me or do you still have doubts?" Pause.

"Okay mumma, I have a lot of work now, my boss is calling. Okay now, bye!" We heard her disconnect and bump into someone – a hug, most probably.

"What a nice presentation! Her mom thinks her daughter is in office, working hard, but who knows how hard she is working in the hotel room!" Joy whispered.

Soon, people started moaning from beyond the wall.

"Okay, that's it," I moved away. I asked Joy to move too, and we slowly left the room as quietly as we'd come in. On closing the door behind us, Joy looked at me and started laughing. I didn't know whether to laugh or not, as we started down the staircase, towards the lobby.

****

"Hey guys, what's up?" I asked, with a plate of food in my hand, standing in an aisle in the cafeteria during our lunch break.

"What? Nothing's up," Joy looked up at me, and laughed. I kept my plate on the table between Shantanu and Rudra. The cafeteria was almost full, with more girls than boys, their conversation creating cacophony. Today's menu had chicken curry, mutton curry, *aloo gobi, daal, chapatis, parathas,* and salad. There was a menu chart hung on the far corner. A huge television was fixed in one corner of the wall, screening the latest cricket match. Where one wall had a wooden box with today's menu inside, another wall proudly displayed the employee of the month, employee of the year, the birthday boy/girl and the new joinees for the month.

"How is today's food?" Shantanu asked.

"Not bad. Good, but not very good," Joy said. Shantanu looked at him and wondered why he'd asked in the first place.

"Everything is okay, but I think there should be some changes to the menu. We can't have the same menu every week." Rudra took a bite of his roti and looked down. Shantanu looked at him but kept quiet.

"Chef, please change some options on the menu. The food also tastes different every day, almost as if a different person cooks the meals every day. Like what we get at the local *aunty* for forty bucks," Joy pointed out to us.

"Lots of menu options." Rudra agreed.

"A little *bhaji*, 3 *chapati*s, and a small portion of rice that's not even enough to fill an empty stomach. You need to pay more if you want to have more. And yet you like that food. Here you get a different menu every day with vegetarian and non-vegetarian options, unlimited refills to your heart's content, and still you prefer that *aunty's* food over this free food," Shantanu snapped, clearly stung by everyone's criticism.

"Chef, this is not free. We get this after spending twelve to fifteen hours on our feet. Don't say we don't pay for it," I cut in.

Joy took another bite and looked at me. "Good. You're working hard. Keep it up."

"Chef!" someone called out from the table behind us, "No dessert today?" he held up an empty food container.

"You go have your desserts at home!" Shantanu snapped back. He kept quiet again, and tried concentrating on his food.

"Chef, is there something missing in your kitchen? You should fix some procedures for everyone to follow," Joy recommended.
"Yes, of course, we are all working only for this!" Rudra rubbed his stomach and said, "If this isn't happy, nothing else will be good!"
"Oh shut up, *bokachodu*!" Shantanu gave it back to Rudra. Rudra stopped eating and looked at him.
"What are you even saying? You eat here in the cafeteria only once a week, and the other times you eat out of the banquet. I know you very well, so don't try to act smart with me."
"Chef, leave it," Joy tried to pacify him.
"What leave it? You people keep saying whatever comes to your minds. Have you ever seen or bothered to know how I manage to provide food for all of you? Do you even know what the budget for one meal is? Do you have any idea how much pressure I have to handle to get this food here? Do you even know how I have to make the best of the small budget and prepare good food for the entire staff?" Shantanu thundered. Everyone became silent after listening to him talk about the non-existent budget. Joy, Rudra and I couldn't swallow another morsel. I looked down at my plate full of rice, chicken and curry, thinking how all this was a product of the budget.
"You know what? All this," Shantanu gestured to our plates, "is not even in the budget, and yet I am serving it." An awkward silence fell between us, broken by Rudra slurping his *daal,* indifferent,and all of us watching him in shared silence.

Chapter 14

25th November was the date of Mr. and Mrs. Khurana's 10th wedding anniversary. Khurana sir hailed from Gujarat, but Mrs. Padma Khurana (nee Padma Acharya)belonged from Rajasthan. Whatever the occasion be, every time we'd meet Mrs. Khurana, she'd invite us over to their house and offer us some *dal bati* – a famous Rajasthani dish. Since Alibaug isn't a big city, our world revolved around the hotel and our accommodation.

We'd constantly miss home, especially when it came to food. If anyone invited us for lunch or dinner, it'd become a much awaited event for us, and we'd never miss it. Godi, Joy, Rudra, Shantanu and I from the Club House, and a few more colleagues from Marteen House were ready to go to Khurana sir's house. Godi had an M80 bike, a famous model from the 80s, which was handy in emergencies. As much as it would help us, it would also sometimes create problems for us. We never knew whether we'd be on time or not when on it. It would randomly stop in the middle and never start, and we'd have to push it to our destination. While the others got on other bikes, Rudra, Godi and I sat on the M-80, anxious about what might happen this time. Khurana sir's house was bang in the middle of Alibaug. With some contribution from everyone, we bought a gift and a bouquet of flowers.

"Good evening, ma'am," I greeted her as she opened the door.

"Very good evening *bacha*," she smiled at us.

"Wishing you a very happy wedding anniversary ma'am!" we chorused.

"Oh, thank you so much *bacha*, thank you so much! Please come in, please," she ushered us inside. Because of the massive age difference, she was calling us *bacha*; children.

"Wow, this is a very nice house ma'am," Rudra said, looking around.

"Really?" she laughed. "You can choose any place to sit, don't be so formal, just take any seat and think of this as your own house." Soon enough, we occupied the entire room.

"Thank you ma'am, we will think of this as our home only," Rudra grinned at her.

"Sit here, *bacha*," she patted at the seat next to her, for Godi was trying to sit on the floor.

"It's okay ma'am, I am fine."

"Not okay, *bacha*. Sit here."

"I am okay ma'am, please don't worry. I will manage," Godi said as he finally sat down cross-legged.

"You must be from the sales team." Everyone looked at each other incredulously as she said this, and Godi, feeling attacked, immediately moved to the sofa. She had somehow managed to recognise his department of work just by his behaviour.

The house looked like any other normal set up, with limited furniture, and spic and span floors. There was a framed award hanging on one wall. I looked around some more, and noticed a picture of Khurana sir receiving the Best Human Resource Manager award, another one with an older man receiving a military honour, and yet another, with Mrs. Khurana holding an award for the Best Hotelier. Did this mean she was from this industry too?

"Sorry guys, your sir is out for some time. There are cold drinks and snacks here, please help yourselves. I'm sorry I am going to have to head to the kitchen. Meanwhile, my dad will join all of you. Just call me if you need anything!" she got up and left the room.

"Hello there, how are you?" We turned around to see a retired officer walking out of the washroom. I recognised him from the picture on the wall. Major-General Surendar Acharya. He must have been around sixty, but had the physique of a young man, and walked towards us as effortlessly.

"Hello sir, we are good. How are you?" Rudra and I answered in a diminished voice.

"No *dum*. I asked all of you and only two of you answer."

"No sir, actually," Rudra started.

"What actually? I am an army man. I don't like people who aren't direct. See how even at this age my voice is so much more powerful than yours." We started looking at each other furtively.

"C'mon now. Don't be so tensed, just relax and enjoy your evening with me." We continued to look at each other, still silent.

"Oh, what happened? C'mon now. Today's generation is much too complicated. Especially you hoteliers. You live your lives without any meaning, without any entertainment. It's horrible. You know, the more you think, the more stress you take, the more it decreases your life expectancy. It increases your stress levels to such an extent, you forget to *live* your life. And what happens at such a young age? Problems like diabetes, blood pressure, heart problems begin. Look at me at this age, I still look and feel like a young man, I can easily fight all of you."

"I don't think we'll require any *dal bati*,"Joy whispered to me.

"What happened, gentleman? Why are you mumbling into his ear? Speak loudly, let everyone hear you."

"Nothing sir," Joy said.

"What nothing? C'mon, what a boring evening, I don't like this. You are all young. Behave like real men. I like to enjoy every second of my life because I can never get these moments back." We were all silent. None of us knew how to make small talk with an army man.

"How many of you are married?" he asked.

"Only me," Shantanu raised his hand slightly.

"What, only you? Are you sure you are all unmarried?" he looked at us in surprise.

"Any doubts, sir?" Joy broke the silence after a minute.

"Yes, I have my doubts about all of you." He shook his head slightly and said, "What is this? No entertainment, no enjoyment, you are all behaving like a newlywed bride – so demure and shy."

"No sir, we are all giving you respect, because you seem like an old man," Rudra said.

"Shut up! Rascal, what do you think of yourself?"

"What happened, sir?" Rudra asked fearfully.

"What happened? Do I look like an old man to you? Look at my arms, my physique, and my face. From what angle do I look like a staggering old man? Don't call me old. I still have my army body. I can still go and can fight at the border." He took off his vest and glared at Rudra, who was now petrified.

"Then why did you retire, sir?" Joy asked him delicately.

"It was just a formality, this retirement. I wouldn't have left the army if I'd had my way. I'd still be there, carrying my ammunition, ready for battle. Never judge anyone by his age, always see his strength." He looked around and spotted Godi. "See this man, you might think he is older, but I think he is not more than thirty. Am I right?" Godi looked at us quietly.

"You know why this has happened? Because you think too much, because of too much tension, because there's no entertainment in your life, because you're all thinking about your futures and not living in the present." We sat silently, absorbing everything he's just said. He was right.

"You are right sir, without entertainment there is nothing in life," Joy nodded.

"So you like enjoyment?" he asked Joy.

"Of course."

"Oh, thank God, I at least found one man who shares my thinking," he laughed. "Don't think too much, let life go on as it has to. Become like water, very flexible."

"You are right sir," Joy agreed.

"How many of you are drinkers?" That seemed like the best question to ask us. But we were still quiet.

"How many?" He asked again, thumping his hand on his thigh. "No one? Too bad. But today you will all drink with me. Today everyone will take a small peg with me without any excuses." He headed to the fridge and took out a bottle of soda, some ice, and moved towards a mounted mini bar on the wall. There were all types of whiskies, rums, wines, and vodkas. Everyone's eyes were glued to the open treasure.

"What would you guys like?"

"Sir, just a few beers and Red Bulls," Joy answered.

"Red Bull? Who wants that?" he turned around. Joy and Shantanu looked at me.

"You," he looked at me and laughed. "Really, you are unbelievable. Okay now, how many of you want a whisky, rum, or vodka?" Godi, Shantanu and Joy's hands immediately shot up.

"Only three, and how many of you like beer?" All hands except for Rudra's and mine went up.

"What about you guys?" he looked at us. "I don't have Red Bull."

"It's okay sir, we don't need anything," I said.

"If you will not take anything then I will give you something from this," he gestured extravagantly at his collection.

"We are okay with beer sir," Rudra said, still fearful, and I looked at him.

"Okay now, the thing is, I don't have any beer here. Someone will have to go get it. So let's not waste any more time, it's already 9 o'clock. Let's go and bring some chilled beer. I don't know much about this place. Who is coming with me?"

"He knows the best," Rudra pointed at Joy.

"Okay, don't just think. Stand up and come." He took his car keys, quickly wore shorts, and came out.

"Padma, we will be back in some time," he called out.

"Dad? Where are you going now? It's time for dinner."

"What, are you mad? It's only 9! Our evening has just started. You have dinner if you want to, we'll have it after the party, right gentlemen?" Seeing no other option, we nodded. After such a long time, we were finally going to have home cooked food, but this army man was adamant on delaying us that pleasure. Joy, Shantanu, Rudra and I went along, in a navy coloured jeep. More than half of the shops we were crossing were closed. Normally, all the wine shops would close around 9 p.m., and this irked sir no end. He kept comparing this to his city. It felt like we were walking in a deserted town, where he wouldn't stop comparing Alibaug to Rajasthan. According to him, one could always get a drink in Rajasthan, regardless of the time. After much exasperation, Joy and Shantanu remembered a shop that they'd visit near the beach. But that too was about to shut. They both ran like professional sprinters, and soon returned with a case of beer and Red Bull.

By the time we returned, Khurana sir was back too, absorbed in a discussion with our other colleagues.

"Dad, where were you? Let them have their dinner, they need to go back and return to work early tomorrow," he said to his father-in-law.

"What you are talking about? They have not even started the evening yet, and you are talking about tomorrow."

"Dad..."

"Nothing doing. Please don't interfere in our party. If you want to join us, please do. But let me enjoy this beautiful evening with these gentlemen," he smiled at us.

"Dad what is this?" Khurana sir asked him as we kept the beer bottles on the table.

"You don't know what this is?" he mocked. "This is beer, and this is soda," he opened the cupboard and took out two bottles, "... and this is whisky and rum. Which one do you want to try?"

"Dad..."

"You've started again. Can't you just stay calm and join us?" He was now shouting at Khurana sir, and all the others could think of was the drinks they were waiting for. All except Rudra and I, that is.

"The *dal bati* is ready guys, are you?" Mrs. Khurana emerged from the kitchen.

"Padma, wait now, we have just started the evening. Please don't disturb us, both of you. We will take time," he looked at us expectantly.

"Yes ma'am, we will have dinner later," Joy said.

"Dad what is this?" Mrs. Khurana had spotted the drinks on the table.

"Oh my god, how many people will ask me what this is? I just explained this to your husband. Please ask him, and please don't disturb us until we're finished." With a little help from Joy, he started serving the drinks.

"Would you like a drink?" he asked Khurana sir.

"No! No, thank you."

"You always drink with me. What happened today?"

"Dad, please try to understand. They are all my juniors. They need to get back to duty tomorrow morning. They just came here for some *dal bati* and not what you are offering them."

"Listen. Don't try to teach me how to live my life, just because you haven't done anything in yours."

"What? What have I not done, dad?" All this while, Mrs. Khurana was trying to stop them both from creating a scene.

"You have done nothing but work," the Major-General glared at Khurana sir, but then softened his tone. "Try to enjoy life. Try to spend some time with your loved ones. Don't be shy to express your happiness with anyone. Come and sit now."

"Dad please try to understand sometimes," Khurana sir said.

"I don't want to understand anything. You HR people have complicated both your professional and personal lives." After much persuasion, Mr. and Mrs. Khurana sat down for a drink. Ma'am and I took a Red Bull, Khurana sir and Rudra took a beer bottle each, and the rest were content with whisky. Everything settled into a comfortable calm. Soon enough, I had finished one can, and the others had downed three glasses each. Never before had we got the time to relax and unwind together like this. Everyone was drinking without any fear as our HR was with us too. Slowly, apart from Rudra, ma'am and I, everyone started getting drunk. Whenever any of them would offer us a hard drink, we'd show them the cans we were holding.

"You hoteliers are very complicated. You never understand others' pains, and forget how to live. You never try to understand what is going on beyond your lives." The Major-General was back to demeaning us.

"It's not like that sir. We are not how others think us to be. We are different." This time, it was Godi who replied as the alcohol got to him.

"What would you know? You are like a new born baby. You don't know anything."

"You are from the army, sir, so how would you know how hoteliers function?" Godi argued. I poked him hard in the ribs, begging him not to, but he was clearly not in his senses.

"How do I know? Good question. First, from my daughter, who worked in the Housekeeping department. You can see that picture," he pointed at the framed photo on the wall. "Everything was fine till her graduation. But as soon as she joined IHM, everything changed. I never realised when she completed her course and became a part of your industry. One day she went for her internal IHM training and brought this gentleman as her husband. I have never understood this man, but she always said I have. I don't know half the things you say, but only an hotelier can understand another hotelier."

"Yes sir, no one else can understand," Rudra nodded vigorously.

"Dad, please be careful," Khurana sir got up and held him up as he swayed, now tipsy.

"Don't worry. I have faced worse things, this whisky doesn't affect me. I am okay."

"Yes, you are right sir." Godi kept his empty glass on the table and waited for the Major-General to pour him another peg.

"I think out of all of you, you are the only person who likes to talk. I think you should've become a lecturer," he pointed out, pouring the drink. Godi chuckled.

"What happened gentleman? Why are you laughing?"

"You know, it's always been my dream to do something different. When I graduated from college and my parents asked me what I wanted to do, I said I wanted to do something different. My dad said he wouldn't give me a single rupee from his monthly pension if I continued saying that. I was scared. They cut my wings off before I could fly. They made me feel like I couldn't do anything. My dad's friend suggested him to send me to IHM. Without asking me he chose this path for me, and now here I am." He'd never told us any of this. This was his fourth peg talking.

"So this means this isn't the life you'd have chosen." Godi nodded.

"So, why did you not try to make your dad understand? Since you wanted to do something different," the Major-General asked.

"I tried. Dad said I didn't understand anything." Godi seemed nervous now, with all of us engrossed in their conversation.

Sir laughed. "Dad tells his son that he doesn't understand anything. A wife tells her husband that he doesn't understand anything. Goddamn it, I will never understand one thing. What is the age for a man to understand things finally? Can anyone tell me at what age he becomes mature?"

"You are right," Rudra agreed, a little tipsy, on his second beer.

"Dad, are you okay?" ma'am asked.

"Yes, I am okay," he said softly, and looked at Khurana sir. "Being a son-in-law, you have never made me miss out on not having a boy. I could never understand you, but you always understood me. Thanks for that, and a happy wedding anniversary to the both of you."

"Dad…," Khurana sir mumbled and hugged him.

"Can we wind up now?" ma'am asked.

"This is our last."

"Yes, yes ma'am, this is our last. Sir, please," Godi said gestured to the bottle.

"Why did you stop? Continue and tell us what your dream was, and what that different thing was, that you wanted to do."

"My dream was to join an insurance company," Godi replied.

"What?" We were all shocked.

"I thought you had something better in mind, but this is completely out of the box. So why was that your choice?"

"Yes, it is. You never know if you will be successful or not, but you will definitely make others' lives better. It's been my dream to be a part of that, and one day I will definitely achieve it."

"And what about your IHM degree, and these years of experience that you have?"

"Once I'm fifty, lying in bed after retirement, who will ask me? You are an army man, so you get some pension. But what about us? Everything will have changed. Nobody will come to ask me what degree I have then. The only thing that'll save me is if I have insurance." This got us all thinking. Really, he was different.

"Dad, it is eleven now. I think we should stop this and sit for dinner," ma'am broke our trail of thought.

"Yes, you are right. We should move now. Okay gentlemen, thank you for this evening. I will always remember this night, especially you, Mr...," he looked at Godi, trying to remember his name.

"Godi! Godi Dsouza," Joy quipped.

By the time we finished everything, it was almost twelve, and time for us to head back. Apart from Rudra and I, everyone else was sloshed. Godi and Shantanu were almost toppling over. Joy, Rudra and I enjoyed dinner so much, we couldn't thank ma'am enough. The others might have liked it too, but they were in no state to be grateful.

"Ma'am, such an amazing dinner!" Godi seemed to have forgotten the name of the dish. "Yes, *dal bati*. What a dish ma'am! I will only marry a Rajasthani girl who will make this for me every day!"

Laughing, she humoured him, "Even if you don't get a Rajasthani girl, I will teach the other one to make it, don't worry!"

"Oh, thank you ma'am," Godi said. "And, yes sir!" he saluted the Major-General dramatically.

"Are you okay Godwin?" Khurana sir asked.

"Yes, I am okay." He looked over to Shantanu who had slipped down his chair, "Chef! Please be careful, you should drink within limits."

"I am in control, you behave yourself," Shantanu snapped.

Ma'am called me into the kitchen in the midst of this scuffle, to help her with the cake.

"Okay guys, it's cake time!" I propped the cake on the table.

"Oh, a cake! Whose birthday is it?" Godi sniggered. We ignored him, since everything he was saying was only because he was drunk. I handed the knife over to ma'am and Khurana sir, and as soon as the clock struck twelve, they cut the cake with us clapping in the background. Khurana sir picked up a piece and fed half of it to ma'am, and the other half to his father-in-law. After such heavy drinking and dining, there was no space for cake, but Joy and I took a small bite of it, and handed the rest to Khurana sir.

"No space at all, we're overflowing with *dal bati*, drinks and sir's lectures," Godi said, and all of us started laughing.

"I think we should move now," Joy said, once everyone was done with the formalities.

"Yes, it is past twelve already," I agreed.

"Yes of course, it is twelve, you should move. Or if you want to, you can stay here," ma'am offered.

"No ma'am, it's okay. We will reach safely, don't worry," I assured her while pushing the others out.

"Ma'am, once again, thank you so much for the dinner, and sir, thank you for your time," we chorused.

"Oh really, the dal bati was amazing, and this party was unforgettable!" Godi put his two cents in.

"Okay, thank you. Thank you so much for coming to my house."

"Sir! You are great. You are a genius. You are not a man, you are Superman! You are Spiderman!" Godi started again. "I don't have words to describe you! This is for you." He then proceeded to lie down on the floor, with both his hands folded towards the Major-General.

"Hey! What are you doing?" he moved back, shocked.

"Godi, are you okay?" A slight hint of worry crept into Khurana sir's tone.

"This is *sashtang namaskar* to all of you from me," his voice muffled. We didn't understand what was happening to him. This was the first time that he was drunk in front of us. None of us knew this side of him.

"Okay, okay, please stand up now," sir helped him up. "Are you okay?"

"Yes sir!" he saluted again.

"Now it's really too late, I think you must move," Khurana sir shook his head.

"Good night guys."

"Good night sir!" Gogi managed one last salute as we pulled him along with us.

Chapter 15

The toughest things in the day of a life of an hotelier, are the things that can't be explained to anyone. Sometimes it happens like magic, or it feels like we are magicians, but it happens on its own. When two hoteliers meet, their way of thinking should be the same, or it will definitely create problems. We are the ones who care the most for the people in our lives, from our family to our loved ones, but when we can't give them time, we come in a bad light. There could be a thousand reasons that make life tough, but nothing's tougher than when it comes to asking your bosses for leaves. If we work for more time than necessary, our bosses are elated, but when the topic of asking for leaves comes up, to them we become nobody of importance. It all started with a call.

"*Beta*, where are you?" I answered *maa*'s call, lying in bed. I was talking to her after twenty days. Thanks to my schedule, whatever little time I had free, I'd spent running to get some rest. On most days, I didn't get the time to do that either.

"Sleeping *maa*," I replied groggily.

"Do you know it's been twenty days since I've spoken to you? No call, no message, nothing from your side. What are you doing *beta*?"

"I know m*aa*."

"What do you know? You don't know anything." She sounded so hurt.

"*Maa*?" I said tentatively.

"What *maa*? You don't think of calling me a single day, you don't even miss home."

"So sorry *maa*, I am really sorry."

"I don't want your sorries, now listen to what I am saying. You do one thing, take a leave for a few days and come home immediately. I have a surprise for you." She sounded like she had something on her mind.

"What?" I sat up. "What is it *maa*?"

"Nothing, you come first. It's a surprise for you." She's calling me to join Hitler's business, I thought. Was she thinking of looking for a job for me close to home? Or was it something else? Whatever was in her head, I wanted to know.

"*Maa*, please, can you tell me clearly what the surprise is?"

"I said it's a surprise *na*. You know how one never spoils a surprise right?" she laughed.

"I know *maa*, but there are no hidden things with us, so please tell me."

"No, sorry."

"If you will not tell me, I will not come. So please tell me what it is." This was the only way she'd answer.

"Manav!"

"*Maa*, please."

"Okay listen, your dad thinks you should get married to Mathoor uncle's daughter. She will come to meet you once you are here. We are all waiting for you."

"What? *Maa*, what is this now?" I was fed up already.

"It is nothing, you just come I will explain the rest to you."

"But *maa*, how will I come?"

"I don't know how. You know your ways better."

"*Maa*, please try to understand," I implored.

"I don't want to understand. Why do I have to compromise with you every time? You need to too sometimes. I don't know anything. You have to take a leave and come as soon as possible."

"Leave, now? Not possible, I have a very busy schedule."

"Busy schedule?"

"Yes and my boss will not give me a leave right now."

"What do you mean *not possible*? Are you doing a job or have you signed your entire life away to those people? Almost a year has passed since you visited. You forget to call your mumma, someone you'd never leave alone before. What busy schedule? You don't have time to have food on time, take proper rest, and now you are saying you don't have time to come home." She was furious. I remained silent. I knew she was right. What was I doing?

"*Maa*, please, I won't get a leave. I promise I will try next month."

"You expect me to believe anything you say? No, not possible. You take leave and come fast or I will call your boss. Then don't ask me why I did that later."

"*Maa* please, not now please," I requested.

"Sorry for this. I will wait for your call." She disconnected the call suddenly. I sat staring at my phone for a minute. She was right. My behaviour with everyone had changed. I had never been this way before. I was just realizing how much I had changed, and just how much that was affecting my relationships.

"What happened? Why do you look so upset?" Joy entered my room.

"Nothing."

"If nothing happened, then why are you so upset?" he tried to make light of the situation, and looked at Shantanu who was standing by the door.

"Can you stop joking?Not everything is a joke," I argued, my voice cracking.

"I like cracking jokes and laughing. I thought you knew that." He came closer to my bed.

"What do you think of yourself?" I pushed him back. "You think everyone is like you, no tensions in life, no family headaches, no future planning, just remain as you are. Do you think all our lives are as useless as yours?" He looked at me silently.

"Tell me why you are quiet," I continued. "I have a thousand problems that need to be solved, and thousands of dreams that need to be fulfilled. I'm not like you. You came into the world without a purpose and will leave it the same way. No goals, no achievements in life. Only jokes and laughter are not enough to be a good person or a successful man!" My voice echoed around the bare room.

"Manav, please calm down brother," Shantanu pacified me.

"Chef, can you keep quiet for some time?" I said and looked at Joy.

"I never said I don't have dreams, but that doesn't mean I need to keep telling everyone about them." Joy said softly.

"Oh really?" I laughed in mock amusement. He nodded.

"What is your dream?" I asked him rudely.

"Never share your dreams with anyone, it's not something to be flaunted."

"Oh great. Really great. You know what your problem is?" I said and took a pause, breathing deeply. "Let it be, you will not understand this."

"Yes, no one can understand me."

"That is your misconception. There are thousands of people in the world better than you. There are people who live every day just to achieve their dreams. Not everyone is like you. Not everyone thinks of their dream as a joke. You can't do anything but joke. Wait, no, you can break rules too. You can show the way to people, but have you ever thought what path you are on? Have you ever once thought that this is not a life that you are living here? There is so much more, but you will never understand."

"Yes, I said no one can understand me."

"No, that's wrong. You are not worthy enough for people to understand you," I grumbled.

"Manav! Enough is enough. You are crossing the limit. Apologise to him," said Shantanu, coming towards me.

"Apologise for what? Why should I say sorry? It's not like I slapped him," I laughed in mock amusement.

"Manav, dude please," Shantanu requested.

"Do you understand now how it feels when someone laughs at us?" I looked him in the eye, unblinking.

"All I am saying is apologise to him. He is our brother."

"You realise brothers always care for each other, they're not like him." I was almost shouting.

"Manav what happened to you, brother? Are you okay?" Shantanu kept a hand on my shoulder.

"Yes I am fine. Just tell him to mind his own business," I replied, removing his hand.

"Brother, calm down."

"I am here to be a good man. Every second I think about my future. Every moment of my life I ask myself what I am doing. Every day I spend just running to achieve my dreams like a good, decent man."

"Where is all this coming from?" Shantanu asked.

Lighting a cigarette, Joy walked into the balcony. "You are right, I don't have a dream. I don't have parents, and the one I think of as family, stays across the seven seas. I don't even know whether she still considers me family. If I don't have anyone, then what do I have becoming a good man for? When I was ten, my dad left me. I have spent my entire childhood with mom. When I became mature, she left me and I became alone again. You don't know the pain of being alone. You don't know what you go through when you live alone. You should be thankful you have parents and dreams, unlike me. You have something I don't. Don't forget how something is better than nothing." He blew the smoke inside the room. I suddenly realised I'd said a lot of hurtful things to him.

"Hey Joy, forget him brother. I apologise," Shantanu pushed past me and went to him.

"Today I don't need your apologies Chef. I say sorry," Joy looked at me seriously.

"Sorry dude," I said softly, and went up to hug him. Shantanu couldn't wait for his turn, and joined us.

"It's okay," Joy said as I looked at him and laughed. "First you tell me not to laugh and then you laugh yourself!" I feigned seriousness and hit him on his chest.

"Ouch!" he chuckled. "By the way, the day is wasted when you don't laugh!"

"Sorry dude, I was fed up with mom. She is asking me to take leave and come home. I was trying to make her understand that I can't," I sighed.

"Take a leave and go," Joy said.

"What?"

"I said take a leave and go," he repeated.

"You really think it is that easy to pack up and leave? You think Suri sir will grant me leaves in such a busy schedule?" I asked.

"Even if everyone is busy for the whole year, it doesn't mean you can't take leaves."

"You want leaves?" Shantanu interrupted. "Okay, take and go."

"Will you sign my leave card?" I asked. After a second, I told them about the rest of the conversation. "There is one more problem. *Maa* is forcing me to get married, but I don't want to marry another girl. I want to settle down first, and then marry Suhani."

"Do your parents know about Suhani?" I shook my head.

"And you don't want to marry another girl," Joy pointed.

"Yes."

"Listen, I have an idea. You take your leaves, go home and meet mom and dad. Take some days to relax and come back then. No issues."

"What about the girl *maa* told me to meet?" I asked.

"Don't worry; you just go meet her formality's sake, for your mom. And the girl who is coming to see you, will definitely reject you." Shantanu and I looked at him incredulously.

"How do you know she will reject him? Do you know her?" Shantanu asked.

"Because we are hoteliers. And only an hotelier can understand another hotelier's plight. So there is no point in accepting her proposal," Joy explained.

"Yes, you are right. The same thing happened to me too. Three girls rejected me." Shantanu added. "They were nurses. They asked me when I'd have the time to look after our children if I cook the entire day. Finally I got married to a housewife."

"All that is fine, but what about my leave? How will I get that? Whom should I go to, Khurana or Suri sir? I am so confused," I said.

"Don't be confused. Just listen and do what I am saying and you will get your leave." Joy cupped his mouth near my ear and started whispering.

"What? Are you mad? What are you trying to say? No, sorry, I can't do this. I don't want to lose my job!" I exclaimed.

"If you want a leave then you have to do this, or forget your leave. Call your mom and tell her you can't come," Joy said, handing me my phone.

"Sorry I can't do that either," I shook my head. "Any other ideas?" He shook his head, as Shantanu looked at both of us in confusion, with no idea what was happening.

"Hey Manav, here you are here. I've been looking for you everywhere." Rudra entered the room and stilled our discussion.

"Yes Mr. Flatterer," Joy greeted him.

"Hey you shut up, don't call me that!" Rudra erupted.

"Joy, can you please not?" I looked at him pleadingly. "Yes, what happened?" I asked Rudra.

"I am going on a leave for ten days. I just came to inform you that I am leaving tonight. Tell aunty I won't be coming for dinner, and I'll tell her once I return." He didn't realise this was exactly what we were fighting about.

"You are going on leave? Who sanctioned your leave?" I asked.

"Suri sir."

"What did you have to do to get it?"

"Nothing much, I just filled out the leave form and took Suri sir's signatures, and gave it to Khurana sir," he replied.

"Did Suri sir say something while sanctioning the leave? I mean, did he easily sign it? Did he ask you something before approving?"

"No, he signed it very easy, and didn't say anything. I'd even filled the application for seven days, but sir gave me ten days' leave." I stared at him with eyes wide open, then turned to Shantanu and Joy.

"Why, what happened?" Rudra asked.

"You asked for a week and sir gave you ten days. He even approved it easily!" I exclaimed.

"Yes, okay now I am getting late. I'll see you later." He stumbled out of the room leaving me dumbstruck.

"I was mad! Why was I behaving like a fool? Why was I thinking so negatively about Suri sir?" I hit the back of my head in disbelief.

"What, you think he will give you leaves as easily?" asked Joy.

"Now shut up. You just heard about Rudra right? He gave him

three extra days! I just need a week. Even if he gives me extra days, I will reject them." I was finally hopeful.

"Oh my god, what do I say to him now, he's gone mad! Chef please, you make him understand," Joy said to Shantanu.

"First let him try then I will also apply for the same." Looking at me, "You carry on and take his signatures. Just let me know what happens."

"What nonsense are you talking? Do you honestly think all bosses are the same? None of our fingers are the same either!" I thrust my hand in front of them dramatically.

"How am I to make you guys understand this? Don't forget, every boss has one special person and that special person happens to be Rudra. That's why he got it." I kept quiet and pondered over what he'd just said.

"Let's see tomorrow?" I finally said, as the room slowly enveloped in cigarette smoke.

****

After the morning meeting the next day, I went to Suri sir's office to discuss my leave. Suri sir was in the good mood I had hoped he'd be in, after the meeting. It is these little things that we need to keep in mind about our bosses when approaching them for personal favours. Their mood is one of the main things to be kept in mind before discussing such things, especially when it comes to leaves.

"May I come in sir?" I opened the door to his office slightly, my left hand forming a knock on the door, and my right holding the leave card behind my back. He was preoccupied so I repeated myself. "May I come in sir?"

"Yes, please come in gentleman. I can hear you properly, no need to repeat yourself," he beckoned me inside, looking at me from behind the laptop.

"Sorry sir," I walked in and stood in a corner.

"Yes, tell me."

"Sir," I lowered my voice, worried I was intruding on his work.

"Yes, please speak gentleman," he continued typing.

"Sir, I am Manav," I replied, doubtful he'd recognised me.

"I know you are Manav Kapoor, gentleman. I may be working with my eyes but my ears are concentrating on you," he looked up at me.

"Sir, I thought I'd wait for a minute since you are busy."

"So what if I am busy? I am always busy, but that doesn't mean you will wait for me to finish my work. You should always speak up. I can multitask you know," he looked at me and laughed. I felt like I was trying to talk to the world's busiest man.

"You are great sir," I returned his smile.

"Oh really, thank you so much," he grinned at me. "Now, will you keep smiling or tell me what you came here for?"

"Sir," I didn't know how to proceed.

"Yes, tell me."

"Sir, I wanted a leave for seven days."

"I thought you came here to discuss something work-related," he grinned manically.

"No sir, I have some work at home, and need to take a leave urgently."

"Yes, we always take leaves when we are needed the most. All these emergencies seem to happen at the last moment."

"Really sir, I do have some urgent work," I said softly.

"Oh really?"

"Yes sir."

"Do you know why we should take leaves?" he asked me out of the blue. I couldn't figure out whether he was serious or not.

"Pardon me sir?"

"I asked you why we should take a leave. Because I don't know why," he smiled crudely.

"Sir, I think we take leaves for some rest, or sometimes people need to take a break from work." I tried giving him the answer he wanted.

"Oh yes, so you mean to say you want to run away from work. My dear, work is the biggest part of life we need to accept."

"Sir that's not what I meant," I fumbled.

"You meant just that."

"Sir, sorry sir," I mumbled and kept quiet.

"Sorry for what? Since you want a leave, you should know why."

"Sir I don't know why, but I know the meaning of it," I said, remembering what Joy had said. "The word roughly translates into letting all employees enjoy their vacation."

"Oh, so now you are trying to act smart with me." He leaned forward with his hands on the table. "Don't be over smart. Now tell me, why do you want a leave? And who will do your job in your absence?" He moved on to yet another problem. What the hell was this? I felt like I was a solider asking his superior for a long leave, while a war ravaged the country. He was behaving like that. There were so many things I didn't know yet, but asking for leaves was proving to be the most dangerous experience in my life.Joy was right all along; I didn't know anything about our bosses.

"I am asking you something!" Sir shouted when I didn't reply.

"Sir, I don't know who will work in my absence, but it's very important for me to go home."

"Why? What happened?"

"Sir, I am going to meet the girl I'm to marry," I told him the truth.

"What? You want to get married? Are you mad?" He almost sounded concerned.

"Why? What happened sir?"

"What happened? You want to get married and you're asking *me* what happened?" he laughed.

"But sir, there's nothing wrong with getting married."

"Do you not want to progress in life, or become a successful man?" he asked out of the blue.

"Sir, I don't understand what you are saying."

"My dear, you understand so little right now, and after you get married you'll understand nothing. Everything will become a mess, all your juniors will move ahead and you will be stuck here."

"You mean to say married men never become successful," I offered.

"Look at me. If I would've got married early then I wouldn't have been here. Don't you want to sit here?" He gestured at the chair he was sitting on. "Forget about me; take the world as an example. There are thousands of examples of people who became successful without marrying. Even they say that had they married, they wouldn't have been where they are now. They created history because they had no other responsibilities. Don't you want to create history?"

"Of course, sir, I do."

"If you get married then how will that be possible? If you want my suggestion, you can take some time to think."

"No sir, I have to go. It's very urgent." I said, remembering *maa*'s dejected tone.

"Are you sure? Here, take some water and think for a minute." He filled a glass and slid it towards me.

"Yes, sir. I am sure. Thank you for the advice," I said with finality.

Finally, after such a heated discussion, he agreed to grant me seven days' leave. No one else could have possibly imagined what I had had to endure for a simple signature. I thanked him and hurried out, with him wishing me luck as I closed the door. The discussion bore fruit. I finally got the sanction. It felt like someone had just handed me an Olympic gold. Like I'd become a superstar overnight.

Chapter 16

There was no reason for me to wait a single day in Alibaug. I'd completed almost a year in the city, and the happiness I felt on finally going home was evident on my face. Joy and Shantanu dropped me to the bus stand, wishing me luck for the journey.

With the rains lashing down, and the lush greenery outside my window, I relaxed. As the entire year's memories flitted in and out of my mind, I started wondering. Why was *maa* in such a hurry for me to get married? Why did she think I needed to get married right now? How would I dissuade her from marrying me to this other girl? Was this the right time to tell her about Suhani? What would dad say? Would another drama start? As these thoughts clouded over, I started thinking about a few years back.

It was the hardest night of my life. Love, the world's most dangerous yet tempting poison had entered my life. Suhani, and my one-sided love story which had come to a halt in the campus garden. I had fallen in love with a girl who didn't believe in the concept. The hardest thing for me was to convince myself of how she'd always see me as a friend. Apart from physical intimacy, we shared an equation of people in love. The only difference was the way we perceived it.

That night proved unbearable for me. The clock on the wall seemed to be ticking away so fast, and my heart begged it to slow down. I dialled Suhani's number but disconnected it before the ring. I tried to call her again and again, but would keep disconnecting it. I couldn't get her out of my mind the entire night. I wanted to talk to her. I wanted to show her my love. My head sank to my chest, dejected. *What happened? Don't cry, man.* The voice in my head said.

"Thank god you're back. Please help me," I said in a pained voice.

Don't worry, all will be fine.

"Why not to worry? Please help me disclose my love to Suhani. I can't be without her. She is moving out tomorrow. How will I live without her?" I sobbed.

This is exactly your problem. If someone is friendly with you, you fall so deeply in love like you've known her for ages.

"Please?"

What do you think of yourself? She met you just a few days back and thinks of you as a good friend. Just because she shares every problem with you doesn't mean she should become your girlfriend. Don't forget these things you share make up a friendship as well. Every girl who smiles and talks to you, doesn't necessarily love you. I have always warned you not to fall in love. First, focus on your career. Your journey has just started.

"What do I do when my heart refuses to understand this?" I said miserably.

Give her some time. Let her get to know more things about you, let her come to the realization of whether you are perfect for her or not, herself. Let the right time come.

"When will this right time come?"

That only the heavens know.

"God, please bring me my right time. You can feel my despair, you can feel my love." I folded my hands and faced the skies.

Your love is not wrong, he said soothingly. *But it is one-sided. Such loves rarely succeed. Do you want your love to fail? Do you want to reduce your love to a missing page in your story?*

Do you want this love to remain only in your memories?
I shook my head in despair.
So, be calm. Give time to your love. Every story is bound to end well, but because we rush into things, we fail. If she is meant to be your partner for life, then you don't need to worry. She will get back to you anyhow.
"Do you really think all will be fine?"
Trust me.
Meanwhile, my phone rang. It was Suhani. *See, didn't I say the right time will come?* He slipped back into my consciousness, and I smiled.
For a minute, I looked at my phone ring. I realized then that if I were to have my love reciprocated, I wouldn't know the value of it. It's only after a lot a struggle, compromises and complications that you do.

"Hello," I picked up the call.
"What hello? Can you not see my number or have you deleted it?" Suhani asked harshly.
"No actually..."
"What actually?" she thundered. "You always have excuses for everything."
"No it's not like that," I mumbled.
"What no? Forget it. Anyway, listen. I am coming to pick you up in a minute. You come down quickly without asking any questions."
"Where are you taking me this time?" I asked nervously.
"Don't be scared. And I said no questions!"
"Okay." I said just as she cut the call. I looked down at my phone and smiled. Of course I couldn't ask her questions, but she had all the rights to. It was fast becoming the best evening of my life. I had just wanted to talk to her on the phone but she was coming to meet me!

I wore a pink shirt she had gifted me earlier, and was downstairs in the next five minutes. Soon enough, her red Mercedes came to a halt outside the boy's hostel. I opened the door and sat next to her. After a few minutes' drive, we parked the car in a corner and started walking, ice-creams from the local parlour in hand.

"You look amazing in that," she pointed to my shirt.

"Thanks to you," I replied.

"Me? For what?" she asked, amazed.

"For this gift."

"Oh yes, and I am still waiting for my gift!"

"I know. I will give it at the right time." I replied.

"Really," she laughed. "I was just joking."

I suddenly gagged.

"What happened? Are you okay?" She asked, patting my back.

"Yes, I am fine."

"No, you are not fine."

"Yes, I am fine." I repeated forcefully.

"If you are fine then what was that?"

"I'm not used to having ice-cream in winters."

"I am really sorry. If you don't have the habit then leave it."

"No, it's okay. I can't leave everything because of my habits, and this is your treat," I looked at her.

"Sorry, because of me you have to suffer a lot. You are so nice, thanks for being in my life and supporting me," she looked back at me.

"Don't say thanks and sorry," I said.

"Oh yes, never say sorry or thank you to a friend!" she laughed out loud.

I couldn't get my eyes off her. She looked even more beautiful than before. I looked up to the heavens, smiling.

"Are you looking for something?" she asked. I shook my head.

"Okay, let's change this topic. You know, you're the first person

I'm willingly going to share my ice cone with," she gave me her cone.

"Suhani, can I ask you something?" I interjected.

"Of course."

"If you really fall in love with someone, what will you do?"

"That day should never come in my life."

"But what if you feel you are in love?"

"We love a lot of things on Earth but that doesn't mean we bind ourselves to them all."

"Like what?" I probed her for details.

"Like, I love this evening, I love this moon, I love nature but I can't *be* with all of them, right?"

"If you are in love with all of these then I have to be part of them," I said cheekily.

"If you are there then I will be too." She looked at me seriously.

"Why don't you like love?" I stopped walking and kept some distance from her.

"Why do you want to know?" she turned around to face me.

"You said I am special to you, so I think I should know about it."

She sighed. "I don't have a problem with love but I don't want to ruin my life being with the wrong person. You know my parents had an arranged marriage, but my dad still misses his first love which is something I don't like and don't want for myself. If I love someone, then I will marry only him, otherwise I don't want to fall in love."

"And after you're married, if your husband loves someone else, then?"

"That's what I don't want."

"So it's better to fall in love and get married," I concluded.

"It is very difficult to find the right person," she replied.

"You try, and you will."

"God creates very few good people on Earth. Like, you are one of them."

"Oh really? How do you know I am a good person?"

"My heart says so," she said looking at me. We both looked at each other unblinking. She followed this up with an impossible question. "Manav, are you not in love?"

I remained quiet for a second before answering, "Yes of course I am in love." I broke the silence that followed with a smile.

"Oh really, so why haven't you told me about this before?"

"I told you, but you took it as a joke," I looked at her.

"I am so sorry, but please tell me now. Who is that lucky girl and what is her name?" As she said this, I looked away.

Wait, give her some time. Your time hasn't come yet. The voice in my head warned. I understood what I had to do.

"Manav, Manav?" she shook me to elicit a response.

"It is a one-sided love," I replied.

"Really, and who is that lucky one?" she pressed.

"Let the right time come. I will tell."

"Manav you are hiding things from me. At least tell me who she is, what her name is, where she stays!" she insisted.

"I am not hiding anything from you Suhani. Someone told me to let the right time come. I promise if my time comes sooner than anticipated, I will tell you first."

"Who asked you to wait for the right time?" she asked.

"Someone who looks out for me." As I said that, she looked around.

"Manav what is this? What is going on? Who asked you to wait for the right time?"

"He said God writes our stories, and if people are really made for each other, one day they will definitely be together." I derailed, "And if you really deserve it, then you have to wait for the right time to come."

"Manav, I don't know what you are saying," she shook her head in confusion.

"Forget everything and listen to me. Today is our last night together for you are moving to Goa tomorrow. Just concentrate on completing your training in these six months and come back fast."

"Please come to Goa with me," she said, looking at me nervously.

"Suhani you are not going for a holiday. You have to complete your training and come back. It's just six months then we will be together again," I tried making her see reason.

"Is this training even compulsory? I don't want to be alone."

"Yes it is. Unless you'd rather fight with our professors here every day," I laughed.

"Don't laugh!" she chided. "I am asking you seriously."

"Yes Suhani, you have to." I repeated.

"But I don't want to," she turned her back to me.

"Suhani please?"

"Just leave it and be quiet." Her face turned beet red in anger. I waited for a minute then held her from behind.

"Don't worry. Everything will be fine," I whispered in her ear soothingly.

"Don't leave me alone." She closed her eyes and leaned back, resting her head on my shoulder.

"It is just six months." She immediately turned around and hugged me, and that's how we remained for a while, in embrace. By the time we headed back, she was still upset. She dropped me at my hostel gate and left in a huff, without saying goodbye.

****

"Did you reach safely? How was your journey? Did you face any problems?" I asked once Suhani answered her phone after coming out of the Goa airport.

"Manav! Can you please ask me one question at a time?"

"Sorry," I apologised and asked again, "Was everything okay?"

"If things aren't okay, what will you do?" she snapped.

"If nothing is okay then I will make it okay for you," I replied calmly.

"Nothing is okay here. I am waiting at the airport, so come and make it okay." She was steadily losing control.

"Suhani, what happened?" worried, I asked.

"No, you just said if nothing is okay then you will make it okay for me. So come and do it now. I am waiting."

"Why are you so upset?" I asked.

"No! No!" she screamed. "First you come here and make things okay, only then will I answer your questions."

I became quiet. Every time she'd get this angry, I'd shut up and give her space. Like she'd told me, she had her dad's temper. Regardless of her anger, she'd still look as beautiful as ever. But I wasn't with her to look at her then.

"What happened now?" she asked once she realised I wasn't talking.

"Suhani, I know how you're feeling but it is just a six-month long training session. You won't even realize how fast this time will fly, and then we will be together again. I promise I will never ever leave you alone in the future," I replied earnestly.

"But I told you to come with me. Why didn't you come then? I need you now. I want you now. I miss you. You will never understand my feelings. What will I do without you planning my future for me?" Her voice cracked as she said this.

"Suhani, listen to me and please don't cry," I waited for her to reply but she didn't. "Are you there?" She simply sniffed. "Okay, I promise I will be there with you very soon." I promised her without thinking of the consequences. She remained quiet.

"Hello, Suhani? Are you listening?" I asked, equally upset.

"Yes, I am listening."

"Please trust me."

"Okay," she started. "Let's see when you fulfil your promise to me. Now I have to go. I will call you later." She put the phone down once I'd said my goodbyes.

This was the first time distance was playing such a huge role in our relationship. I was heartbroken, feeling helpless and alone. I couldn't help but remember our initial days together. There wasn't a single day that we'd spend apart. But now, I was the summer and she, the winters. One heart, split into two seasons and cities.

Chapter 17

The most trying time for an IHM student is the IT, or the Industrial Training. The training is a headache for him and for others around him as well. Anyone can come and screw things up for him, treating him like he is a waste of space. One can't share their problems with anyone; they can't share their pains with anyone. Learning from how they were treated, when they become seniors they do the same to their juniors. It's a vicious cycle of contempt and disregard.

"Your session will be in the Housekeeping Department for a few weeks then I will transfer you to the Front Office and other departments as per the requirement," said the HR, as we stood outside her office.

"But ma'am, my interest lies in the Front Office department. It is mentioned in my college letter as well," I said, confused.

"Yes, I know that, but due to staff shortage you have to work there."

"But ma'am...," I said then kept quiet looking at her. "Okay ma'am, no problem." I wanted to explain to her how I didn't want to waste my time training in housekeeping. But as a mere trainee, I couldn't afford to argue with the HR on my first day of joining.

As some staff passed through, wishing her, she said, "I hope you will complete your training with full interest and fulfil the requirements of your seniors."

"Of course, ma'am," I assured her. "You just give me one chance. You will only hear positive reviews about me."

"Oh, I really hope so. Keep it up," she smiled at me curtly. "Do you know anything about housekeeping?"

I replied, "Ma'am in theory I know a little, considering how big a lesson it was, but not as well practically."

"Okay. You will learn how to do things practically here. That way you can add an extra training point as well."

"Okay ma'am," I said, thinking about getting that extra point in the trainee register to be filled by the HR, which we had to submit to the college as our training record. Finally, walking through four to five corridors, meeting some staff in between, we reached the small housekeeping cabin.

"You wait here for a minute. I will be back," she said and went inside. I was being trained in a five-star hotel in Shimla. Standing alone, I started looking around. To my right were a uniform room, laundry, and a flower room. Some staff members were busy working there. Some of the staff members going to and from the cabin, looked at me like I was a different kind of creature waiting outside the cabin. I looked down, trying to convince myself of all being okay.

"Fresh meat?" one staff member said to another, looking at me. "I think so," the other replied and they both burst out laughing. I was there for something new, and instead of people helping me, I was being made fun of. It hurt me considerably. After a painful minute, the HR came out and confirmed me for the night duty.

****

"Good evening sir, ma'am," I rushed in to greet them, interrupting their briefing.

"Who are you?" One of the supervisors asked me.

"Sir, my name is Manav. I am from IHM College Dehradun. Today is my first day as an industrial trainee." I introduced myself stressing on my college's name, since our teachers had taught us to do the same. This was considered the professional way of introducing oneself.

"So what? Answer only as much as is asked of you. You don't need to act smart here," a female supervisor fired at me. She looked like an odd mixture of both genders, and her voice was deeper than a man's.

"Sorry ma'am, sir asked me, which is why I said that," I replied, looking down.

"If you try to act smart with me again, I will punish you with a double shift and you will have to handle a three-staff area without a single mistake." She threatened me with more work then continued to speak to the staff member next to me. Her voice resonating around the room, with an aura of authority.

"Where were you yesterday?"

"Ma'am, I suddenly got sick," the guilty staff member said in a low voice, sinking in his seat.

"Oh, really? And you became fine in one day?" she asked.

"Yes, ma'am. It happened suddenly."

"Oh, how sad, what had happened to you?" she asked snidely.

"Ma'am, cold, fever and a headache." It seemed like he had forgotten exactly what had happened to him, so he named all possible symptoms.

"Did you think who would work if you get sick?"

"Ma'am, I'm sorry it all happened suddenly."

"Shut up!" she shouted.

"What happened ma'am?" he asked, startled.

"Every week after the weekly off you get sick for no reason. Do you think we are fools?" her voice thundered across the room.

Ashamed, he muttered. "Sorry ma'am, this will not happen again."

"Sorry for what? And do you think if you say sorry I will forget it? You take us for fools!" She turned to the supervisor and said, "Make him work in the public area alone, let him do the deep cleaning."

"But ma'am, how will I do that alone?" he asked in a soft, defeated voice.

"You can make a fool of us easily, but this you can't do," the male supervisor said curtly.

All of us became quite after hearing the punishment, the guilty staff especially so. The lady supervisor completed the tasks in the register before her. She took our attendance, read the briefing points, and allocated work, while the male supervisor started checking our grooming. He moved from the left side of the room to the right, crossing off parameters like shaving, hair setting, black socks and black shoes, maintenance of the uniform and more, before joining the lady in front. Before starting a shift, all this was mandatory. Since it was my first day, I was just observing everything.

As the male supervisor came to each of us one by one, we were expected to show him our nails to ensure the length was acceptable. We also lifted our trousers to let him confirm the socks we wore were black. He then moved on to our hair, to see whether it was cut neatly, and then the worst part, he would caress our faces with his hand, checking for stubble. All the men were supposed to shave every morning.

"Why haven't you worn black socks?" he asked me.

"Sorry sir, I didn't know about that. I will follow the same from tomorrow," I replied, as the lady supervisor looked at me from her stand.

"Oh, you have not shaved either. Very good," the male supervisor said.

"Wow great! Are you here for your reception? Is this your wedding?" the lady asked harshly.

"No ma'am. Sorry ma'am," I stuttered.

"Keep your apologies to yourself. Why did you not shave?" she shouted. I was quiet. She didn't stop there, but started cursing under her breath. "If you don't come in properly groomed tomorrow, then don't come at all. Sit at home."

"Yes ma'am," I replied, and looked down.

That was the day I realised the importance of grooming. I was being shouted at on my very first day. Sorry, okay, and thank you. These were all the words we used to keep our seniors happy. During our training, if our seniors were happy, it meant smooth sailing for us, topped with a good remark in our college note. More than our work, we were graded on the respect we showed. Slowly I understood this unspoken rule and started following it. But I was scared of Leena, the supervisor. If my housekeeping results were in her hand, then I was definitely going to fail.

As a trainee, we had to think of our college's reputation also. Professor Chaturvedi would always say that wherever we go for training, we don't go alone. We carry with us our college, professors' names, and their reputation. We played a big part in preserving the reputation of our college. We'd always have this label on our head.

Present Day, Shimla

After hours of reminiscing, I finally reached Shimla. Exactly a year back I had left home, and in this one year a lot of things had changed, but the happiness of coming home remained the same.

"Oye puttar tu aa gaya, aaja puttar aaja," *maa* wrapped me in an embrace once she saw me at the entrance. I was standing in front of her after a year. Silently, we both immersed ourselves in the hug.

"I missed you so much, my son," she said.

"Me too, *maa*."

"You didn't."

"*Maa*...," I started.

"What *maa*, don't you eat anything? See how you were and how you have become now," *maa* pointed to my body, now much slender than when I was home.

"*Maa*!" I said, exasperated.

"What *maa*, don't those people give you food to eat? See, you look so weak. I don't know where you are working. You don't miss me. You forget to call me. Ever since you left the house you've changed. I let you go for your job, but I didn't know this was the price I'd have to pay."

"*Maa* you never get anything without sacrifices," I said calmly.

"Don't shrink so much, otherwise there will be nothing left," she said seriously.

"*Maa*? Did you call me home for this? I've come home after a year. Please don't shout at me now."

"I don't know what more I'll have to see in the future. I thought after your graduation everything would settle down and you'd be happy," she sighed.

"*Maa* I am happy. Look within me, not my health."

"Look at yourself *beta*, at least don't lie to me."

"But *maa*... please don't react like dad."

"Then show me your happiness."

"How can someone show their happiness? Isn't it just meant to be felt?" I countered.

"Leave it, you will not understand," she sighed.

I tried to change the topic, "My dear *maa*! Don't worry, I am okay. Now you forget all this and tell me what you've cooked for me."

"It is useless to tell you since you anyway don't need to remind me what you like. I've made a special dish for you," she said.

"Thank you so much *maa*. You know I have been craving

homemade food all year round. I miss it thrice a day. So now, please no more discussion. First we will have food then sit to speak," I said and smiled.

"Okay *beta*, you go and get fresh. I will get the table ready for you," she said, finally smiling back.

"*Maa*, where is dad?" I asked as she served me *khir-puri* on a plate, once we were home.

"He is in office and he promised me he will come home early today because he knows you are coming." She overcompensated, to prove dad cared for me.

"*Maa*, why do you have to do all this? I know he doesn't care about me. He's always loved and cared about his work and meetings more than me," I said, frustrated.

"It is not like that, Manav," she replied softly.

"So, how is it *maa*? Can you explain?" I asked.

"He cares for you. That is why he is your dad and you are his son."

"Sometimes dad doesn't seem to love you either," I muttered.

She took offence. "Who said your dad doesn't love me? He has always cared for me and for you as well. Just because he was rude to us, doesn't mean he doesn't love us. He is your dad. Why would he hate us?"

I bit my retort back, and said simply: "You know better than me."

"Yes, I know better than you."

"Why don't you try to understand *maa*?" I tried again.

"Why don't you try to?" When I kept quiet, she continued, "And listen, as per our discussion, Mathoor uncle's family is coming to meet us, so you be ready and please don't refuse."

"*Maa* I am not interested in getting married right now. I need some time. I've just started my career, I have lot of things to do, and...," I trailed off.

"And... what Manav?" *maa* asked. For a minute, I was blank as to what to say.

"Look Manav, you requested us to let you work so far, and I made your dad accept your decision. Only I know how I've managed last year. And now your dad's only decided to get you married, so please don't refuse him," she said, serving more *khir* on my plate.

"What? Dad thinks I should get married? But why? And without my permission?" I stopped her from serving me.

"Yes," she simply said.

"But *maa*, what about my future? And how did dad even think I'd be ready for marriage without my permission?" I asked.

"Now should your dad ask you for permission before doing everything? He is your dad and you are his kid. Don't forget that."

"But *maa* why does dad think I should get married *now*? I need some time to get settled." I was frustrated.

"Your dad's home. It's better if you ask him only," she signalled to a car honking outside.

"No then I better be quiet. Let's see. But *maa*, I am not interested in marrying now, and all this that I am doing is for you only. So sorry, but I can't say yes, even though I am meeting that girl for you, I will not say yes."

"Don't forget, you chose this job and your college on your own, against your dad's decision. If you refuse now, he will feel bad."

"What? Do I need to get married just to make dad happy? I need to say yes only because I joined IHM without his consent. What is this, *maa*?"

She seemed to think for a minute before replying, "He thinks you will leave your job and join him in his business."

"I know *maa*. Anyway, the entire last year dad didn't even remember me. I haven't received a single call from him. He's not even bothered to ask me how I am!" I exclaimed.

"And how many times did you call him? Every night before he falls asleep, he asks me about you. How many times have you asked or called?" she rebutted, walking towards the door to welcome dad home.

I was speechless, trying to digest what she'd just said to me.

"You're here," I heard her say.

"Yes of course. You still remember me. I thought you'd have forgotten me now that your son is home," dad taunted her.

"He is your son too," she smiled.

"Yes, I know that." He looked at the table and exclaimed, "Wow! Your son's favourite food today!"

That's when I came forward. "Hello dad, how are you?"

"I am okay *beta*," he replied. "You tell me. How is it going with your... what do you call it? Aah yes, an hotelier life."

"All well," I replied.

"Good, so what is your plan next? When are you joining my business?" he asked suddenly.

Even though I was half expecting this, I was taken aback. "Not yet," I replied.

"So, think now and come join me from tomorrow. What are you waiting for?"

"I am okay as an hotelier, dad."

"Oh great, you are happy working under someone but you don't want to join your own ready-made business. Great idea." He shook his head in disbelief.

I retained my cool. "Dad, I just started my career. I have my whole life in front of me; I didn't get an IHM degree to join your business. I also have my own dreams. I also wanted to do something different."

"Being an hotelier, there's not much of a difference that you can make. At the most, you will become a General Manager one day. Not that it's a bad job, but in any job you will always have to work under pressure. If you want to do something different, come join my business," he smiled at me.

"Dad, there are thousands of people who are happy being hoteliers. They also manage to live their lives on their own terms. They also have their own dreams and they fulfil them. They have not joined their dads' businesses. I also want to do something different for myself. Please, dad?" I urged him to understand.

He looked at me steadily. Then, "You don't want work in our family business, but you can work under other people."

My patience was wearing thin. "Dad, not all jobs are the same. Even if I don't become a General Manager, I will be happy as a Manager. Thousands of people work on their own terms. Are they all bad?"

"Now, enough is enough," he stopped me. "I don't want any more excuses. Mathoor comes with his daughter tomorrow. You have to meet her and agree to the union. We will fix the wedding date." Before I could say anything *maa* gestured at me to remain quiet.

"Dad, I don't want to marry right now," I said still, getting up from the table and moving towards my room.

"Look at what he is saying!" I could hear him as I left the room. "I am telling you not to embarrass me in front of my friends. Now you speak to him. He went and got an IHM degree and I did not say anything. He chose his own job and I didn't say anything. But this time I will not be quiet. Come what may, he has to say yes. Don't forget this."

Chapter 18

"Oye Mathoor, please come my dear. How are you?" dad welcomed the Mathoor family, among whom was Sunaina, who I was about to meet after fifteen years. I busied myself in my room, thinking of excuses to reject Sunaina. In India, the boy's family goes to the girl's, but in my story it was the opposite.

"*Oye yaara*! I am good, how are you?" Mathoor uncle hugged dad. They were childhood friends. *Maa* also welcomed them in, meeting Mrs. Mathoor and Sunaina. Finally, as the Mathoor family settled down with the intention of converting their friendship into a family relationship, nobody quite knew what the future really held. In a country like ours, the family tends to get even more excited with the prospect of a wedding, than the potential bride and groom. The big Indian family drama in the form of a conversation started in the hall, and I could hear them laughing. Their friendliness agitated me, and I started pacing the room again, trying to find the perfect excuse to reject Sunaina.

"Where is Manav?" I heard Mrs. Mathoor ask *maa*.

"Manav!" *maa* immediately called out. I ignored her.

"Manav *beta,* look who's here!" dad screamed out. With no other option, I walked out into the hall where everyone was looking at me like I were on exhibit.

"*Namaste,*" I greeted them formality's sake with a smile plastered on my face.

"Hello *beta*, how are you?" Mrs. Mathoor asked, smiling prettily, like she was already seeing me as her son-in-law.

"I am fine *aunty*, how are you?"

"Good, very good *beta*. How is your job going?"

"As of now all's well. I hope in the future too it remains okay." As I said this, everyone looked at each other.

"Oh sorry, I forgot, just give me a minute, I'll bring out some snacks." Everyone laughed at *maa*'s attempt at changing the topic.

"Hi Manav, how are you?" Sunaina held her hand out to mine.

"Hi," I answered as normally as I could under the circumstances. I could see her happiness on meeting the person she wanted to spend the rest of her life with.

"Dad, if you guys don't mind, can we discuss something in private to understand each other better?" Sunaina asked dad fearlessly. I was astounded. As I looked at her talking to her dad, I realised I'd never had such courage.

"Why not *beta*. He is all yours," my dad answered. He'd never behaved like that with me!

"Thank you, dad."

"Manav, I hope you don't mind this?" she asked.

"Actually," before I could say anything else, *maa* interjected, "Why will he mind? He is just shy because he is meeting you after such a long time. Also, this is the first time he is going to get married." Everyone was stunned.

Sunaina replied with composure, "Aunty, this is going to be my first marriage too."

"Oh, I am really sorry *beta*. I forgot."

"*Maa*!" I whispered, horrified.

"What *maa*, don't give me any excuses. Now go with her and understand each other well."

"Yes *beta*, later don't tell us we didn't give you any time!" Mathoor uncle made the room laugh.

I led Sunaina to the terrace, since I too was waiting for the right time to talk to her.

"Don't be formal with me now," she said as I offered her a seat on the sofa. She held my hand and we sat together. I smiled at her, and she did the same. It was a quiet, awkward moment for us both. "Say something," she finally broke the silence.

"It's better if you start."

"Manav, I don't like behaving like Laila – Majanu, Shahjahan – Mumtaz, or Heer – Ranjha. I don't like to be confused. So if you want to ask me anything, you can." She gently kept her hand on mine.

"Actually Sunaina," I started.

"Wait, Manav! Before you say something, I want to clear a few things which I feel are very important for you and me. I have a few questions that you need to answer."

"Answer what?"

"Manav, I know this is very awkward for you. We've been friends, and that's fine. But now our relationship is going to change. And according to me, we have to think a hundred times before choosing a partner, because it'll be for a lifetime. I think you will support me in all my decisions." She looked at me like I was forcing her to choose me as a partner. I sat quietly.

"Manav, what happened?"

"Yes, please, continue," I said.

"Are you sure?" I nodded.

"Okay then, my first question is why do you want to get married?" she asked.

"I don't know," I replied honestly.

"What? Manav, what do you mean by that? You are going to marry me, we are going to spend our lives together and you are saying you don't know why you want to marry! Are you joking with me?"

"No, it means I don't know why I want to marry." I said, trying to be as passive as possible so she'd feel bad and refuse to marry me.

"Manav what are you saying? Are you okay?" she asked.

"Yes, I am okay."

"Okay. Anyway, leave this. We'll discuss this later." She went on to ask, "My next question is, do you love anyone?"

I stayed quiet.

"Manav, please reply to me. You can't be quiet at all times. Please." She forced me to answer. I was in love with someone, yet couldn't acknowledge it in front of her. If I told her the truth, then the reason would definitely reach my dad, who'd start off again.

"No," I replied.

"Okay good. I haven't fallen in love yet either. But I know I will love my husband very much."

"Oh really, nice thought," I said shaking my head, and we laughed.

Suddenly, "Are you a virgin?" she stopped laughing and asked. I looked at her with my mouth wide open. She couldn't possibly be serious.

"What kind of a question is this?" I asked.

"Manav, we are in the 21st century, the Hindu *Kalyug*. It is very difficult to differentiate between what's right and what is wrong. I don't know about the others, but I should know whether my future husband is a virgin or not, because it is important to me since I am a virgin." She asked me to be open enough to divulge such details. I listened carefully as she continued, "Manav listen, I am a very straightforward girl, I like to live honestly I dream practically, and the person I am going to get married to, should share my dreams. He should always listen to me. He should always understand my needs and fulfil them without any demands. In a day, he should spend at least 13-14 hours with me. Nowadays no one spends time with their loved ones, which then creates misunderstandings, because of which the relationship doesn't last. I don't want such a relationship. These are my basic needs and conditions."

"And what if he doesn't do all this?"

"If he isn't like this, then I will not marry him," she said simply. Her requirements were such which couldn't possibly be fulfilled by an hotelier. I thought she'd definitely reject me. I looked at her still expecting an answer.

"Are you sure you are looking for a husband?" I mocked.

"Why, don't I have the right to find the kind of partner I want?" she answered smoothly.

After a small pause, I answered her previous question. "Yes, I am a virgin."

She looked at me in disbelief. "Oh, thank god," she let out a sigh. "Okay last question," she continued. "I am a software engineer with Microsoft. My working hours are eight, and I earn anywhere between sixty to seventy thousand, depending on the extent of my work. If I put in extra hours or work extraordinarily well, then my earnings cross eighty. But I get at least sixty every month. I think my future husband's salary should at least be a quarter more than mine." Her words fell like a hard blow. It hurt to realise that forget earning more than her, I couldn't even compete with her salary. There was a stark difference between what our families think we earn, and how much we actually do. I'd just started my career. Even after a year of being there, my salary was barely a quarter of hers. This was the perfect chance to get out of marrying her, but the fact that she earned so much more than me, really hurt me.

"What happened, Manav?" she asked, patting me on my back.

"Nothing."

"By the way, what is your job profile? I mean, what company do you work in?" I kept quiet, still mulling over her salary.

"Manav?" she shook my shoulder. "I asked you something," she waited for my answer but I remained silent. "Manav, what happened?"

"Sunaina," I started. "I am an hotelier. I have an IHM degree and am working as the acting Front Office Manager in Alibaug."

"What?" she looked shocked, as if I'd said something very bad.

"What happened, Sunaina?" It was my turn to ask.

"Manav, are you sure you are an hotelier?" she asked, turning to my side.

"Yes, I am sure. Why, what happened?"

"Actually Manav, I am really sorry. I don't want to make my life hell. I don't want to make my life meaningless. Sorry, I can't marry you," she said, not looking at me directly. She rejected me and I heard what I wanted to. Even though I was happy with her decision, I wasn't happy with her reason.

I acted like her rejection stung me. "Sunaina, why are you saying this?" What I really wanted to ask her was, are all hoteliers that bad?

"Manav, I know hoteliers very well. They work for more than 13-14 hours every day, have no personal lives, no time for their family, less increments, rare promotions. You know, when I joined Microsoft a few months back, my salary was thirty-five thousand. I was just an assistant then. But in a few months, my salary doubled as I took on the post of a software engineer. Will it be possible for you to manage a miracle like me? Not more than me but can you at least earn as much as I do?" She was asking me something that was not in my hands. I didn't know how to respond. "Manav, please reply. Can you earn what I expect?" she repeated.

"I don't know," I said honestly. "Maybe not."

"See, if you don't know yourself and are not sure then what can I expect from you? I don't know what you think about me. You can remain a good friend of mine, but I'm sorry but I can't make you my life partner. Sorry, you are not the one for me." She got up as soon as she'd said this, and left the room.

Just the thing that I'd wanted happened. But I hated the way it happened. Thanks to this experience, I realised how others perceive hoteliers. Giving my profession as an excuse, she sat down next to her parents. Mathoor uncle sympathised and urged me to sit next to him. "Don't worry. Everything will be okay. She will be ready soon. I will take care of it. You don't worry." Soon after, they left.

I turned towards dad and found him furious. He looked at me like I'd stolen all his property. *Maa*, on the other hand, remained quiet. She sat as if she'd expected something like this to happen.

"See, now do you understand or do you have something more to do?" dad pointed at me. I sat quietly.

"I had told you to not listen to those bastard friends of yours, and not get into IHM, but you didn't listen to me. What had you said? 'My future will be bright. I will do something of my own.' Where is your bright future now? What have you done by yourself now? At least open your eyes now." His words thundered in the room, as I sat listening quietly.

"Can you tell me now?" he asked. But I left the room.

I didn't even stay there for the remainder of my leave. I took permission from *maa* and came back before my official leave ended. I was being pulled apart from all angles. My job, my family and my personal life were all tense. I was fed up with all of them. But through all of this, one question kept cropping up. Had I done anything wrong choosing this field? If I was wrong, then were all the thousands connected to the hospitality industry wrong too? And if all of us were wrong, then what should we all be?

Chapter 19

That night was the first time I drank. I'd never tried it before, but because of the tension that plagued me, I became addicted. Every single day can't possibly be the same, yet we are expected to enjoy every moment. I didn't realise that would be what everything would lead to, the night those bastards came home and convinced me to join IHM. It was funny how one ridiculous night changed my whole life. Once we decide on what we want, we just think of the things we have to be, but we never realise what we have to sacrifice to get there.

Even though I was immersed in my life as an hotelier, a few questions still remained; questions that would disturb me every waking hour. Did I choose the right path? Will my future really be bright? Will I really get what I want? I knew my destination was still far, and when I looked back, everything had changed. I had chosen this life, and the price I paid was my dad hating me, more problems finding their way into my life, distancing myself from *maa*, and a girl rejecting me only because I was a part of this world. I was walking blindfolded, with no idea what the future would hold.

Shantanu, Joy, Rudra and Godi were enjoying their Saturday, drinking and snacking. In some time, Rudra also joined them with a drink. They were enjoying, and I was drinking away the tension of the last few days.

They couldn't stop laughing after I told them what had happened. One by one, they started cracking jokes at my expense.

"Dude, you made fun of the whole industry," Shantanu said in Bengali, blowing smoke in the air, a glass in his other hand.

"What did you do man, you shamed us in front of a girl!" It was Rudra who spoke up this time, laughing aloud.

"Guys, please don't joke now," I warned them. In a few minutes, I had downed almost two pegs. The tension inside me, clubbed with their teasing angered me. That's when the alcohol took its effect. I didn't understand half the things that were happening there. My emotions mixed together.

Shantanu looked at me and said, "We are just joking, my dear friend. You made a joke out of us too."

"Please Chef, don't say anything. It's better if you keep quiet."

"Oh, so you go and spoil our names and we have to keep quiet."

"I didn't do anything, it was just…"

"What?" Rudra looked at me.

"Nothing, leave it."

Joy offered me his glass. "Take some more, this is the best medicine in the world. It makes all your problems disappear. Everyone will come and give you a shoulder to cry on in your bad times, but only this will give you love."

Rudra thrust his glass forward and said, "Oh really? Then give me some more. I am frustrated too." After taking his share, he continued. "Bro, whatever happened was horrible. You embarrassed us in front of a girl, like we're worth nothing." He moved to my side and laughed.

"Shut your mouth!" I lost my cool and shouted. "I'm sitting here with you foolish guys making fun of me. I will kill you, you rascal! Shut your mouth! My life has fucked me over and you are making fun of me." I picked up an empty beer bottle and tried hitting him with it, but Joy stopped me.

"Manav! Have you gone mad?" Joy took the bottle back.

"Yes! I am mad, I'm a fool!" I waited for a second to gather my thoughts, but started crying inconsolably instead. Everyone immediately dropped what they were doing. "Hey Manav, c'mon bro...," Godi muttered.

"Hey Manav, what happened? Don't worry all will be fine, don't take it seriously bro," Joy said sympathetically.

I despaired. "I am really sorry, but what do I do?"

"Bro, just think. Whatever happened was in the past. Forget about it. Try to live in the present and concentrate on your future. All these things are a part of our lives. All will be okay dude. Don't worry, everything will be fine."

"Nothing is okay, Chef. Ever since my first day at IHM, I have only been listening to people say, 'Don't be an hotelier, your life will stagnate.' I was a blank slate before I entered this industry but I readied myself to be a part of it. I wished to be successful. I am so far from home, my dad hates me, all because I am an hotelier. I can't do this, and I can't do that, just because I'm an hotelier. But things don't stop there. After all this, a girl come and rejects me because...," I sighed. "What is all this? Is what I do a crime? Or just a huge mistake? What's *okay*? Nothing and never will anything be okay in our lives, Chef." Everyone listened carefully to what I had to say. The night's silence enveloped us, but was then broken by Joy.

"Hey dude, please you calm down. Don't cry like a girl. Don't spoil our reputation." His phone rang, and the screen showed Ketaki calling. Joy cut the call and turned back to me. "See, this is the first time I've disconnected your sister–in–law's call. Only for you. I'm requesting you bro, please stop crying like a girl."

"Hey bro, please don't request or else I will end up crying more," I said. "These aren't just tears. This is my pain that I am trying to explain to you."

"What do you think? Is this your problem only? This is a

problem the whole world faces. Every human struggles with this problem, and this problem exists in all fields. The Prime Minister of the country has to tackle problems of the entire country. Doctors have critical situations with their patients. Bankers have issues with their customers. Engineers have their own problems. Lawyers have problems with justice. Do you think this is the only industry with such problems? Bro, it's the same everywhere. You need to make yourself strong to fight this, not cry over it. You see, if you ask anyone from any field, no one is happy in their own field. This is not because they have chosen the wrong field. We feel others are happier than us, but what we forget to respect is, what we have, the others don't."

I looked at him in confusion. "What exactly are you trying to say?"

"What I mean is, instead of thinking this way, look at the other side and change yourself. Bring more ideas to your work. Work smart. Let your work speak for you."

"You think I am not strong?" I countered in my drunken state. "Every day I work for more than 12 hours without a break. I take a break for food and tea, and most of the times I end up having to miss that too. I should make my work speak for me, you said. So do I have to work for 24 hours now? I've sacrificed a lot of things to be here, do I need to sacrifice more? I am so far from my family, what else is there to compromise?" I asked.

"This is the problem," Joy had his rebuttal ready. "To be a success, you don't have to work 12-hour shifts. You don't have to spend your entire life in office, always tensed. If you really want to be successful and want to do some different things, then do some smart work also. Always think of doing that one thing that no one else can. Give yourself challenges.

Complete your 12-hour work in nine hours. Bring good ideas every moment." He finished his fourth peg, as Rudra, Godi and Shantanu looked at us conversing intently.

I fell silent for a minute before commenting. "Bro, I think I work smart only, because others are very happy with my work. Even Suri sir appreciates my work."

Joy laughed and shook his head. "*Oye* you dumb man, don't make others happy! First make yourself happy then see how the others will automatically be happy. If you are not happy and worried about others' happiness then there is no use. Then you are the most foolish person in the world. Because others will only be happy as long as you're working. Then when you leave, new bosses, new places and new job descriptions will force you to repeat. But if you make yourself happy first, then your work will be easy and effective. It's your happiness after all, that will help you grow, nothing else. Before you start any work, sit for a minute and think if what you are doing will give you happiness. Never work only with your mind. Sometimes you have to listen to your heart too. Try to do something new. We don't bring any new ideas. We don't bring any speciality in our work. We don't work smart, and then feel like we are failures. You know the field we're in requires us to promise people we've never met before, that we'd meet them again. We put our faith in them and ask them to visit again. Why? Because we want them to return to further our business, and promote us. If we will not be perfect for them, how can we expect them to return and promote us?"

We all sat quietly, letting his speech sink in. "You mean to say, this is the key to success," Shantanu's lilting Bengali voice joined the conversation. Joy nodded.

"I don't believe in all this," Rudra mumbled.

"Someone once said, 'A dream is not that you see in sleep, but is something that does not let you sleep.'" Joy said, looking at us, and finally, at Rudra.

"Also don't forget this basic truth; if you don't sleep for a minimum of 7-8 hours a day then you will be ridded with illness. And if you fall ill, how will you be successful?" Rudra replied to Joy's jibe.

"All this is okay, but what about me? I am almost a year and a half into this industry, and I haven't received either an increment or promotion. What should I do?" I asked.

"How do you think you will get it?" Joy asked me. "You never knock on the HR's door to discuss this. If you want it that bad, then you should have the guts to ask for it." I nodded, understanding what he getting at.

"Don't think about the past," Shantanu piped in. "Think only about the future, but live in the present and enjoy your chilled beer for now."

"What rubbish are you all talking about? Talk about something else," Godi finally opened his mouth.

"What *something different*? You are a sales person. You don't need to think too much." Shantanu waved his hand over Godi's head, to everyone's amusement.

Godi snapped back, "Hey! Don't talk nonsense! Working in sales is a different type of art. We can do things that others can't, and don't forget, our role is very big."

"Oh really, then why do you want to change your profession?" mocked Joy.

"I am not changing my profession," Godi replied calmly. "I am just changing my way of work from this industry to an insurance company. I want to make myself proud, since like you said, we should keep ourselves happy."

"If really you wanted to work in an insurance company, why did you join this industry and waste three years on an IHM degree?" Joy asked.

"I have not wasted a single day. I try to learn at least one thing a day. I'm always ready to learn something new, each and every moment. I always try to accept the challenges life throws at me. Only one thing I realised today, after all of this, is that this industry is not made for me."

"Oh really, but sorry bro, I don't like insurance people," Shantanu laughed. "They're so scary. They decide your death, plan for your family like you don't care for them, and promise you a future where you might not be alive."

"It is called family security. You know, the insurance companies give better returns compared to banks. They never think of today. They always think about your future and try to secure your family. Especially when it comes to your kid's education or wedding. It works on your behalf, as a strong shoulder for your family."

"Can I ask you something?" Rudra asked, taking a sip of his beer. "See, every insurance company cares for every family, and all the companies promise to secure your life. Instead of waiting for twenty – thirty years, I will pay the entire policy amount now, and you pay me the amount that you'd have paid me later, now itself. What do you say?" Rudra said, looking at us with a lopsided smile. Everyone but Joy laughed.

"This is the first time I have met an insurance person who doesn't judge my future. Everyone else decides how many years I have left to live," Rudra's beer started taking its toll on him.

"I think the world's toughest job is selling a company's product."

Godi took a cigarette from Shantanu and blew smoke in the air. "You know, we are all millionaires here, we don't feel it and never recognise it, but you are a millionaire too. If you look at things from my perspective, you will realise I'm right."

"I think you are very drunk, we should stop here," Rudra tried to take his glass away.

"You shut your mouth."

"But…"

"I said shut your mouth."

"Okay now I am quiet, please carry on. Everybody please keep quiet and put your fingers on your lips. Nobody will say anything, just listen." Rudra staggered and tried concentrating on Shantanu and Godi's conversation.

"What were you saying about all of us being millionaires? There is only a negligible amount left in my account and all my pockets are empty! How can I be a millionaire?" Shantanu asked.

"If you see from your perspective, then you definitely aren't. But if you see from the point of view of a sales person, then you are," Godi pointed.

Joy wasn't having any of it, though. "*Oye* don't take us for fools, don't talk nonsense."

"No wait, let him finish," Shantanu said, and asked Godi to continue. Godi finished his glass of beer in one sip and banged the glass on the floor. "Till now, I was talking from the point of view of an hotelier. Now let me explain to you as a sales person. So, listen." As we looked at him in expectation, he swivelled towards Shantanu. "What is your average salary?"

"Around fifty-five thousand," replied Shantanu.

"Okay," Godi continued. "So if we calculate it annually, your salary will be around...," he closed his eyes to calculate.

"It comes to around six lakh, sixty thousand or something," Shantanu answered.

"Oh, nice. Good mathematical powers," Godi smiled at him. "So, how much experience do you have?"

"Twelve years."

"So, my dear chef, can you please calculate your annual salary clubbed with your total years of experience?"

After a slight pause he answered, "Seventy-nine lakhs and twenty thousand." We all looked at him stunned.

"So, my dear friend, you already have your answer. You know this better than I do. Twelve years of working have earned you around seventy-nine lakhs, which is equivalent to being a millionaire." Smug, Godi crossed his arms and leaned back. Shantanu sat still, absorbing what he'd just been told.

"*Udi baba*, how didn't I realise this!" Shantanu exclaimed, putting his hands on his head. "Hey Joy, see!" he called, "I am a millionaire! Manav look, I am a millionaire but I never realised it! My money is right here. Thank you, thank you so much! You don't know what you have done. You've opened my eyes!"

****

"We will miss you buddy. And sorry for everything. If we said something bad or did something wrong, please forget it," I said to Godi.

"Yes bro, really sorry if we did anything wrong," said Joy.

"Hey guys, please don't make me cry. I am only leaving this organisation but I will always be in your hearts. I will miss you guys too," Godi replied, wiping his eyes with the back of his hand.

"Don't forget, or else I will start coming in your dreams then you won't be able to sleep well either," Shantanu said and hugged him. Joy, Rudra and I also joined in. We were in the Club House, sending Godi off. He'd finally resigned from his duties to join an insurance company. That was the day I realised how very easy it was to get close to someone, and how equally difficult it was to bid him goodbye. Even though all of us felt bad, we knew he was leaving for his future's sake. He was going out to achieve something. After coming to Alibaug, this this was the first time we were sending someone away.

"Whoever comes must one day leave. This is for you from all of us," Rudra opened a small box and took out a Titan watch with a golden dial, and all the hours in silver. Godi was taken aback.

"Oh, thank you so much guys. Don't worry, I will not forget anyone. And how can I? You guys have given me a gift that will always be with me, and whenever I see this, I will miss you."

"Thanks for making me a millionaire," Shantanu said, and we all laughed.

"Don't just thank me, now that you've become a millionaire, I hope you will take some policies from me, it will help me achieve my yearly target!"

"No worries bro, confirm a family policy for me," Shantanu replied in good spirit.

"Are you sure?" Godi confirmed, being a typical sales person, he worried about completing his targets.

"A hundred percent."

"What about you guys?" Godi looked at Joy, then me.

"Is one each okay?"

"Okay," I replied.

"And you?" Godi moved to Joy. "You take two separate ones. One for you and the other for your *gori* madam."

"Okay confirmed," Joy grinned, fist-bumping him.

"Okay guys, now please allow me to leave. Thank you for everything," Godi came up to us and hugged us all. When he reached Shantanu he said, "Chef, special thanks to you for your food. I'll definitely miss it thrice a day!"

On reaching me, he said, "Really, if you feel you should get a promotion or a higher salary, don't hesitate to walk up to the HR's office. And if you don't get a raise, raise your voice."

When he reached Rudra, he thumped him on his shoulder and said, "Hope I will see you in a different blazer very soon."

"Of course."

"Okay guys, bye, take care." Saying that, he left us thinking about a very important friend we'd just lost.

****

The whole conversation around increments and promotions confused me. Was this really something we needed to ask for, or would it be given to us? Even though these things were the most important aspect in every employee's life, was it really necessary to improve your salary at one time? I just wanted to be clear before walking up to the HR's office.

Khurana sir let me in after I knocked thrice. As I stood inside, he was on the telephone with someone and gestured at me to take a seat.

"What is your salary expectation?" he asked to the person on the other side.

Pause.

"That is too high; I need to take my budget into account as well."

Pause.

"But don't just look at your salary! Think about your future! Our facilities! You will get a chance to work in a 5-star hotel, which will be beneficial for you in the future." Pause.

Sitting in front of him, listening to his conversation made me feel like a fool for coming. Oh really? I did not realise the facilities I was getting would help secure my future as well.

"Okay listen, do one thing," he continued. "Come for an interview. We'll discuss and finalise things then. I will let you know the date and time soon."

Pause.

"Okay bye. See you soon." He hung up. Taking a breath, he sipped some water and looked at me.

"Hello sir, good morning," I said when I had his attention.

"Oh, very good morning. Sorry Manav. What to do. Lot of work pressure, and I need to deal with different kind of employees every day," he smiled, fidgeting with his tie as usual. I smiled back as he continued, "Anyway, such is our work. So, how are you? And is everything okay?"

"As usual, fine sir. But... something is not okay. So I thought of coming to your office and discussing it." I said, starting the conversation in a soft voice.

"Oh! Thanks for coming then. Is it anything serious? Is everything okay at home? Are you okay?"

"No sir!" I exclaimed. "Everything is okay at home. My mom is very happy with my job."

"Great, anything personal then?"

"No sir, it is related to my job."

"Are things alright with your department? Any issues you're facing? I know we are short of staff, but we will fill the vacant spots soon. Apart from this, anything else?" he smiled, his palms facing the ceiling. It was almost like he understood what I wanted to say.

"Sir, can I say something?" I asked delicately.

"Of course, why not? My office and I am always available to you guys. Please, go ahead."

"Sir, actually today's the day I complete 18 months and 25 days in this organisation, which comes to almost a year and a half." I pushed myself to start from somewhere small, to move on to the bigger things.

"Oh really! Is it?" Khurana sir looked at the calendar lying between us. "Manav that's great! Thanks for reminding me. Actually, I also joined a few days before you. Even I didn't realise how fast time flew. No issues, I will speak to Suri sir to arrange an 18-month success party for all the employees. Thank you again for reminding me. Due to so much workload,

I miss things sometimes. But don't worry, I will do something."
He smiled at me, as if I was the idiot who'd come to ask for a
party in my honour.

I shook my head in response, and said, "Sir, I didn't come to
talk about the party. I am here for another reason."

"Please Manav, go ahead. I am sitting here to help you only."

"Sir, as you know now, I have completed almost a year and a
half here, which was the most valuable part of my life. Now
that I think about it, I feel that my salary should increase,
and I should get promoted." I adjusted myself on my seat
and continued, "It's not just about the time either, sir. I have
to move forward in my life, I want to reach the top. I have
some of my own goals and plans for the future. And sir, I am
especially unhappy since I can feel the financial strain increase
every day. So, I feel that my salary should increase, since I am
working for far more than what I am getting."

"Okay this is the main reason you came to my office. No issues,
this will be sorted out," he said and smiled. I felt a weight lift
from my shoulders, like my work was done and I'd get what I
wanted.

"Strange. We are both on the same track," said he. "You know,
even I am not happy with what I am getting here. Not a single
rupee worth increment has been done in the last 18 month
for me either. What to do, we have to run our lives so we are
surviving as it is. But you know one fact about human beings?
We can never be happy with what we get. We always want to
grow and achieve more with every step."

"But sir, if we don't go after what we want, there is no meaning
left in life."

"Yes, that is also true. Especially in this industry, we must get
everything on time."

I agreed wholeheartedly. "You are absolutely right sir."

"Okay, now before we take this forward, I need to just go back in time with you and calculate how much time you've spent working here. I'll then raise this issue with the top-level people."

"Sure sir, why not," I said confidently.

"Okay let me see now." He pulled out a pad of paper and a pen from his drawer, and started writing. "How many days are there in the year?"

"365 or sometimes 366 days," I replied politely, wondering why he'd ask me something like that.

He continued scribbling, "Do you come to work on the weekends?"

"No sir."

"Okay, so how many weekends do we have in a year?"

For a minute, I sat quiet, trying hard to calculate. Noticing my confusion, Khurana sir moved the calendar towards me.

"Including Saturdays and Sundays, it comes to 104 days," I said. Khurana sir nodded and jotted it down.

"Okay, great. Now, if you take out 104 from 365 days, how many do you have left?" "262 days, sir."

"Okay, and how many hours make up a day?"

"24 hours."

"How long do you work in a day?" A small smile spread over my face. He was finally asking me the most important question.

"Twelve to thirteen hours, sometimes 15 hours."

"What? But as per the rules your duty hours are between nine and ten, right?" Khurana sir asked.

"But sir, our tasks hardly ever get done in 9-10 hours."

He looked up at me, "You should complete it in the stipulated time only. That is why the company hires talented managers."

"But sir, if we have responsibilities of all the work, it is not possible to manage everything in such a short amount of time.

We don't even get to know when our shift ends. For the last 6 months, I haven't been outside because I enter the hotel before sunrise and leave after sunset. You can check my attendance which proves I work more than 12 hours a day."

"You are the manager, my dear Manav. You should know how to manage your work in 9 hours. If you can't manage it, there is no point of being a manager." The way he smiled at me then made me squirm in my seat.

"Sir, it is very easy to say that, but it's not possible in reality," I measured my answer. "There is a big difference between the theory and practical aspect of this." He looked at me for a moment, lost in thought, then asked, "Should we move ahead with the regular duty timings?"

"Yes okay," I said, seeing how I didn't have any other option. "Nine hours, but if we count your lunch and tea break, your work hours become eight. And what fraction of those eight hours do you work?" he asked.

Frustrated, I said, "Sir please, it's better if you only count it."

"Listen Manav, these are very critical situations. As Human Resource people, we never play hide and seek. We are always clear about everything."

"Around a third, eight hours out of twenty-four," I replied.

"Excellent Manav, now what is one third of 262 days?"

"87 days."

"Great. Now, we give you sick leave for two weeks, 15 days of casual leaves, 5 days of optional leave, 30 days paid leave, so if you take those 64 days out, how many do you have remaining?"

"23 days left," I said, looking at the paper in front of me. All this calculation was going over my head.

"Do you work on festivals?" I shook my head, since there was no point to explain any more.

"In our country, we have 20 festive holidays in a year," he continued. "This is not the case anywhere else in the world. So, how many days without them?"

"3 days," I mumbled.

"Do you work on Republic Day?"

"No sir."

"Do you work on Independence Day?"

"No sir, only one day left, and I don't come to work on New Years either. So now you tell me what you want to explain, sir!" I was frustrated now. My head hurt, and I knew exactly where he was heading.

"My dear manager," Khurana sir turned the paper to my side. "If you know the calculations so well, what are you claiming for, my dear?"

"I have understood, sir," my voice barely audible. "I didn't realise I was stealing the company's money on all these days…"

"Anything else, Manav? Tell me so I can help you smooth your worries out."

"No, sir. Thank you for your support." I stood up and walked towards the door, turned back and said goodbye, and left the room.

A few days back I was content, imagining I could do magic, since being an hotelier wasn't short of being a magician. What I didn't realise was there were better magicians than me here. In the HR's office I met the world's greatest magician who turned the tables around instantly. I knew then, never to go to an HR to discuss your salary increment or promotion.

Chapter 20

The Housekeeping and Front Office department are like the two sides of a coin. Mistakes and misunderstandings were a regular happening. Our industry is a service provider, 24/7. Every hour of every day is the same for us. We work at night, when the whole world sleeps. It is not possible for the person who works through the night to give his 100% at all times. But our job is such, everyone expects us to give our 100% all the time.

I was at my night shift in the Front Office.

"Hello, is anyone here?" A guest walked in at 03:30 am, and called out.

"Good morning sir, how may I assist you?" A receptionist came out from the back office and welcomed him.

"Hey gentleman, due to some emergency I need to check out. Can you please complete my check-out procedure fast?"

"Sure sir, why not. We are happy to help you. May I know your name, sir?"

"Michael Roy, room number 1214." He handed his room's keys over.

"Thank you, sir."

"Can you please tell me what the outstanding amount is?"

"Sure sir. Kindly allow me some time to check the details." The receptionist bent over his system.

"Of course, but make it fast. My cab is waiting."

"Okay sir." As he pulled out the details, a bellboy put the guest's luggage in the cab. "Your final amount due is Rs. 5,500, sir."

"Okay please clear it," he handed his card over, paid the amount and left.

"Good morning. Housekeeping!" In a sleepy voice, the housekeeping staff picked up the call. As a Front Office employee, on must inform the Housekeeping department of a check-out as soon as it's done, so they may get the room ready for the next guest.

"Room number 1214 is empty," said the receptionist.

"Pardon?"

"Room 1214 is empty," the receptionist repeated.

"What? Room 1412 is empty?"

"Brother, listen carefully. 1214 is empty, not 1412. Do you understand?"

"Yes, I understand now." The Housekeeping staff member cut the call and rushed to check the room. There is a strict protocol that needs to be followed before entering a room. The bell is to be rung thrice, with a ten second interval in between. Sometimes, in a state of exhaustion, a staff member enters a room without ringing the bell. This then creates a lot of issues between the bosses, managers and employees.

The staff member stood in front of room 1214. Unfortunately, rooms 1214 and 1412 were facing each other. He looked at both the rooms in deep confusion. He thought of confirming the number with the receptionist again, but his ego didn't let him. He waited for a second, looking at both the doors, then walked towards room 1412.

He opened the room without ringing the bell, and walked into a pitch-dark room. Everything except the AC was off. He could never have guessed what would happen next. As he switched the light on, a horrible scream pierced the air. Shocked, he saw a man and a lady on the bed, with the man yelling at him. "Hey! Who the hell are you? What are you doing here?"

The staff member stood frozen. He couldn't say anything and didn't understand what to do.

"Hey, bloody fool! Who are you?" the guest thundered, covering both himself and the lady next to him with a duvet.

"Sorry, I am really sorry sir," he stuttered.

"Sorry for what? What the fuck are you doing here? Get out of here!" Irate, the guest threw the TV's remote at him. "Who the hell are you? What are you doing in my room?"

"Sorry sir, I am the housekeeping staff. Actually sir, I came to check the empty room across this one, and entered this room by mistake. Again, I am so sorry sir."

"Go, get out of here, you bloody bastard." The guest stood up, wrapped the duvet around himself and walked towards him threateningly. The staff member ran from there and came out, closing the door behind him.

"Wait, where are you running? I will kill you, you bastard!" the guest screamed from behind the door. "What the bloody hell is going on here! Don't you people have any manners?" he shouted into the telephone picked up by the receptionist.

The next day, this incident became a huge issue, because of which, the day took an ugly turn for Suri sir, Joy and me.

****

Hospitality is a type of industry where we get global experience in one place. We get the chance to meet different people every day. We need to deal with different kinds of guests every day. We meet the world's biggest liars and the world's most sincere people as well. Sex, enjoyment, happiness and sadness are all a part of our lives, without which, our lives are useless and meaningless.

Today's generation is different. Our expectations are bigger than our necessities. Instead of searching for love in the most obvious places, we try our luck in places we' have never expected. We go in search of happiness in another corner of the world, when happiness resides within us instead.

"Sam, what is our plan next? What do you think, what should we do?" A girl asked a boy sitting across her in the basement of the coffee shop, next to the lobby.

"Soniya, I love you so much. You know well how things are going on. I try from all angles, but dad is not ready to accept our relationship. He always says our caste is different and we can't accept a daughter-in-law from a different caste. He says, if you want to get married for love, find a girl within our caste. He is very strict when it comes to religion. But baby, you don't worry. I will only marry you, no matter what happens," the boy sitting across her said.

She seemed nervous, and pleaded. "But Sam, I'm twenty-three and you're almost twenty-eight. We can't be like this forever. We have to stop all this at some point. I also spoke with mumma, but it's the same problem there. She also doesn't want my future husband to be of a different caste. I don't know what to do. Please do something!"

"Hey honey, don't worry. Everything will be fine, you trust me *na*?" She nodded.

"Please trust me. We will be together very soon."

"It's only because I trust you that I am with you."

"Should we elope?" he asked her. "Because I don't think our families will support our decision."

"Honey, I also think the same. But what's the point if we've done nothing wrong? I don't want to hurt our parents. I think we should wait some more and convince them. I hope they will agree. We will prove to them we are not wrong."

"Do you think they will agree?" he asked her, unconvinced.

She took a moment to reply. "I don't know… You've always asked me what my biggest dream is. It is for us to get married happily, with our families' blessings. I don't want people to curse us for our love. This is what I hope for."

"Don't worry. If our love is true, then the gods are with us. Nobody can separate us."

They soon paid their bill, stood up and moved towards the lobby.

My receptionist, Neha Tandon and I were in the lobby, like we always were. Neha had joined my team a few days back. Known as the DVD girl, her work was as perfect as her resume had been. Soon after joining, she'd taken charge of the entire front office team, and would even help me out in my absence.

As the couple came towards the reception from the coffee shop, Mr. Singh, a regular guest accompanying a young lady walked in from another side.

"Daddy?" Sam exclaimed, on seeing Mr. Singh.

"Sam! What are you doing here?"

"Daddy, forget about me, what are *you* doing here? And who is she?" Sam looked at the girl standing next to his father.

"Oh, she is my colleague."

"But daddy, what is she doing here with you in this hotel? And you both just came out of a room!"

"No Sam, you are taking this in the wrong sense, she is...," he looked at the lady next to him, and said, "We're here for a business meeting."

"In a hotel room," pointed Sam. "What kind of a business meeting, daddy? Can you tell me what kind of a business meeting takes place in such privacy? Meetings are meant to take place in conference halls. Your office is big enough, what do you require this private place for?"

"No Sam. Actually, our office people booked some rooms for our entire team to freshen up, and we are coming down from different rooms," he explained, and turned to the lady to confirm what he's said. "Right Riya?"

"Riya! Who's Riya?" she asked, taken aback.

"Oh sorry! Look how tired I am. Sorry Rita, can you tell my son the truth?"

"Really, you want me to tell your son the truth?"

"Yes," Mr. Singh blinked forcefully, trying to ask her to lie for him.

"For your information," she started, "I am Sayali. Not Riya or Rita, I don't know how many more names you have. Take this key and let me go please." She thrust the room's keys in his hand, and turned around to face both son and father. "And don't forget to tell your son that we had no conference or presentations to attend to. We were lovemaking in a room. Also, don't forget to tell him that we were in a live-in relationship for a year."

Mr. Singh become completely silent once the truth was exposed. He looked at Sam pleadingly, as the lady walked out of the lobby.

"Daddy! What is this? What are you doing? I'd never expected this from you."

"Hey my son, listen, it is not like what you are thinking. You are taking this the wrong way."

"So it's better if you explain."

"Sam...," Mr. Singh looked at Soniya as if he'd just noticed her. "Hey, you are Soniya right? Please make him understand *na*."

"Daddy please talk to me. Don't get her involved. Now tell me, what is this? You both came out of one room. That lady said you've been in a live-in relationship for a year. If that isn't the truth, what is?"

"Sam, you are my son, I will not lie to you, but please try to understand."

"What do I have to understand daddy? You say you are here to attend a conference, but you spend your time in a hotel room."

Mr. Singh stood silent.

"Daddy, say something, don't be quiet."

"Sam, I accept my mistake. But please trust me, this was my first and last time. And she is lying. I am not in any relationship with her, please try to understand."

"What do I have to understand? You should understand. Mom loves you more than anything else in the world. Have you thought of what she will feel when she'll get to know about this?"

"Hey Sam. Please just leave it and forget it. I promise this will not happen again. Please forget it here only. Don't let your mumma know. Please *beta*."

"Daddy..."

"*Beta* please?"

For a second Sam kept quiet, looking at Soniya just as she looked at them.

"Listen Sam, you don't think anything," Mr. Singh pleaded. "And please don't tell your mumma. I will do whatever you say. You want to marry this girl? I will convince your mumma. But please, my son, leave it, forget it. One mistake even god grants you. I am your dad, and this is my first and last fault."

"Daddy, for the time being, I will forgive you. But one day anyway mumma will come to know. Just think of what she will feel once she does."

"Listen Sam, you forget this now. Don't go to your mumma. If you don't tell her, she will not get to know. And I promise, this is my first and the last mistake."

Sam looked at Soniya and kept quiet.

While they were busy with their conversation, we were busy watching their story unfold. One of our housekeeping supervisors went to them and addressed Mr. Singh. Neha was trying to stop him from interrupting them, but he went anyway. "Excuse me sir," he held out a ring. "This lady's ring was kept in the Lost and Found department on your request, since you asked us to keep it securely the last time you were here. I hope ma'am will be happy to get this ring back now."

"Oh, this is mumma's ring. She was asking you about this and you'd said it's lost in the office somewhere, so then how come it's here in this hotel now?" asked Sam, his eye on the ring in his father's hand.

"Sam, listen…"

"Sorry daddy, this is too much. After this if you ask me to forget this, then I am sorry I can't. I am ashamed of calling myself your son!"

"Sam please, Sam I know this is my fault, but…," Mr. Singh trailed off.

"What? Daddy, this is not just a mistake. You play with mumma's emotions and you break our trust. How can you call this just a mistake?"

For a moment, there was pin-drop silence in the reception. Mr. Singh couldn't figure out what to say. Everyone looked at each other in nervous anticipation.

"Mom!" shouted Soniya all of a sudden. Everyone turned around to see another couple walking down from the opposite end. The lady, Soniya's mother, stopped on hearing her daughter's voice.

"Excuse me, you can finish your conversation. I'll be waiting outside," said the man standing by the mother, before excusing himself from the lobby.

"Soniya." Her mother slowly came towards her.

"Please, mom, don't take my name," Soniya shook her head in disgust.

"Soniya!"

"What, mom? Who was he?"

"Soniya, it's better if we speak once home. I will explain everything to you."

"What will you explain to me, mom?"

"Soniya, please understand and come with me," said the mother on reaching her.

"No, I want to know here itself."

Her mother dropped her head in resignation, and explained, "Okay so listen, he was my classmate. We've been in love since eighth grade. Is that enough or do you still want to know more?"

"What are you saying, mom? If you've loved him since eighth grade, then why'd you marry dad?" Soniya's scream could be heard all the way to the reception.

Her mother replied calmly, "Because he is from a different caste and my dad wasn't ready to accept him as my husband."

"I couldn't have ever expected you to do this."

"Soniya…"

"You told us you wouldn't accept someone from a different caste. Which is why we were thinking of ways to better the situation without hurting you. But little did we know the people we were trying to protect, were the ones with horrible secret lives." Soniya took Sam's hand. "Shame on you, mom. At least we're not like you."

"Soniya! What are you saying? Come home with me now," her mother held her other hand and pulled her towards herself.

"Please leave me, mom!" Soniya shouted, shrugging her mother's hand off.

"My dears. Both of you, please try to understand," interjected Mr. Singh.

"You know what, uncle?" Soniya looked him in the eye. "Sam and I love each other so much. But unlike you, we think about how our actions will affect you, before we do anything. We think about our parents first. Sometimes we think of eloping, but we stop ourselves only because of you. We were just talking about ways to convince you of our love, but how can we possibly convince you now that you've broken our trust?"

"Don't say this, we are still your parents," Mr. Singh stuttered. "Mom," said Soniya, looking at her mother directly. "You always told me you wouldn't accept Sam as my husband, since he's from another caste. We love each other more than anything in life. We trust each other enough to know we won't have to resort to your methods. And now I feel that we don't need your permission or blessings anymore."

With this, Soniya grabbed Sam's hand and led him out of the room. Mr. Singh and Soniya's mother looked at each other then immediately looked away. They couldn't even face each other in their embarrassment.

Chapter 21

"What is this?" asked Joy, as Rudra came in and threw a couple of pages on the table we sat around.

"Your birth chart," he replied sarcastically. I picked it up and started reading; it was Joy's resume.

"What do you want to prove?" asked Joy.

"You are making a fool of everyone. How can this be possible?"

"What do you mean?" I asked.

"We are all getting degrees and struggling to make a mark in hospitality, but this guy wants to prove we are nothing."

"I didn't prove anything," Joy said.

"What rubbish are you saying," Shantanu interfered.

"Yes, my rubbish will prove what's real."

"Can you stop beating about the bush and come to the point?"

"Ten years, eight jobs, with so many promotions. How can this be possible without a single degree? Can you explain this?" Rudra pointed the resume out to Joy.

"Nothing is impossible," Joy replied, smug.

"Oh yes, I forgot man. You are the person who makes impossible things possible, right?" Rudra looked from Shantanu to me.

"It's not like that," replied Joy. "But yes, if we decide to achieve something, nothing can stop us."

"Can you show me how to stand on a needle's edge? Can you touch the sun?" Rudra asked incredulously.

"I said *sometimes*. Do you have a problem with me not having any degrees, or with me?"

"With both."

"So please explain why you changed so many jobs in ten years. Is this the key to your success? And if it is, I've never heard how changing so many jobs in such a short time can be the key to success. Let me also learn what magic you did."

"That is my own business. I don't need to explain anything to you."

"Nothing is your own business, Mr. Joy Dharmarajan. I know you can't perform any magic tricks, but you sure can make a fool out of everyone, like you did here."

"I have not made a fool out of anyone. I just…," Joy stopped before completing his sentence.

"What? Please go ahead."

"It's my personal problem."

"Nothing is personal here. We are all from the same field. You don't need to worry," Rudra pointed out.

"Rudra what are you doing? Leave it. We are not here to force people to say what they don't want to," said I.

"No, you just wait and watch. He will tell us." Rudra turned to Joy expectantly, "By the way, today is the day I take my revenge from you. You remember I'd once said I will? You've always hurt me. I've suffered a lot because of your behaviour. Every dog has his day, and today is mine."

"Hey, mind your language Rudra. Behave yourself!" Shantanu reproached him.

"My dear Chef, Mr. Mukherjee, you mind your own business and keep quiet." "Rudra, enough is enough!" I wanted to stop him before thing escalated. "What is going on? You should think before pointing at someone else. Don't utter a single word now."

"Why are you not trying to understand, guys? He is making a fool of us!"

"I have not made a fool of anyone, do you understand?" Joy snapped, holding Rudra's collar. "Don't say that again."

"So, tell us the truth," Rudra repeated calmly.

Joy let go of his collar and went quiet for a minute. Then started, "Yes, I changed so many jobs in my career, but that doesn't mean I made a fool of people. I haven't made a fool of anyone and nor am I one. It was my own decision to reach here without a degree."

"I've always seen people fighting with their own decisions. I've seen people wandering around helplessly for a job, in spite of having a degree. So, I decided to reach here without one. Is a degree that important to be successful? Even in my career, the ones who started working with a degree have reached the same position as I have. With or without it, we all seem to get less than what we should. This I've seen of every IHM student, this happens to all of them."

"Every year, thousands of students graduate and end up running around for a job. Go and ask them what they feel like after having done all that, and they are still jobless. Forget about them, ask yourselves, did you really get what you wanted? Are you really happy?"

None of us could say anything to that. Rudra too kept silent, and looked at the floor. "You got yourselves degrees, but you're still struggling. You are experiencing the same things as I am, the only difference being, I'm experiencing this without a degree."

"You mean to say a degree has no value," said Rudra softly, still looking down.

"No, it's not like that. Of course it has huge value. You can stand in front of and alongside people anywhere in the world. I am not against getting a degree. But just think for a second, can your degree prove how good you are? Can it show how capable you are? Can it tell one how much you've struggled in your life? If you go anywhere for an interview, people first look at your degree and not you, because they are only interested in that piece of paper. It's become more important than the worth of a human. A degree is important, but it can't prove what you are, and I don't think any degree is required to be successful. Numerous successful people have made history without a degree to their name."

"So, you're one of those people, is it?" Rudra asked.

"No, but I am one of those who can do something by his own merit. At least I can say I have achieved something in life. And whatever it is, at the end of the day I am a happy man."

"So, we're not happy, is it?"

"Ask yourself the same question," Joy pointed out, and looked at Shantanu and I. "Chef, are you happy?" Shantanu remained quiet.

"See, for the last ten years, even he isn't happy," Shantanu laughed. "I am just making my guests happy, but whether I am happy or not, I can't say. You are right, though. Our degrees are valued more than us. Everyone asks us how many years of experience we have, and how many degrees we've earned, but nobody has ever asked us how happy we are. They're all selfish. Everyone wants to get their work done. Where some of them get it done politely, some fuck us over. It's nice, at least you are happy."

****

Every hotelier celebrates their annual function in different ways. This year's theme was the Blind Annual Function. They wanted to see how capable we were, blinded. We could do a lot with eyes wide open, but delivering clients blindly was going to be the challenge. Every department was to conduct their own activity on-stage, blindfolded.

The function started with the HR team announcing a new joinee's name, the birthday of the month, and finally, the names of the promoted employees. My team conducted a skit with some of us enacting guests, and a few became receptionists. The receptionist communicated with the guests perfectly, in spite of being blindfolded. It was hard, but an incredible experience.

Joy's team presented their skit – making the bed, creating origami out of towels, and cleaning the area, all blindfolded again.

Shantanu's team had the hardest time, but managed to conduct their skit perfectly - chopping vegetables and creating animal art out of fruits.

****

One gets promised the world, on their last day of college. We promise people to remain as we are for the rest of our lives, as if we know what our next step will be. In the end, only our shallow promises remain.

"What is your plan next?" I asked Suhani as we walked the college corridor towards the main gate. She was in her patent red *kurti* with black leggings, and looked as beautiful as always.

"Dad wants me to go to London for a few years. He thinks me working out of the country for a few years before settling back in India will do me good. He wants me to start my career in India on the perfect note."

"And what do you think?" I asked her in a low voice, without looking at her.

"I think dad is right. I have to learn something abroad so it helps me grow fast here." I stopped mid-walk as she said this. She turned back, noticing I'd stopped, and said, "What happened? Don't be sad *yaar*. Wait for some time. I will call you from there." I laughed.

"What happened?"

"Really, you will call me from there?" I asked her in disbelief.

"Of course I will. Why won't I! You are my best friend, and…"

"And what, Suhani?"

"Nothing," she shook her head. "Would you like to work out of India?" she asked instead.

"Yes."

"You never told me."

"You never asked me."

"Thank God I asked you everything on the first day of college! Had I not, I don't know how many years you would've taken to tell me all that," she said, making us both laugh.

It was hurting me, and I think it was the same with her too. We had almost finished our course, and the time to set out in different directions was fast approaching. Our lives seemed to be playing some perverted version of chess with us. There was one rule it seemed to not be following - you can play any move you want, but you can't kill your own people.

I wanted to stop her. I wanted to beg her not to go, not to leave me alone. *Please listen to what my heart is saying*, I screamed internally. *You've spent three years with me but you still can't understand what it wants. You are my best friend. No! Not just a friend. You are so much more to me. At least understand and listen to what my heart is saying today.* I wanted to propose to her. I wanted to tell her how much I loved her. Manav was a lost cause in her love.

"Suhani?" I gently called to her. She turned back and smiled at me. Oh, that smile. *Let her say she loves you first*, said the voice inside my head.

"Why? Has my right time not come yet?" I asked, pained. I felt him smile in comprehension and disappear.

"What happened?" asked Suhani, coming close to me.

"Nothing," I shook my head.

"I thought you called me to tell me your love's name," she teased. I smiled.

"Is it not your right time yet?" she asked.

I ignored her question and searched my bag instead, out of which I took out a gift-wrapped box.

"Suhani, this is for you."

"Oh thanks! At least I got my gift at the right time."

"Yes, and Suhani please don't open it until I ask you to."

"Why?"

"You girls and your never-ending questions," I laughed.

"You boys never say things clearly either, *na.*"

"Oh really?"

"Has there been any progress with your one-sided love?" she asked.

"No," I replied softly.

"It hurt you so much when I moved to Goa for six months, but today I am leaving the country. Don't you feel anything?"

"Yes, I do. But this is for your career and I don't want to come in between you and your career."

"Manav, please can you tell me the girl's name, the one you're in love with?" I stayed quiet.

"Okay, I will not force you, but if she said no to you, please let me know."

"Why?" I asked, curious why she'd want to know.

"Nothing, leave it," she said, her voice breaking.

"Suhani, why are you crying now?" I asked her, and pulled her into a hug.

"Please, promise me you will not leave me alone. Promise me you will always be my best friend," she sniffed.

"Yes, I will."

"You will not forget me after you get your girlfriend *na*?"

"No, I won't." She tightened her grip around me. We stood there in comfortable silence, broken suddenly by the honk of her car.

"I think I should go," she pulled apart, wiping her eyes.

"You will really call me *na*, Suhani?" I asked earnestly. She didn't reply.

"This is for you," she took out a half-eaten butterscotch ice-cream cone from her bag. "I finished half of it, and the other half is yours. I know you don't like it, but please this one you have to have. Don't throw it. This is my last treat." She put the cone in my hand, turned towards her Mercedes waiting outside the gate, and left.

"Suhani!" I called out to her again, but this time she didn't turn around.

Her car started, and slowly moved further away. I stood there waiting for her to see me, but she didn't. I ran after her car, calling her name like crazy, but the car doubled its speed in response, took a turn and vanished from view. I looked at the empty road before me, feeling utterly alone. Just me, with the ice-cream cone in hand.

Chapter 22

"Good afternoon, this is Joy," Joy picked up the telephone in his office.

"Hi Joy, this is Khurana," said Khurana sir from the other side of the line.

"Hello Mr. Khurana, how are you?"

"Fine, fine. Joy listen, I am sending one guy for your assistant position in your department. Please take his interview and let me know your suggestions. He has a good five-year experience and has a degree from a reputed college as well. The only thing is, he has been jobless for the last six months. He needs a job. Please update me as soon as possible."

"Sure, why not." He cut the call.

A knock on the door announced the interviewee's arrival, a few minutes later. "Excuse me sir, can I come in?"

"Yes, please come in," Joy replied, taking off a file from a cupboard mounted on the wall.

"Hello sir, good afternoon," said the man on entering, as Joy still faced the wall.

"Hi, good afternoon." Joy smiled back, turning around to face him. As soon as he did, both the men stood stunned for a moment. The interviewee took his hand back without shaking Joy's hand, as Joy still looked at him with the file he was looking for in hand.

"Sorry sir," the man, now completely flustered, turned back to the door.

"Rohan, wait," Joy stopped him.

"It's okay, and really sorry. I didn't know or else I wouldn't have come for the interview," said the guy in a soft voice.

"No problem, sit down," Joy gestured at the seat, smiling at him. "I hope you remember me."

The man sat down, still red in the face. "I am really so sorry sir."

"Not sir, I am Joy Dharmarajan, and you can call me Joy." The man sitting across him fidgeted, and looked everywhere but at him.

"Don't worry, just calm down and relax. I will not treat you like you treated me." Joy's tone hardened perceptibly.

"Sorry, it was my fault. If you can please forget it...," said the man in a pleading tone.

"Sorry for what? You were only doing your duty. But I wasn't wrong either."

"Yes, I realised it later and tried to contact you, but…"

"No worries. Our industry is as round as the world. One day, at some point, we meet our colleagues again. Like us today. Even after a few years, here we are face-to-face again, with only a slight difference between us."

The man laughed and said, "Not a little bit, sir. Sorry, Joy. It is a huge difference."

"What matters the difference? Our hearts should be clean and clear, and then all becomes well one day. To get the work done from our juniors we treat them like they're worth nothing."

"I think you are taunting me," said the man across Joy.

"No, I am telling you the truth."

"But the same way we get treated by our seniors as well."

"That doesn't mean you should do the same. Look at me. I've had the worst seniors but I don't treat my juniors the same."

"Maybe you are right. Maybe that is why you became successful and reached here, and I am still where I was."

"And I have not forgotten a single word of what you said and how you treated me. But I should thank you for that. It's only because of that that I have reached here."

"Can you forgive me?" asked the man.

"Do you remember what you'd said?"

"Please, leave it."

"I am not repeating that for you, but I'll always remember it."

"I agree I shouldn't have said that. Believe me, later it hurt me too."

"I know you were my supervisor and the most senior person, but I was just…"

"I think I should go," said the man, half-rising from his chair.

"'A villager, an uneducated, bloody fool. A bastard who can't do anything in life, someone who will always remain a cleaner.' This is what you'd said to me, right?" Joy spat, and the man facing him sat back.

"You know," Joy continued, "I cried for six months. Every second of my life since then, your words have echoed in my head, making me feel like I'd committed a crime. You know I haven't slept for five days straight. It took me a year to come out of my shell. I still haven't forgotten anything. But you can see where this villager is now." Joy took a deep breath to calm himself before saying, "Even though it hurt me a lot, I will not let it hinder this interview. Let your work speak for yourself."

"I am really so sorry," said the man on realizing what he'd put Joy through.

"Your apologies can't change the past. I can't forget things, but don't worry, that will not come between our work. I know what it feels like being jobless for six months. You can work with me. I don't have any issues. But before you join us, please keep your ego out of the premises, because I refuse to work with egotistical people."

"It will be my honour to work under you."

"Excuse me, nobody works under me," clarified Joy. "We all work together because we are one team."

"Thank you Joy," said the man, his eyes twinkling, finally being able to look Joy in the eye. "Till today, my knowledge and degrees have taught me how to work and how to be professional, but you have taught me how to be human. I thank you from my heart."

"Thank yourself, not me." Joy extended his hand to shake his. The man hesitated for a minute, before putting his hand forward too.

Chapter 23

Emergency meeting. This was the first time I was hearing this phrase professionally. I had heard of emergency numbers, emergency exits and emergency calls, but not this. This is something we can't experience sitting in our office; one can only know what the meeting will entail once one attends it.

I reached the meeting room. Everyone but Suri sir was already present. I slid in and quietly took a chair next to Joy.

"For what've they called this emergency meeting? Has anything happened?" I asked Joy.

"We are all here for the meeting together, aren't we? How would I know?" Joy replied seriously.

"No, you are the most knowledgeable person here, hence I asked." I smiled, pulling his leg.

"Yes, the world's richest men are coming to stay here and you are to welcome them," he joked right back.

"No jokes today, please," I said, feigning anger.

"Life is too short. No need to be serious all the time."

"Good afternoon, sir!" we heard people around us chorus suddenly.

"A very good afternoon, everybody," Suri sir replied, taking an empty chair in a hurry. "Okay, I know what you all must be thinking. You must be wondering why I suddenly called for this emergency meeting." He glanced at us, opened his diary, then looked back at us. "Can anyone guess?"

We shook our heads collectively.

"Okay, let's not waste any more of your time and come to the point. The reason for this meeting is, we have an unexpected function for the city's richest family – think of it as a VVIP's function – set to take place next Monday. I know it's going to be a challenge for us, it's going to seem impossible, but I feel like we can make this possible. The function's footfall is around 800-1000, we're not sure of the exact number yet. The function will be held on the terrace attached to the banquet hall, and we'll require all the rooms. Everything happened so quickly, and got finalised just this morning. Guests will be pouring in from all cities. I know it is a very difficult event to manage, but I don't want that function to go from our hands. I want to make it successful. So, without wasting time, let's work on it and make it a smooth, successful operation." He looked at us to gauge the effect his words had had on us. "Now, does anyone have any questions?"

"No sir," some of replied.

"Joy, are you ready?"

"Yes Mr. Suri, I am always ready," Joy smiled.

"Okay great, then let's move ahead," Suri sir looked at all of us. "Okay, since I know this is last minute, and we will all have to work doubly hard, one by one could you all share all your department requirements and issues?" Khurana sir had meanwhile taken out his diary, and was ready to note down all the requirements.

"Yes Chef," said Suri sir to Shantanu. "I think your department will play the most important part, so please go ahead."

"Sir, I need to work on this. Please give me a day's time. I will let you know all the details by tomorrow," Shantanu said.

"Sure."

"Excuse me sir," Shantanu said, before Suri sir could move on to the next manager. "Sir actually, I have a shortage of staff.

I've informed the concerned department multiple times, but this issue is not yet sorted. I will require more staff to run the operation smoothly, especially for this function."

"Khurana, why is this still pending?" asked Suri sir. "What is your plan of action? I need to close this before the function."

"Sure sir, I will close this as soon as possible." Like a typical HR manager, his voice conveyed no emotions. Satisfied, Suri sir moved on to the next person.

"Does your department require anything?" he asked Rudra.

"Sir, I too have staff shortage in my department, but I can manage for a few more days. But sir, I will require some Out-Door Catering staff to manage the function. I think, not only I, every department requires ODC staff for the function. We don't have sufficient staff members in any department."

"Great, good idea. I think all you guys should think about each other's departments as well. I like this idea. Very good job," Suri sir thumped him on the back. "Now all of you please give your requirements for ODC staff to Khurana, so he can take care of it."

After giving him the requirements, Suri sir moved on to me. "Yes, Manav."

"Sir, I can manage with my current reception staff, however, I'll need a few bellboys. At least till the end of the function."

"Yes, that we'll close with the ODC only."

"Okay sir, nothing else then."

"Guys please listen carefully," Suri sir turned to face everyone. "As you all now know, this VVIP function is going to be held in our hotel. I don't want a single complaint from them. We have to give our 100% to the function anyhow, because I don't want to lose business from them in the future. And always remember, when it comes to the company's business, we have to sacrifice a lot. So let's work together and make this function as successful as possible. And before I forget, please brief your team as well. Till the function doesn't end, no leaves will be approved, especially for you guys. So please avoid visiting my office for leaves. Guys, it's time to get serious and work immediately – get all your needs and requirements in order. I don't want anyone waiting till the last moment. Is this clear with everyone?"

We nodded in agreement, as Suri sir, Khurana sir, and the Purchase Manager walked out of the room.

****

The day of the function was finally here. Ever since we'd been told of this day, we'd been kept busy like never before. In spite of being in one room, we didn't get the time to talk to each other. The function's schedule had also increased our duty hours. We ended up sleeping in the hotel for a few hours before going back to work again.

Flowers decorated the hotel, right from the parking to the banquet hall and around the hotel. Lights hanging outside the building gave it a lavish look. The parking was jam-packed, with all types of old and new cars. The hotel itself was full to the brim with VVIP guests. Inside the lobby, two receptionists along with two ladies, dressed impeccably in matching *sarees*, gave out roses to all the guests, under the supervision of Neha Tandan. The lobby too was adorned with yellow, orange and white roses, symbolising joy, purity and energy.

The terrace banquet, where the function was to be held, was on the 5th floor. Not used to holding so many guests, every department's immediate needs were accommodated on the ground floor, and the things that didn't fit there, went to the terrace. The most frustrated were Shantanu and Rudra, since the most important departments were the Food Production and

Food & Beverages. So hyper were they, no one could talk to them normally, as long as the function was on. Because of the resource distribution, all the guests' food and beverages were being brought up from the ground floor.

The function started at 08:00 pm with the place almost packed to capacity. The guests, all VVIP, donned the world's most expensive jewellery, clothes and perfumes, but we had no time to gawk.

"Excuse me, can you please send some snacks and cold drinks this side? We've been waiting for a long time," one of the guests stopped me to say.

"Sure sir," I replied, and immediately called a white-shirted F & B staff member to serve him. I then went up to Shantanu and Rudra, where they were busy discussing the set-up counter. "Rudra, I think you should have some more staff members serve snacks and soft drinks," I suggested. Rudra shook his head and laughed.

"What happened? I am not joking."

"Yes, I know bro. I am still waiting for my ODC staff. They haven't come yet. Once they join us, I will do that," he replied with a maniacal grin.

"But how is this possible? The function is already underway. They should have been here before it started! Did you have a word with Khurana sir?" I asked.

"Yes bro, more than ten times. He said the ODC staff is on its way. I don't know where they are coming from. They've been on their way for the last few hours now," said Rudra, arranging a counter with Shantanu and screaming at a pantry chef who on his way to moving fruit animal-art to a table, had ended up dropping them. "Hey be careful you bastard, we are not free here. We're already tackling a lot of problems, so do your job properly."

"Sorry sir," he frantically apologised.

"Your apologies will not work here, just concentrate on your work, okay?"

"Hey what you are doing?" shouted Shantanu at the same time. "Please don't make any mistakes today."

"Rudra, some of the guests are shouting in the banquet hall. There is no one to serve the snacks. Can you send one staff or ODC member?" Joy repeated the same plea as he reached our table in a hurry.

"Can you please tell him what I said?" Rudra asked me, busy pushing the table himself.

"What happened?" Joy asked, looking at all of us.

"The function has started but not a single ODC member has arrived. Did you get any ODC member for your department?" I asked.

"No, not yet. And what rubbish are you talking man? I called Mr. Khurana and he told me they are on their way."

"They've been on their way for hours now. I got the same excuse," said I.

"Can you please call and ask him again?" Shantanu looked around at the chaos. "If they're done with their trip to Mount Everest, ask him to send them here. Such bullshit's happening here."

"He is not answering any calls," said Joy, his phone to his ear. Shantanu sighed, "I don't know what will happen. I don't have that many staff members to manage everything. How will we manage? We'll have to pick up and serve everything from the ground floor to the terrace ourselves. We have to serve more than 30 dishes to a thousand people. In our current situation, this is not going to be possible. I don't know what's going to happen in the next couple of hours." We all shared his frustration.

"I don't think the ODC staff will come," said Rudra. "Forget it. We'll have to manage this ourselves."

"Hey wait! Mr. Khurana is calling! I think the ODC guys are finally here!" Joy's expectation was palpable as he picked up the call. "Hello Mr. Khurana!"

Pause.

"Mr. Khurana, the ODC staff members for my department aren't here yet. The ones for the Kitchen, F & B and Front office aren't here either. What happened, sir? Is there any problem? Because the function has started, and we really need all the staff we can get. I don't think we can manage without them."

Pause.

"But Mr. Khurana, where are they coming from that it's taking so much time? How long will it take? Rudra and Shantanu are saying you said the same thing to them a couple of hours back as well. This is really not the way. This is a VVIP function and we still have not received a single ODC member. How will we run the function? Sir, please try to understand."

Pause.

"I don't think any ODC staff will come," said Joy, disconnecting the call. "We will have to handle this ourselves. Don't worry, if the moment arises, we are all here and we will all work together. I will put my whole staff here if required. At the end of the day, we are one team."

"No worries, I will be here too," I quipped.

"Hey guys! What is going on? Who is the manager here?" An elderly man came up to us from the banquet hall.

"Hello sir! I am the manager here. How may I assist you?" asked Rudra.

"What assist? There is no assistance we are getting from your end. The function has just started and we have to wrap it up by the morning. I don't know how you guys will manage it."

"Sir, please tell me the issues you are facing. We are here only for you. And don't worry, we will manage," Shantanu politely appealed to him, calming him for the moment.

"For the last half an hour we've been asking for snacks and soft drinks, but no one has come. I can't even see for a single server," the guest put his issue across.

"Sir please look there," Rudra pointed in the opposite direction. "More than ten staff members are serving drinks and snacks. Please look at them."

"But there are so few of them."

"The others are on the other side, sir," Shantanu pointed further.

"But I can't see them," the guest looked confused, looking into the crowd.

"Sir, how you will find them in such a crowded place? We will serve you directly," I came in front to answer him.

"You are all managers?" he asked. Joy nodded.

"I think you have more managers than staff members. Anyway, please send someone with me immediately."

Rudra called in one staff member from the F & B department, and ushered him to the guest. "Is this fine sir? Please enjoy the party and I will send one more staff member in a minute."

"Oh thank you so much. Can I have your number please? If there's anything else required I will call you directly."

Unwillingly, Rudra gave his number and the guest went back to the banquet hall.

"Excuse me, I want to meet Rudra sir. Who is he?" a couple of men came up and asked. All of them were in full-sleeved white shirts and black trousers, with their hair reaching down to their ears, looking like young, upcoming Bollywood superstars. Not going by their intimidating appearance, I asked them who they were.

"We are the ODC staff members. Khurana sir asked us to meet Rudra *ji*," one of them said. I looked them down from top to bottom, wondering whether they'd really come to work here or attend a dance competition.

"Have you worked in a hotel before?" Shantanu asked.

"No sir," one of them replied. "Actually, we work for a catering company. Since we were free today and got a call for this catering job, we came here. We've come to such a hotel for the first time. Nice arrangement this is; is it a wedding or an engagement function?"

I looked at them in shock.

"What happened sir? Any problem?"

"Really? Are they seriously going to work with us? This is a VVIP guest function, don't forget!" I mumbled into Chef's ear.

"Don't worry sir, this is nothing for us," a third person who'd heard me, said. "We attend functions twice a week, and all of them are VVIP functions."

"Oh, really?"

"Yes, you know who the richest person in India is? We attended his wedding as well. And now they call us for every function."

"Great, and who is that person?" Joy asked.

"What do we know?" they said and laughed. "We only know our caterer who calls us and gives us the address."

All of us looked at each other, judging their behaviour. It was highly problematic, but we didn't have any other option.

"Okay now forget all this and go with this guy. Get to know what your work is," Rudra said, pointing at one of the F & B staff members.

"Wait *na* sir, let us enjoy the function for a while first."

"*Oye*, shut up! Don't try to be over smart here!" snapped Joy. "You've come here to work, not to attend the function, okay? So keep quiet and start your work."

"Excuse me sir, don't shout at us. We are not in the mood to work today. We were free at home when we got a request for this job, so we came here. If you don't like this or have no need of us, please tell us and we will move from here. No issues. But don't shout at us."

"Okay sorry, leave it now and go with this guy. But please don't leave us today, we need all the help we can get," Rudra said, then looking at Joy, sneered. "What are you doing? Khurana sir's already fucked us over. Now you don't fuck us and create issues here. I am already very frustrated."

"But they are trying to be our bosses!"

"Please, no jokes right now," Rudra folded his hands to Joy and requested. "If you don't help, it's fine, I will manage. But no jokes today, please."

"Rudra leave it. Guys, please be alert. We have a lot of things to do, and we have to do our best," I said, quickly changing the topic.

Slowly, as the crowd increased, so did our problems. Compared to the crowd in front of us, and basis what we'd been promised; only 25% of the ODC staff had arrived. Khurana sir was still waiting at the staff entrance to welcome the ones still on their way. Meanwhile, all us mangers were working with the staff provided. Soon enough, there was no any difference left between our staff, the ODC members and us managers. It was around this time that Shantanu and Rudra's situation became worse, and things started spiralling out of control, in spite of the fact that we were giving it our best. Soon enough, the time for dinner arrived, and a lavish buffet opened for the guests. From salad to dessert, there were almost 25-30 live counters open at once, which still seemed insufficient to serve a thousand guests. More than 200 guests were queuing up, and almost all the staff members were running around, bringing up food from the ground floor, emptying it and scurrying back down. The staircase and elevators were choc-a-blocked, with people running up and down like crazy. All us managers were at the live counters, serving all the guests. We'd volunteered to handle the buffet without any complaint. That was the first time I felt like we were all a team; working without any egos in our hearts. Joy, two more managers and I were handling the buffet, while Chef and Rudra sent the food containers from the kitchen, while keeping constant communication with us. It was not easy, what we were doing, but neither was it impossible.

"Hello! Excuse me, who is the manager here? What is this nonsense going on?" the same guest who had taken Rudra's number started shouting at a restaurant manager.

"Yes, sir how may I assist you?" the manager asked.

"There are only problems in your service."

"What happened sir?"

"We have been waiting for rice for the last 15 minutes, and we have still not got it. All this food has become cold, there is no *paneer* in the *paneer* curry, there is no chicken in the chicken curry, the salad is over and nobody's bothered to refill it, we are getting *naan* without butter because your staff doesn't have butter!" Irate, he lay out his points. "This white shirted staff of yours, if we ask them something, they say they don't know anything. What is going on? I have been calling your manager for the last 30 minutes and he's kept his mobile off. Call your manager right now! I want talk to him."

"I am really so sorry sir. Don't worry, just give me five minutes and I will solve all these issues. And sir, we've been continuously serving food, we have not stopped anything. Have a look sir," the manager pointed at the staff members walking in with food containers from the kitchen.

"He is just carrying two containers with some food; we are more than 500 guests, what will we do with that?"

"Sorry sir, I will clear this issue and refill all the empty food containers right away." "I don't want your apologies and excuses. Go and bring your manager right now, I want to see him," said the guest, his voice getting louder.

"Sir, that manager is busy in the kitchen. This is our second manager, you can talk to him," he pointed me. Immediately, my expression changed as the guest started coming towards me looking angrier than ever.

"Hey you, come here!"

"Hello sir, what can I do for you?" I asked politely.

"There is not a single thing happening here and you are asking me what you can do! What is all this bullshit going on? If you people didn't have the capacity to manage this function then why you did you agree to it? Are you making a joke of us in front of our guests? Don't you have manners?"

"Sir! Please forget whatever has happened. You just give me some time and I'll fix everything."

"You have all only been giving me excuses since the function's started. All of you are just making a big fool of us! You're not even capable of managing this function! I made a big mistake choosing this hotel."

"Sir," Joy said cautiously, "You chose the right hotel. See, all your guests will be happy with our service. It is not a function for 50 odd people sir. We have more than 800 guests here. Some ups and downs are bound to happen in all our services. After all, we are also human, and we can't be perfect. But I assure you, we are doing our very best, sir."

"And who are you?" the guest asked him.

"Sir, he is another manager here," I replied.

"Oh great, you only have managers here, no staff. I can't even see a difference between your staff and managers."

"We are all one team, sir," Joy replied.

"I am not here to see your team spirit. Please give us your best service and don't let me down in front of my guests."

"Sir, we won't let that happen."

"But it is happening! See all my guests waiting in queue."

"But sir, that's only half of them! The other half have finished their dinner and see, they are now resting and enjoying the evening."

"But no one is happy here."

"I agree sir, there have been some problems, but overall they are all happy."

"Do you think I am lying to you?" the guest asked, angered.

"No sir, but I am not lying either. Your guests are happy sir. I will show you," Joy stopped one guest and asked him, "Excuse me sir, how was the dinner? We hope you enjoyed yourself. Please give us your valuable feedback."

"Oh amazing, the buffet arrangement was awesome. And the food! I can't tell you how good that was! After we get done I want to meet your chef. And especially you guys, you've been amazing. And thank you so much Mr. Jindal, for choosing one of best places in the city. Next month's my daughter's wedding, and I think I will change the venue to this hotel. If not, I will definitely suggest this hotel to my friends and family. Please guys, after this function is over, can I have your hotel card? I will meet you guys soon to book this place in advance." In an instant, all our problems seemed to disappear. Our guests were happy!

Everything was not perfect, but we'd tried our very best. Especially Joy, who'd held his cool and sorted out all our problems with a smile. By the time the last of the guests left, it was past four in the morning. We'd all served them nonstop, without having a single bite ourselves. Everyone was exhausted, and we could no longer stand on our feet.

****

"What do you think? Will we get positive feedback from the guests? Were they happy with our service?" I asked Joy, a night after the function took place. We were on the Club House terrace, looking over to Valenki Villa, sharing a cigarette. He laughed.

"I didn't ask you to laugh!" I handed the cigarette back to him.

"You asked me a question meant to be laughed at!"

"Of course, their satisfaction is a must. Otherwise, what is the use of all that we did."

"Do you think they are?" he asked.

"No idea," I answered honestly.

"I've always observed this. Nobody is a 100% satisfied with anything. Our juniors aren't so with us, we aren't so with our bosses, and most importantly, neither are our guests, for whom we compromise everything, sometimes doing things completely out of the box. If everyone's a 100% satisfied with everything, then nobody will be troubled by anyone. Since everyone seems to have a problem, that means they are not happy and there's still something left from our side."

"I think what we did for this function was extremely difficult. How is it possible that we still didn't give them our 100%? If we need to do better than this, what else do we have to do to satisfy them?" I looked at him, confused.

"It's midnight, bastard! Can you stop peeking here and go sleep now?" Suddenly we heard a lady scream from Valenki Villa. Rudra was peeping into their house as usual.

"See, even he is also not satisfied with his life," Joy pointed out.

"Rudra close the window!" I shouted, throwing a towel at the window below.

"Hey, you bastard! Don't tell me what to do! You come and sleep. What are you doing on the terrace at midnight? I think I'll have to complain to the HR about you guys disturbing me at midnight," he screamed.

"You come and I will take you to the HR, you bloody fool! I will show you who is disturbing who!" the lady shouted at him, and Rudra closed the window and switched off his light in fear.

We both laughed at the scene. When all was settled, Joy asked, "There's one word called ability. Do you know what it means?"

"It's better if you explain," I took back the cigarette, knowing full well his explanations would be beyond me.

"Ability means," he explained, "the power of a person. The capability of a person that changes the results of hard work. It is a highly powerful word that makes a lot of difference in our lives, but the value of which becomes less when we use it without understanding its meaning. If you see, almost everyone uses this word in their resume, but how many people follow the real meaning of it? I think only a few know, because we're all scared of reality, of the gravity of the word. It is a word that can change the life of a person, if properly understood. But nobody wants to, we're all running to complete our work."

"So should we not use this word at all?"

"We should, but…," his explanation got cut short as my phone started ringing. It was *maa* calling. I looked at the caller ID and switched my phone to silent mode.

"There are more than thirty missed calls from her. Why aren't you talking to her?" Joy asked, pointing at the mobile in my hand that was still ringing. I didn't answer.

"What happened? Why are you hesitating?" I still didn't answer.

"Say something."

"Every time that she calls at this time, she calls me in front of dad. I will talk to her later," I replied.

"So, talk to dad also *na*."

"I don't want to."

"Why do you hate your dad so much?" the topic was fast moving from a professional one to a personal one.

"Tell me," he urged again, when I didn't reply.

"Nothing, leave it. Every family's story shouldn't be disclosed."

"Tell me *na*, think of me as a part of your family."

"I am not happy with dad's behaviour," I said after a moment's silence.

"See, the answer is in front of you only. If you are not satisfied with your dad, someone who is one of the most valuable persons in your life, then how can you expect to be satisfied by another random person?"

"My reasons are different."

"But the satisfaction is the same," he said, looking into my eyes. What he was saying was true, even if I refused to digest it. I looked at him in anger.

"What happened, angry young man?" he grinned at me, then burst into laughter.

"He is not my dad, he is Hitler," I pushed him back and said. "He always hates my decisions. He doesn't like my friends. He doesn't like it if I try something new in life. He always forces me to join his business which I don't want to, because I have my own dreams, my own ambitions. He doesn't like anything. He just wants me to leave everything and join his business."

Joy listened to me and laughed.

"What happened? I knew you wouldn't understand my problem. That's why I never share it with anyone."

"You are the most foolish person in the world."

"I know," I turned my face away.

"Thank God you have someone who hates what you do. I don't have anybody to hate a single thing of mine. You won't understand what it feels like when you don't have your own people with you, when you don't have anyone to share your good and bad moments with. Have you ever wondered why he hates the things you do?"

"Maybe he thinks I am wrong."

"He thinks all this because he doesn't want you to be in trouble," Joy pointed out to me. "You decided what was in your mind, but you have to try to understand what is going on in your dad's mind. You are just thinking of today and tomorrow, but he's been thinking about you since the day you were born. He thinks about what his son will be like at a certain age. He thinks about what you should achieve in your life. He thinks about how your friends are. He wonders if you're going in the right direction. We will never get to know the things he's had to compromise for you. Your mother might've carried you in her womb for nine months, but since the day you were born, and till the end of his life, he has been and will continue to carry double his weight on his back. One is him and the other is his son. We'll never come to know what he did during your childhood; sometimes he became a horse, sometimes he became a donkey, and sometimes, he became nothing to you. If ever he wanted to buy something, he'd first buy it for his son, and then if he had any means left, he'd buy for himself." Joy's pain and love for his lost dad was clearly visible on his face. I could see it now. "That's the thing about time; once it's gone, it will never come back. Even a stopped clock shows us the right time twice a day, but life gives us only one chance. My dear, you still have time. Don't waste it, make it useful."

"Do you think he is right?" I asked softly.

"What does it matter if he is right or not? Whether he is okay or not? Whether he is perfect or not? But he is one of the most valuable persons in your life. Don't forget, it's only because of him that you are in this world, busy judging things." I couldn't look into his eyes. Everything he's just said filled my head, and I felt like something was eating me up from the inside.

"What should I do?" I asked.

"We don't value the things we have, and when the same things go away from our lives, we feel their absence. Don't waste time. Life is too short. And if you want to know what it feels like when we have no one in our lives, ask me. Don't waste a single second. Call and speak to your dad, you'll see how much lighter you both will feel once you do." He was asking me to do something I'd never thought of in the last couple of years. I didn't know how right he'd be, but it was true that it was my ego that had been stopping me. I'd only been thinking about myself. I'd never thought what my dad would think about me and what his expectations were of his son. Joy was telling me to do the toughest thing I'd ever done.

"If he doesn't speak to me, what then?" I asked furtively.

"A son can be angry with his dad for a long time, but the dad can't be angry with his son forever. Even if you don't understand him, he will understand you. Don't worry."

Everything he was saying brought up a thousand questions in my head. I closed my eyes and stood in silence. The voice inside my head came back to me. *Hey, everything is fine. Now I feel like you don't need me anymore. You've got a good friend who will always be with you. He will understand you better than me. You don't need to worry. Even if you lose something in life, you'll have this best friend who can teach you right from wrong. He is right; speak to your dad. Your dad's also been waiting to talk to you. Now it's time for me to leave. But if you ever want to see me again, just choose any star in the sky, and I will be at your disposal.*

The voice disappeared. I opened my eyes and saw Joy still smiling in front of me, waiting for me to speak to dad. The voice inside might have disappeared, but he'd left me with the best friend I could have ever asked for; Joy. Joy handed me the phone.

Was this correct what I was doing? Would dad really accept my faults? Would *maa* feel happy? The mobile in my hand, and a lot of questions in my mind, I dialled the number, but disconnected it before it could ring.

"From where should I start?" I asked Joy.

"Speak from your heart. Ask your heart what it wants and say that." Again, I called, and disconnected it after one ring.

"If he asks me why I want to talk to him after such a long time, then?"

"Say you've always missed him, but today you couldn't hide it anymore." After another minute of indecision, I called again. This time, I let it ring, and dad picked up.

"Hello," he said. I remained quiet.

"Hello," he said again.

"Who is it?" I could hear *maa* scream from behind. "Give it to me. I was trying to call Manav."

I cut the call and turned to Joy. "I can't do this."

"Try from your heart."

"But...," I started, when my phone started ringing.

"*Beta* Manav, where are you? Where is your mobile? Can you see how many missed calls there are? Are you that busy?" before I could've answered, *maa* started.

"*Maa*," I said, my voice soft. I looked at Joy who was gesturing at me to talk with confidence.

"Manav is everything okay? Can you say something please? Don't be quiet *beta*."

"*Maa*, I want to talk to dad," I said. *Maa* became quiet. She couldn't believe what she'd just heard. "Manav! What happened? Is everything fine? Do you need anything *beta*?"

"*Maa*, all is okay. Now can I talk to dad? You always ask me to speak to him right? Now today I want to. I just want apologise to him. I just want to ask him if he can forgive me."

"Manav…," her voice betrayed her confusion.

"*Maa* please, I know dad is next to you. You just keep the speaker on."

"Okay," she said, and did just that.

"Dad, I am really sorry. Can you forgive me?" the sentence came out both soft and fast. Joy, standing across me, smiled at me sympathetically, and on the other side, my parents were quiet. "I have taken the responsibility of being a son for *maa* but now I want to take the responsibility of being a son to you. Will you allow me to? I want to tell everyone you are my idol, will you allow me this? I want to tell everyone you are the first person who came into my life as a teacher. You are the only one who wants me to go ahead of you. Dad, you taught me how to walk, but I couldn't walk with you. You taught me to speak but I couldn't sit and talk to you. I don't know how many dreams of yours you might have given up for me, and I couldn't even fulfil one dream of yours. Whenever I wished to fly, you gave me your wings, but I never tried to fly with you. You did so much for me, but I haven't done a single thing for you. I am really sorry dad, please forgive me. Today I realize my mistake. It was entirely my fault," my voice cracked, and I found myself crying. With my head on Joy's shoulder, and the phone in my hand, I awaited his response.

"Manav! Hey Manav, *beta*," after such a long time I heard dad say my name.

"Dad, I am really so sorry," I whispered.

"Hey *beta* please don't apologise again. Now, enough! If you say it again, then I probably don't deserve to be your dad. It was my fault also. I didn't understand what you wanted to be in life. Being a father, it was my responsibility to understand and support you and your dreams. It was my duty to help you at all times. You are my son. I'm sorry *beta*, I will never again ask you to join my business. My business is my identity, but moving ahead in life I forgot you also have to build your own identity. That is your right."

"I want to meet you, dad. I am coming home," I said. I couldn't bear the thought of not being with him.

"You don't need to come *beta*, I will come to meet you. And listen, from today don't call me dad, call me Hitler. It sounds better."

"Dad!"

"No dad. Hitler," he corrected, and I tried to smile with the tears drying on my face. After a while, we cut the call. I looked at Joy with my eyes still glassy, and without a second's warning, I hugged him. I was hugging the world's most foolish guy, but he'd become a best friend to me.

Chapter 24

The morning meeting the very next day wasn't a usual one.

"After informing you several times, you guys still failed to attend the function. Mr. Jindal, the owner of the function had huge complaints and negative reviews about our service and set up. This was not expected from all of you. Compared to the guests' expectations, the F & B service was the worst, and more importantly, the Front Office only had two receptionists to handle 400 guests." Suri sir looked directly at me. "I had told you guys how important this function was. I'd asked you to take care of everything, but everything got messed up and we failed. I could have never even imagined this would happen with me. This is the worst moment of my career. Over the last fifteen years, I have never failed as bad as this. I have never brought my company shame, but today I've failed because of you guys. I feel like such a loser only because of you, and all of you are responsible for it. Especially the man who argued with Jindal sir. Who was that bastard arguing with Jindal sir?" he exploded in anger, filling the room with dreadful silence. He looked at us one by one in hope that someone would reply to his question.

"Reply guys, tell his name! I am not going to be quiet today." We remained silent, looking down at our shoes.

"Hello, are you listening? Don't be quiet. I want an answer. Tell me his name or I will punish all of you. I will fire everyone. Do you have any idea who Jindal sir is?" he looked at us in disgust. "He is one of the richest people in the state. That's who you made a joke of. You argued with him. Who is that bloody bastard?" A few of us looked at each other, but nobody had the guts to answer.

"I was not arguing with him," Joy broke the silence.

"Oh, so you are that smart guy. Who gave you the permission to argue with the guest?"

"I was not arguing, Mr. Suri. I was just trying to tell him that we'd been working non-stop for them. Mr. Jindal was trying to say that we are not capable enough for the function, so I was trying to pacify him by showing him our efforts. He was not happy with our service so I was just showing him our efforts with the help of other guests, and really, the other guests were very happy."

"You came to know in a minute which guests were happy and which weren't? Don't you think you've become too smart for your own good? Do you think you're the General Manager of this hotel? Do you have any idea what you did?"

"I have done nothing wrong."

"You never do anything wrong. We are wrong, the ones sitting in this meeting room are wrong."

"That's not what I meant." Joy's voice was soft.

"I know very well what you meant."

"No, but the guest was trying to show us how wrong we were."

"I think you know how the guest is always right, right?"

"That I agree with, but that doesn't mean we were in the wrong."

"Every hotelier must respect the guests."

"Of course we should respect the guests. And I'm sorry Mr Suri, I agree our guests are right but we can also be right sometimes. At the end of the day, we are all human beings."

"Don't act smart! What do you think of yourself? And who told you to interfere in the F & B department's service, that's not even yours. There were other people there to manage the guests. It was not your responsibility. How did you involve yourself, and with whose permission did you fight with Jindal sir?"

"I was supporting our team."

"By fighting with our guest?"

"I was helping our colleagues by working in a team. And if we need to ask for permission to work as a team, then what's the point? Teamwork means we should be ready for any problem, ours or our co–team member's, at any time. And there was nobody there so I felt the need to help them."

"Oh really! Nobody was there! All the managers in this room right now were available. If there was a problem then you should have come and spoken with Khurana or me. The two of us were at least available."

"Mr Khurana was busy with his job! We were waiting in hopes of getting some more ODC staff to join us but no one came. Till the function got over all the ODC staff members were still on their way. I don't know where they were coming from. But as discussed at the meeting earlier, all departments were short on staff members. We still managed a smooth function through all our efforts and hard work. We did our best, and did whatever we could have from our side." Joy addressed the issue for us.

"Is this true?" asked Suri sir, glaring at Khurana sir.

"There were some issues," suddenly nervous, Khurana sir replied. "But I had sent some ODC members with Rudra and Shantanu."

"But they were not as per what we'd discussed," Joy interrupted.

"Chef, I had sent them at the right time, and they worked till the function ended," Khurana sir said.

Before he could reply, Suri sir pointed, "Chef, I think you had only one member short before the function started, so how now suddenly there were 4-5 members short on the day of the function?"

"Sir actually," Shantanu replied, "On the day of the function, two more staff members of mine were absent. One was not well and the other had a loose stomach, so they both couldn't come for duty."

"Very good, I think these illnesses were waiting for the function. I would like to meet all of them. Let me also see what illness they were suffering from," Suri sir said.

"Okay sir."

"What about the Front Office? Did you also have the same issues or do you have another reason?" He looked at me.

I didn't reply to him.

"Yes, go ahead," he urged. "Everyone has a reason, you must have one too."

"Sir, one of my staff member's grandmother was admitted in the hospital, and the other's grandmother passed away on the same day." I told him the excuses I'd got from my staff.

"What the hell is this? Are we responsible for all grandmothers in our country? Do you think I am mad? What do you think of me?" he shouted at us all. I glared at Khurana sir, who was the most to blame for this horrible meeting.

"The VIP guest function failed," continued Suri sir. "The entire hotel's reputation has fallen, and you guys are talking nonsense here. Can we think for a minute what we've done and what we should do now? If you'd concentrated on your work then this wouldn't have happened."

"We gave our best, sir. And we did it with full concentration. It's only because of that that the function even took place," Joy replied.

"Yes, you really did your best. I think there is no other way to explain to you guys the gravity of this situation." Suri sir turned his laptop around to show us a list of guest reviews and comments. "This is the result of your work over the last six months. The guests have shared their personal experiences. Just read this here to see how much you guys have been working and what you're capable of. Please, come here Joy."

Joy went up to him to read the screen. "Are these the reviews?" he asked.

"Yes, and I hope you know the value of them."

"I know how valuable they are, but we can't judge ourselves basis them."

"What do you mean we can't? This is the experience of a guest, through which we come to know our weaknesses and strengths."

"We can't judge or decide anyone's capability with one guest's review. Reviews are okay to find the problems they faced and solve them for the next time, but we can't stick it as a label for bad or good."

Suri sir shifted to face him, "So you mean to say the guest reviews are nothing, and they just waste our time? They stay with us. They observe everything during their stay, and then share their experiences. You're saying that is not important for you."

"That is important. I didn't say that. But we can't put it as a label on our head. One bad review doesn't determine our worth."

Suri sir was having none of this. He said, "I feel your thought process does not match an hotelier's. I feel you should get some rest and get to know more about this industry first."

"Whatever it is," countered Joy, "We've done a lot for this organisation. We could've never thought that after working days and nights, all we get judged on are a few reviews. Instead of being proud of us you are saying we didn't do anything. That is really strange. You should be proud of us for our work and support instead."

"Oh really! I should be proud of you! Do you really think you are that capable enough for me to be proud of you?"

"I am not saying that for me. It's for everyone."

"Shut up!" he screamed. "We are not here to listen to your jokes every single time. Don't forget we are professionals, part of this huge industry that stands on our strong shoulders, and not on fools like you. Do you understand?"

"But Mr. Suri…"

"Keep quiet! Can't you understand?" Suri sir screamed at him before he could've completed his sentence. "Now, I can't tolerate this anymore. I think I should take action against you guys because our hotel's reputation is at stake. I think you should be held responsible for the issues we faced at the function. You crossed all limits, and your behaviour with the client was unforgivable. Your communication with your seniors is not up to the mark either. I think…," he seemed to pause for effect. It worked. There was pin-drop silence in the meeting room, with all our eyes on Suri sir. "You should resign from your duties. This is not a warning; you can take this as my decision." Everyone sat stunned. None of us could believe what had just happened.

"But sir…," I started, before Suri sir's furious gaze rested on me.

"Khurana, all the other managers involved in this are to be given a warning letter, and if you are also involved in this, send in your letter to my office as well. I will sign them all. This letter will be your last warning."

"Sure sir," Khurana sir replied, his voice soft as usual.

"This should serve as an example to everyone. I will not tolerate any funny business in the future." Suri sir immediately got up and left the room. We looked up at Joy as he too stood up. We still couldn't believe what had just happened. I looked at Shantanu, and he looked at Rudra and I, all in stunned silence.

Everything that had happened was highly unacceptable. Today I realized one unspoken rule of hospitality. The one who works hard, works smart, and does things out of the box, will not be liked by his seniors. I was confused. I didn't understand what our seniors expected of us. Asking Joy to resign was unacceptable to him, but it was also appalling to us. As human beings, a lot of things can hurt us in life. If Suri sir wanted to say something, he should have called him into his office, and not shouted at him in the meeting room in front of everyone. That's what hurt more. When your senior fucks you over alone in his office, it doesn't hurt as much. But when it happens in front of all the managers working with you on the same level, it becomes personal. This is something I learnt from Joy. Bosses are bosses, a job is a job, and your personal life is your personal life. There is no way and no need to compromise anything for your personal life. It affected Joy a lot, but more than him, it hurt me. I couldn't believe what had happened.

Joy, Chef and Rudra were in the Club House looking morose. I couldn't see this and took this as a personal affront. Without wasting a moment, I went to Suri's office. This was first time I was taking something other than my own job so seriously.

"I want to talk with you," my tone a little harder than usual, cloaked with a lot of emotions. I'd entered Suri sir's office without knocking the door, and he, as usual, was busy on his laptop.

"How did you enter my office without knocking? Don't you have manners?" Suri sir asked, glaring at me.

"I am sorry, but…"

"Sorry for what?"

"We have manners. We respect you."

"I think your warning letter wasn't enough."

"You hurt more than one person today."

"What do you mean?"

"You know very well what I mean."

"Don't be smart, you don't know me."

"I know very well who you are. You are Mr. Upendra Suri, the General Manager of this hotel and my boss. I am your manager who is no longer scared to tell you the truth." My voice loud, resolve strong.

"Are you okay?"

"What does it matter if we are okay or not?"

"Don't shout in my office! Don't forget I am your senior." I laughed from within when he said the word 'senior'.

"I don't like people laughing in my office. Tell me for what purpose you came here."

"You don't like us laughing, you don't like us working, you don't like anything we do, so what are we doing here?"

"Shut your mouth and tell me why you are here."

"Who are we?" I asked.

"What do you mean?" he looked up from his laptop and focussed his gaze on me.

"Working with you, I have given you almost a year and a half of my life. After all this, what is our worth? What do you think of us?"

"What do you want?"

"My General Manager, the one I've worked with for the last 18 months doesn't know what I want?" I grinned incredulously, and then stood poker-faced to say, "Then, how will the outside world understand me? Who will give me opportunities to move ahead? Who will call me on their path to success to work with them? Who will say I am perfect for them? Nobody. How will I tell them who my boss was?"

"Stop beating about the bush and come to the point." He pushed his chair back and stood up.

"Already life has fucked us over from everywhere. When will you guys stop fucking us too? Till when will we juniors have to agree to everything you say? Till when will we have to demean ourselves in front of you? Till when?! What happened when we worked for 14-15 hours for you guys? What happened when we compromised everything for you, made you more important than our families? We worked like crazy year after year, and today, one guest's review is more important to you than us? Everything we did the last year is nothing, but one guest's review is everything. We built ourselves and had your back, but today our worth depends on one review. One review! One measly feedback decides what we are and how capable we are."

"Shut up, don't talk nonsense! And don't cross your limits. Standing in my office and asking me such hellish questions? Who the bloody hell are you? You will teach me things now? Mind your language!"

"I am minding myself, which is why I am here! If I wouldn't have, then I don't know where I'd have been."

"Shut your mouth and get out of my office! You bastard, you will teach me how to work? You will teach me what's right and what's not?" his face went red with all the screaming.

"Then you tell us how to work. After spending three years we get an A-4 sized paper with a stamp that decides our future for us, and we must keep that with us our entire life, for we won't get a job without it! The person who really deserves the job is nothing, but that paper is important more than him. But it doesn't end here. Even after getting a job, we work for more than a year and the increment we get is like slapping someone first and apologizing later. What about promotions? In all honestly, the ones who deserve to be promoted, don't, and the ones who don't know anything but flattering their bosses, get everything on time. When the time for promotion arrives, everyone asks us what we've done to deserve it. And when the time comes for leave sanctions, everyone asks us who will work on our behalf." One by one, all my frustrations were coming out.

"Are you blaming me for all of this? Am I responsible for all that happens to you?"

I shook my head.

"Do you know how much experience I have? 15 years," he emphasised on the duration. "In my entire career nobody has spoken to me like this. And you, someone who just started working 18 months back, you're now standing in front of me and teaching me what work is and how to work. You are becoming too smart!"

"This is the exact problem sir. If we want to tell the truth, nobody likes it and nobody wants to listen. Everyone's addicted to speaking and watching people tell lies. Working with you, my experience has stretched to 16 years. You are my boss. I should learn things from you, but I have learned more from Joy than you." I watched his face contort but continued, "He taught me how to balance my professional and personal lives. He taught me how to work with a team, to become a part of your juniors' lives, and not to become their boss. He showed me the respect that I should have learned from my boss."

"Have I not taught you anything?" he asked softly, yet rudely.

"I taught you everything I knew. You didn't learn, that is not my fault. Especially...I taught you about teamwork."

"And Joy is getting punished for just that! Just because he worked with the entire team that day!"

"Shut up! Enough is enough. Did you come to speak for yourself or for him?"

"I came to speak the truth."

"Don't tell me what the truth is and what is false. I know that better than you. Don't forget I am your senior."

"What happens if one junior does things better than his senior? Instead of motivating him, we cut his wings and blame him. We say he is not capable enough for the work given to him. If we cut his wings, then how will he fly, and how will the work get done? This warped sense of hierarchy is spreading in us like cancer. If one senior can't make one junior perfect, I don't think that senior is capable enough for his designation."

"Keep quiet!" he shouted. "Just because I am not saying anything doesn't mean you will say whatever you want! Get out of here right away!"

I stood quiet for a minute, looking into his eyes.

"Do you have anything to say?" he asked.

"Take back your decision," I said, unblinking.

"No! I can't. And I will never. In my entire career, I have never taken back my decisions. This is my final decision. Go and do whatever you want to, but that will be my final decision.I will not change my mind at any cost. If you want to work here, work, or else you can also leave."

"If in your entire career, you have not taken any decisions back, do it now. If you don't change today then nothing will ever change. Everyone wants to change the world but no one wants to change themself. If you don't change today, then our coming generation will suffer. And if you live to see that time, you will realise it then. You are also part of a family, but you will not realize the pain of your own people because you've never valued them. Work is a part of our lives, not life itself. How can it be more important than us?" I lay out all my thoughts and emotions in front of him. "I will not force you. As a boss, you know things better than me. Consider this my resignation. I am leaving. I can't work here." I took out a piece of paper from the inner pocket of my blazer, and kept it on the table in front of me.

"What you think doesn't matter to me," he said slowly. "But at least once think; you are putting your career in jeopardy."

With one hand on the knob, I turned around to face him once more and said, "Instead of working in a good company with a bad boss, I would rather work in a bad company with a good boss. And don't forget, if your boss becomes your friend, then everything works smoothly." I banged the door behind me and walked out. This was the first time I had ever argued with a senior in my life. It must have hurt Suri sir also, but sometimes we have to choose the wrong way to do something that would take us to the right path. Maybe the way I spoke to him wasn't good, but I had no other choice.

As I came out, Suri sir was meanwhile grumbling about me being too hyper, when his phone rang.

"Hello papa, what are you doing?" asked his son on the other side of the line.

"*Beta,* I will call you later. I am busy now," said Suri sir.

"No papa, I want to talk right now."

"*Beta* I said I will call you later."

"Papa, but I want to talk now."

"You don't understand what I am saying, or what? Are you mad?" Suri sir shouted into the phone.

"Papa," his son blubbered on the other end, close to tears. Suri sir's wife took the phone instead. "What happened? You can't even talk to your kid properly. You don't have the time to talk to us!"

"Please try to understand," Suri sir reasoned.

"Why are *you* not trying to understand? I know your work is important and we are not. What is the point of that work which takes you away from your family? You don't have the time to come home. You don't have the time to be with us, and now you don't have the time to talk either. After all of this, why do we have to understand everything?"

"Sorry, I was not in a good mood."

"But your kids don't know what your mood is, do they?" she snapped. "They just want to talk to their father who is so far from them and who doesn't have time for us."

"Sorry, I just…"

"Listen," she said, calming herself down. "I know you are busy but please understand what I have to go through. I don't want my kids to also suffer the same. We need you. We need your time, not your money or designation. Don't work so much that you forget your family. One day your work will end, but you have to be with us till the end. Don't forget we are also waiting for you. And once you get the time, call us. We are waiting." Before Suri sir could say anything, she cut the call. Suri sir looked at his phone silently. Tired, he sat back down.

****

"Why did you resign?" Joy asked me seriously.

"For the first time in my life I had taken something for granted," I said.

"Don't think about me. Take back your resignation and re-join."

"No, I will not," I said.

"You have to!"

"I said I will not."

"Don't be a kid. Forget whatever happened. And it was about me. Why are you worrying?"

"Will you forget what happened? And remember, we are a part of a team," I said.

"I will manage. What to do, it's become my habit. Sometimes people don't like me, sometimes I don't like them and sometimes we don't like each other. Because of this I have had to change so many jobs in ten years. But it's okay. I am happy," he smiled at me.

"I know you will manage like always, but this time you are not alone."

"Don't take any decision in haste. Think for yourself."

"I've been thinking for myself only so far. But today I realized

I have to think about others as well."

"But...," he paused, lost for words. "What will you do after leaving?"

"I will go abroad," I said after a moment's silence. He laughed at me.

"What happened? Why are you laughing?" I asked, a hint of a smile on my face as well.

"Because of your joke!" he continued laughing.

"I am serious, not kidding. But there's nothing wrong with it. Thousands of people move abroad to become something, to achieve something. I will also try."

"Don't count yourself in those thousands. Do something of your own."

"Suhani has been calling me. She has a good job vacancy. Going abroad is bound to be challenging. But she is helping me out."

"I hate the people who go abroad."

"Do you even like anything at all?"

"I hate things that have no substance."

"You mean going abroad is not a good idea."

"How can leaving our country and working in another be a good idea? This is the problem with you guys. What's your purpose?"

"Everyone has different reasons. I want to become a better professional and earn some more money."

"You can do that in India as well."

"Here people don't let you live, how will they help you grow?" I shook my head in disgust.

"Don't think about the people; think about yourself, what you can do and what you are doing."

"What do you mean?"

"We're born in India, we live in India, and this is our home.

We study in this country, learn from our fellow Indians, spend everything here, and what happens at the end? When the time comes for us to give back, or achieve something, we seek work abroad. We end up moving to countries we've never been to, and working with people we've never met. And for what? Just to earn some extra money? Or to keep others happy?"

"Maybe to keep others happy," I quipped.

"Keep yourself happy, the world is not happy anyway."

"We get paid less here. My starting salary there is three times more than what I'm getting now."

"Money is not everything and it can't fulfil our dreams. Don't run after it. Just do your job and one day you will get what you deserve."

"What are you trying to say?" I asked, perplexed.

"Don't go abroad. Work in India, even if you get paid less. Because at least here, you're contributing to the country with your knowledge." Joy's advice had always helped clear things out for me. But today his thoughts had put me in a deeper dilemma.

******

I kept rolling around in bed that night. I couldn't sleep. I kept thinking about how one's life can change in a second, and how one decision causes that change. It had been the hardest day of my life. The day had begun with a horrible meeting and ended with a cancelled international plan. And now, I was stuck in bed wondering what my next step would be. The last time a night had changed my life, I had decided to take up hotel management. And tonight again, I was plagued with a lot of thoughts. Had I not decided to take this field that night, I would not have experienced some of the best moments of my life. I knew I had to forget and forgive the ones I'd been blaming for my decision.

I looked at the clock. It was six in the morning, and here I was waiting for sunrise, but it was still midnight in London. Again, my heart seemed to contract just thinking about Suhani. Memories of all the times we'd spent together started coming back to me. From the first time we'd met, to the time her Mercedes left me alone at the college gate. It all felt like yesterday, but it had been almost three years since all this happened. That's the irony of life. Days, months and years may pass, but memories remain as fresh as ever. Of all the aspects of my life, my love life was by far the hardest. The tiny voice in my head had nudged me gently, indicating the time to tell her my feelings was here. But just the thought of it was frightening.

I kept staring at my phone for some time. I called her then, let it ring twice, and then cut the call. But she called back immediately.

"Hey duffer at least let me pick up!" she chided sleepily. "I was in a deep sleep, how could I have known you'd call me at this time? What happened? Is everything okay?"

"If everything were okay, why would I be calling you at midnight?"

"Manav, what happened?" I could hear the concern in her voice.

"Suhani I want to talk to you about something important. Can you wake up please?"

"I am already awake. Now tell me." Her voice hard.

"No not like this. Go wash your face and come back."

"Manav! Are you mad? Do you know what the temperature is like here? I can't even get out of bed and you are asking me to go wash my face."

"Suhani, please?"

I heard her grumble as she left her phone. Soon enough, she was back, her voice clearer now. "Yes, tell me now."

"Suhani...," I still don't know how to begin. "Suhani, listen."

"I am listening. Now say something or I will kill you."

"Suhani would you like to meet my girlfriend?" I asked hastily.

There was silence on her end.

"Suhani, are you there?"

"Manav, are you serious?" she asked softly.

"Just answer me."

"Where is she?" I could hear her anticipation through the phone.

"Please don't ask me questions today, just answer."

"Who is she?"

"Suhani please no questions. I had told you when the right time came, you'd be the first to know."

"Okay sorry, you continue. Yes, I want to meet her, where is she?"

"Near you. And she will meet you very soon."

"Are you sure?"

"Yes."

"Who is she?"

"My girl..."

"Manav, please stop. Sorry, I don't want to meet her. Sorry I just can't."

"Suhani listen!"

"No, no, I'm sorry."

"Suhani, listen I have not asked her out yet! You have to help me."

"Sorry Manav! I can't do this."

"Suhani, please. Please, do this for me."

"Okay, tell me what I have to do," she sounded like she was going to cry.

"Where is the mirror in your room?"

"It's to my right."

"Okay, close your eyes and stand in front of the mirror."

"Manav, what is going on? I don't understand."

"Please?"

"Okay, now tell me what it is," she asked, standing in front of her mirror with her eyes closed.

"Now, slowly open your eyes." She did.

"I love you," I finally said softly. I imagined her looking into her mirror, overcome with emotion.

"Manav…," she stopped before saying anything more.

I on the other hand, continued. "Suhani, I don't know what you think of me, but I have really loved you since our first day in college. I loved you when I saw you in the college garden. I loved you when you left me alone for your training. I loved you when you chose me as your best friend, and even when I was angry when you left me alone and went to London. I don't know what your answer will be, but I really love you so much. I promise I will fulfil all your dreams."

"But Manav…," she started again, but I stopped her. "Suhani listen, whatever your answer will be, I swear we will be friends forever."

"What took you so much time?" she asked, sniffing into the phone.

"I thought if you didn't feel the same way, I'd lose my best friend."

"You're mad; you should've at least told me."

"Do you love me?" I asked, butterflies fluttering in my stomach.

"Of course I love you, you duffer!" she laughed. "But you took so much time."

"I was waiting for the right moment."

"I've also loved you from the first day of college but I was waiting to hear it from you."

The knot in my stomach slowly loosened now that I knew she felt the same.

"When are you coming here?" she asked.

"No, I will not come. You have to come to India."

"What?"

"Suhani listen, I think instead of leaving for another country, I would like to remain here. Please come and join me here. We will live together with our family."

"But Manav…"

"Suhani please, nothing is better than India. And this is my wish, so please come."

"Don't worry I will come there soon."

"Thank you so much, Suhani. I love you."

"I love you too," she replied softly, and cut the call.

Chapter 25

We were in our rooms packing our belongings. Ketaki was back from Zurich and was trying to help out us as much as she could. She was even ready to go and talk to Suri sir but Joy had stopped her. She was forcing me and Joy to go with her to Zurich. I kept wondering how a person who hates people going abroad would agree to go out himself. As for me, I'd left all hopes since Suhani was ready to move back.

Ketaki, Joy, Rudra, Shantanu and I were just going to move in a while, when the doorbell rang. When Shantanu went to open the door, we saw Khurana sir standing outside. Regardless of our feelings towards him, everyone stood up and wished him.

"Hello guys, can I come in?" he asked, entering the Club House. All of us looked at each other in confusion.

"What is going on? I think you're all busy winding up." He'd noticed our packed bags strewn across the room. We remained quiet. "What's the next plan?" he asked.

"Don't worry sir, we will vacate in sometime," I said. He laughed, and we kept wondering at the reason for his visit.

"I meant, what have you guys thought of doing next? Where will you go?"

"First we will leave this place, then think."

"I can understand why Joy's leaving, but I don't understand why you are. What is your problem? You don't seem to value your job." I looked down, ignoring his gaze.

"What has he done for you that you're leaving your job for him? There are a thousand students in queue for this job. If you leave, it won't affect the company much, but it will affect your career. One day you will look back and realise how wrong you were." When we still didn't respond, he changed tact.

"I'm sorry, I did not come here to lecture you before you go. I didn't come here to ask you to stay either. That is your decision, and you'll know better. But before you guys leave, I want to say something. If you guys have really decided to go, I will not stop you. Suri sir sent me here to talk with you. We're organising a small farewell party for you guys. And it is our request that you all attend it. If you come, it will be my pleasure, because I promised them you would."

We looked at each other in shock. He didn't seem to notice, and continued nonetheless. "I know whatever's happened has been very bad. That should not have happened. I can't change the past. But I request all of you to please come and join us. That's the least we can do." After saying what he'd come here to say, he walked out, leaving us all stunned with his audacity.

****

We decided to give in to Khurana sir's request and headed to the farewell, or the "Send-Off Party" as they were calling it. Farewells generally include drinks and music, but we'd been called to the Banquet Hall, where a stage with seats around had been set up. As we entered, we saw Khurana and Suri sirs with some corporate people, sitting on the right side of the stage. The rest of the employees were already seated. Everyone looked at us, smiling at us like we were new joinees. We slipped in, and sat in the front row. When all conversations died down, Khurana sir took the mic, and stood centre-stage.

"Good evening everyone," he said, looking at us. "Without wasting a single minute, I would like to call Mr. Suri here and say a few words," he smiled and gestured at Suri sir to join him. I was a little confused as to what was going on. The person, who had not laughed in the last 18 months, was now grinning on stage. Suri sir joined him on stage, and the hall went even quieter. I don't know what was happening to me. I felt so weird. My right eye started twitching. I remember *maa* had once told me of a superstition - if your right eye starts twitching, it's an indicator of good things to come.

"Hello everyone," a soft voice with a hint of a smile broke the silence. "I don't know where to start." Suri sir looked at us for a moment before continuing.

"We're all human. We all have some limitations. We can't break through them even if we tried. These limitations keep us in control. Even though we're all managers, we have the same limitations. People often misconstrue our reasons. But because of our limitations, it takes us time to understand certain things. We are all a part of this organisation. We are all employees. We can't judge people in a day, or even a month, because we too need the time to understand and process things. Till today, I've achieved everything I've reached for. I fulfilled most of my dreams. Sometimes, I ended up achieving things I'd never even thought of. Like the day I became a General Manager. I remember thinking, now I've achieved all that I had to. I don't require anything else from life. But it's only later that I realised that my actual life was yet to start. And that's when I thought I had the answer to the question my senior at the beginning of my career had once asked me. 'What should I do to be a successful hotelier?' And today, when I look at myself, I still don't have an answer to it. Not because I was wrong, or because my senior was wrong, nor was it because this industry is wrong. It was because the question itself was wrong. Instead, I asked myself, 'What should *we* do, to be successful hoteliers?' Now that's a question I can answer. Today, I stand before you and realise I was wrong. And now, without wasting a single moment, I want to remove *I* from that perspective, and include *we* instead."

He paused to a thunderous applause, echoing through the hall. I sat shocked looking at the person in front. I looked at Joy, who looked back at me, and we both looked at Shantanu. Good sense had prevailed, and the person who hadn't said a single good thing since I'd joined, was now finally speaking sense. It was like a magical moment for us. My right eye was still twitching, but now I was grateful for it.

"Till today I was living with an illusion that I would do everything. I am the best, and nobody can be better than me. Because of this mindset, I forgot what lay beyond. And when you look at history, there was not a single person who won a war – it was always a team. It was always with their people, their colleagues, and their fellow soldiers. And if throughout history, people couldn't fight and win without their team, how can I? If they can't fight wars alone, then how can I? It is not possible for me either. So now I want to put *we* instead of *I*, because now is the time to change."

He looked at us in the front row, and in a low voice, continued. "As someone once told me; change is a must in life. If we don't change ourselves today, then change will never come. During my service, I forgot I too have a personal life, a family life. And there are people waiting for me at home. I realise today that work is a never ending process. It is just a small part of our lives, not life itself. So today, I have decided to go back to be with my family. They need me. My wife, my kids and my house are calling me. They've been waiting for me for a long time, and I'm finally going home." He stopped to wipe the tears now gathering in his eyes. We sat stunned, wondering what had happened overnight. It seemed like the first time that Suri sir had ever paid heed to anyone else's advice. That just happened to be mine. I sat there, proud of myself for managing to bring about this change. And all this credit went only to Joy. As the sound of applause reached a crescendo, Joy stood up, trying to move out of the room.

"Mr. Joy," Suri sir called out. Joy turned around and looked him in the eye. "Today is my last day in this organisation. And with me leaving, all respectable people concerned want you to take charge. Please come on stage and take over from me. You really deserve this. Yes, we should manage our work during the allotted office hours. And yes, we have lives beyond our work. It doesn't matter if we're called mister instead of sir. And it is all of us who come together to build this organisation, not the reviews and comments we may receive." None of us could believe what was happening. Without a second's thought, I stood up and ran to hug Joy. Ketaki and Shantanu also got up to hug him, and we gently pushed him on stage.

He took the stage, slowly walking to the centre. He removed his blazer and placed it on a chair. Left now in a cream-coloured shirt and a red tie, he went up to Suri sir who hugged him and handed him the mic. As Suri sir took his place, Joy looked at everyone in the hall. Soon enough, the applause died down and all became silent once more.

"I think this is our biggest problem," Joy spoke into the mic, looking at his blazer. "The one who wears it, become the boss. Even if he doesn't know his job. The ones without it become the junior staff, even if they know more than him. I don't think the problem lies in us. We are all okay in our places. The actual problem lies in this hierarchy, that's divided by this blazer. It creates a lot of issues and problems between people working on one project, for the same company. After wearing this, we forget our jobs and think of ourselves as superior. This breaks lot of self-respect. And how can a person with a shattered self - respect give his 100%? We must remove this distinction from our mind, because it is just a matter of getting the work done."

"Manager. I'd first heard this word when I started my career. I'd thought it'd mean something different, but I finally understood what it meantwhen I became one. I understand its value every time I encounter problems. This job is not as easy as we think. Only those who are managers can understand this. It's much like how you can tell people about your wound but can't share your pain. A manager is both sides of a coin. Sometimes he becomes knowledgeable for a junior, and at the same time, he becomes useless for his senior. He has to understand his junior's problems and fulfil his senior's requirements. He's one who understands everyone but nobody understands him. I think your boss should be like your best friend. But seeing how things have been going so far, we don't count on the ones who really deserve it. Our degree certificates seem more valuable than the persons holding them. We always find faults in others but never look at ourselves."

"I want to bring changes in our lives. I want to make everyone proud to be hoteliers. I want to make sure everyone feels worthy. But this is only possible with your continuous support. I am nothing without your support. And one more thing, nobody will work under me, we will all work together, and together, we will create history. Thank you so much for your love and support." As soon as he finished, Rudra stood up and gave him a standing ovation. Soon enough, everyone started clapping and the Banquet Hall resonated with their cheers. We took this as cue and rushed to the stage to hug Joy and be with him.

"I thought I'd become a boss very soon, but I realise today how difficult it is. Not everyone can handle it in such a short time. And to be a good boss, I have to first be a good colleague, a good team member. I don't think I deserve this yet, but you do!" we heard Rudra spill his heart out as he hugged Joy.

In no time, I too took back my resignation and re-joined duty. It was an honour to start working with a boss who was also my friend. Chef also moved into a house with his family once they arrived. I moved in with Suhani once she returned, and started working with me. Ketaki also shifted to India, and started working in our hotel as a full-time trainer. And the next month, Joy and Ketaki were to get married.

Maa and dad also came down to visit us. And dad was proud to have Joy as my friend, once he got to know how he was the reason for my awakening.

That was the day I realised how every friend was meant for a different purpose. Some of them represented an ideal to you, and gave you lessons for life. Joy had become one such person.

They say, when one door closes, another opens. Today, I hold no hatred towards the people who left me after I chose this career path. Everything I became was only possible because of them. I may have lost out on a lot in life, but when I look back, I realise I gained so much more.

Everyone has a different way of looking at us hoteliers. Some think we are mad to have chosen this field. Some call us fools. Some think we are nothing. But now that I'm living the life of an hotelier, I know better.

Author's Thoughts

To the Guests

My dear guest,

In Indian culture, guests are treated equivalent to God; Atithi Devo Bhava. And as the entire world knows, we're a country of ardent religious believers. So how can we ever break our God's heart? How can we ever put our God through troubles? How can we ever betray Him? We hoteliers are human too. We too make mistakes, and misunderstandings are a part of our lives. But none of them are intentional. A simple feedback or review might not seem as important to you, but it is the most important aspect in our field. Where the entire world is becoming a slave to their smartphones, and one review can traverse the globe in a second, it has become even easier to decide someone's worth basis a review someone might have written. Until a few years back, guests would pick a hotel basis other factors, but today, people choose hotels basis the reviews they receive.

Remember, we only always try to provide you with the best service. We miss out on milestones and our own happiness to keep you happy. We keep our stomachs empty to fill yours. We work on holidays to give you the service you deserve. We stay away from our homes to make you feel at home. If we are wrong, you can definitely suggest us changes in our services. Human beings learn through their mistakes, and that's the way we'll learn too.